POPULAR TITLES PLAN BOOK NCF

MYSTERY -1

OFFICIALLY WITHDRAWN
FROM THE
HENNEPIN COUNTY LIBRARY

Books by Clarissa Watson

THE BISHOP IN THE BACK SEAT   1980

THE FOURTH STAGE OF GAINSBOROUGH BROWN   1977

THE SENSUOUS CARROT   1972

THE BISHOP IN THE BACK SEAT

THE BISHOP IN

THE BACK SEAT

Clarissa Watson

New York   Atheneum   1980

Library of Congress Cataloging in Publication Data

Watson, Clarissa.
    The bishop in the back seat.

    I. Title.
PZ4.W3386Bi   [PS3573.A848]   813'.5'4   79–2115
ISBN 0-689-11012-X

Copyright © 1980 by Clarissa Watson
All rights reserved
Published simultaneously in Canada by McClelland and Stewart Ltd.
Composition by American–Stratford Graphic Services, Inc.,
Brattleboro, Vermont
Manufactured by Fairfield Graphics,
Fairfield, Pennsylvania
Designed by Harry Ford
First Printing December 1979
Second Printing February 1980

To George
FOR LOVING
LIVING

THE BISHOP IN THE BACK SEAT

1

Gull Harbor, Long Island. A community of gracious mansions, rolling fields, grazing horses, gamboling dogs, perfect children, handsome grown-ups, French *au pair* girls, English nannies, and miles and miles of well-kept country roads and sparkling white fences. Rich. Neat. Well-bred.

The most exciting and violent thing that ever occurs in Gull Harbor and environs is the occasional raising of a voice. Once upon a time, it is true, considerable violence was visited upon the local fox population as the residents tramped and galloped around the countryside accompanied by packs of various-sized spotted dogs, but today the beagle and foxhound packs are disbanded and the hunts nothing but a memory. Most people have taken up bird watching and surrender only occasionally to bloodthirsty bird-shooting sorties into Georgia or Scotland or thundering stag hunts in the châteaux country of France.

What irrepressible violence remains in Gull Harbor today dissipates itself in the swatting of countless balls on countless tennis courts and golf courses. Anyone absolutely bent on additional excitement might go over to Mrs. Sandringham's and watch the clock man wind all her clocks, as he still comes to do once a week, or survey the occasional bottles tossed on the sides of the tree-lined roads to see if the young are still drinking Dom Perignon or have switched to Korbel. Or perhaps he might jaunt over to see if the residents of Gull Harbor's slightly raunchy neighbor, Rum Island, have come to blows yet over the design of their own private flag or have finally sawed through the causeway, liberating themselves from the mainland, and floated out to sea.

Nothing more fierce than that. Until the day armed intruders entered the Waldheim Museum and kidnapped Saskia van Uylenburgh at gunpoint.

February 10, the day that would shatter the tranquility of Gull Harbor and a lot of people in it, began with an unconscionable wait at the airport. Willem de Groot's private jet bearing Willem de Groot's private superstar was unaccountably late. During the long wait for its arrival we could clearly hear the nervous crackling of police radios as they relayed messages back and forth.

The security measures were extraordinary, even for this occasion. Sixteen armed men were stationed around the perimeters of the area where the Gulfstream jet was scheduled to roll to a stop away from the regular air traffic at LaGuardia Airport. These sixteen were a combination of Gull Harbor area police and private Brinks security men hired by de Groot for the occasion. There were also armed plainclothesmen scattered strategically about. I could count eight squad cars and six motorcycle police ringing the place. An armored truck, courtesy of Pierre Richardson's banks, waited nearby. Walkie-talkies squawked and muttered angrily.

From where I waited in my little Mustang with the heater going full blast to keep me from perishing with the cold I could see the seven cars of seven of the richest people in Gull Harbor. Six of them hadn't been able to resist coming to see what the seventh—de Groot—was up to: curiosity is not the exclusive province of the poor. Some of the vehicles were glittering limousines, with chauffeurs (Willem de Groot's included) stationed at the sides, shivering. I couldn't see inside the big cars from my vantage point to sort out who was who, but I recognized the sparkling red Ferrari, the smart little Aston-Martin, and the glove gray type 57 supercharged Bugatti: they belonged respectively to Rosemary Craig-Mitchell, Diantha Lord, and Pierre Richardson. I had seen them before. Other cars, too, sat idling amidst the TV equipment and the motorcycles, but they were wreathed in vapors from their exhaust systems and it was impossible to recognize anyone inside.

All the vehicles, large and small, had their heaters blasting away.

On February 1, de Groot had issued an elaborate invitation to the press for his superstar's arrival, complete with a toney press package that contained four or five lengthy releases. The media had responded enthusiastically—they were all here. As soon as de Groot's plane taxied up to where they waited, television cameras would grind and flashbulbs would flash as the golden Dutchman was captured on film. The beautiful descendant of New Amsterdam's First Settlers would then transfer his charge to the waiting armored truck to be escorted with wailing sirens and roaring motorcycles to Long Island's new Gull Harbor museum, the Waldheim.

The center of all this drama—de Groot's superstar—was not, of course, a person but something far classier by Gull Harbor standards: a painting. Specifically, a $4 million piece of canvas measuring 18 by 24 inches and painted by Rembrandt van Rijn. The painting was a portrait of his lovely young wife, Saskia van Uylenburgh. By nightfall it would be the most talked-about painting in the world.

As we waited for de Groot's flight to arrive, I thought of the events that had brought us here today. . . .

It all began in mid-September which is why, I suppose, I fell into the habit of thinking of them as the September Seven, even though it made them sound like a terrorist group, which they definitely were not. Not, at least, in the popular sense of the word.

It was very hot for September. I was grateful to be wearing one of those dresses that require next to nothing underneath. Even so, I could feel the dampness on my forehead that meant my hair would soon be hanging in dank corkscrews like Medusa.

The temperature inside the library, which has no air conditioning, registered 97 degrees, and they were wilting in the heat like ordinary mortals, which surprised me. It was one thing for me to be hot—I was merely a starving artist, a token member of the group—but seven of the richest, most influential, and most powerful people in Gull Harbor—seven perfect examples of old money, old property, and upper class—ought to have been above such fleshly frailties.

Nonetheless, here they were, wilting just like me. I made a

bet with myself that by next September the Gull Harbor library would be air-conditioned. The Rich get things done when they are personally inconvenienced.

You would not have been able to tell by looking at them that the September Seven were angry: there were none of the usual signs—no raised voices, no gnashing of teeth. But the fact was that the meeting had been called precisely because they were so enraged by a certain H. Caldwell Ringwell that their fondest wish at the moment was to see him summarily drawn and quartered.

This requires a bit of explanation. H. Caldwell Ringwell was the county executive, a politician definitely of the shifty variety, who had a burning desire to be governor. He had the political clout: he was married to the daughter of a big union official. What he lacked was identity, image, class. Like Rockefeller.

Unfortunately, he made the mistake of trying to acquire that class by applying to every exclusive club in Gull Harbor. He should have known better. You don't apply to those clubs—you are born into them. Naturally, they laughed at him. Consequently, when shortly thereafter the state began pondering whether to build a bridge linking Rye and Gull Harbor, Ringwell, joyously aware that it would wipe out the scene of his social humiliation by burying it in a sea of cement, vociferously and in every nefarious way he could think of supported the plan.

While Gull Harbor fought, he gloated. And then one day, while rooting around among the county's more obscure possessions, he discovered that the famous financier, Jacob Waldheim, had bequeathed his country mansion to the county in the twenties for use as a museum. As he had neglected to also bequeath funds and paintings, the big pseudo-French château had fallen on the tragic circumstances of an aging mistress whose protector has reduced her allowance to poverty level.

County Executive H. Caldwell Ringwell leaped upon the aging mistress like a lustful young lover. A museum—now that would give him class. But only if it were done right. He and his trusty henchman, Willam C. Brown, went to Gull Harbor's elite and proposed a détente: they all had fabulous art collections. If they would lend their paintings for the opening exhibition and serve as the museum's board of trustees, he would get the bridge called off. Was it a deal? It was. What else could they do?

The only dissenter was my aunt, Lydia Wentworth, who announced her opinion of Ringwell, Brown, and the rest of their gang in no uncertain terms. "Eyes too close together. Simply *not* to be trusted. Rather give my paintings to the butcher." And, as always, she was right.

Thanks to the investigative work of David Lawless, one of the Seven and senior partner in the aptly named firm of Lawless & Lawless, "attorneys at law since 1863," we had learned that the county executive had no intention whatever of stopping the bridge from coming to Gull Harbor. Or of consulting the board about any decisions. Or even of *telling* us anything—he had already hired a museum director, some man from Europe, without letting a single one of us know. We'd been tricked. Betrayed. Hornswoggled.

So here we all were on a sweltering September night, seated around one of those longish, pockmarked tables one finds in every community library. There was something Last Supper-ish about the gloomy group.

"County politicians, of all things . . . imagine being insulted by people like that!" Old Mrs. Sandringham gave her wheelchair a scornful rattle. Obviously it was a hundredfold more devastating to be insulted by political small fry than by their nationally famous counterparts.

The simple truth was that the big politicos would have had more sense than to treat these people badly. It wasn't just a matter of votes—doubtless Ringwell could make them up by promising money and jobs elsewhere. One did not push these people around. By the most conservative estimate, the bodies in that sweltering room could hurl first-class thunderbolts without visible effort.

"That beastly man. I don't suppose there's any question about it?" Rosemary Craig-Mitchell was twisting her hair into a blond coil and pinning it on top of her head with a big tortoiseshell hairpin. I was envious: it looked cool.

"I'm afraid the evidence is incontrovertible." I wished Lawless wouldn't be so pompous about it. It was too hot for posturing.

"All he wanted was a token board. I can't believe it. We had an *agreement*." Diantha Lord was one of the few idealists left in the world. Your word was your word. It had been that way with everyone once, I suppose.

"Political nonentities—imagine," Mrs. Sandringham repeated, unbelieving.

"So, Lawless." Pierre Richardson, our banker, sat very still, his eyes glittering like flint. "What are our options?"

"I'm very much afraid that he's painted us into a corner, if you will forgive the play on words." Lawless paused for the obligatory polite chuckles, but none came. "He's made sure that everyone knows we're lending our pictures. If we back out now, we'll be branded elitists—you know how politicians love that word. And we can't make a public fuss about his breaking his word because the kind of deal we made with him isn't something we can talk about. Besides, he'd deny it."

"You said he could do it, David. You said 'the right word' to his father-in-law and he could have the project scuttled." Rosemary Craig-Mitchell laughed angrily. "I don't want to wake up some morning and find a bridge over my house. . . . Can't we have Ringwell and his sidekick assassinated? Do you know a hit man, David?" Her laugh was a surprisingly robust ha-ha-ha affair.

"Rosemary—please!" Rosemary always said exactly what was on her mind and David was always despairing about it.

Belle Sandringham snorted. "I don't suppose it would be practical to have them killed, Rosemary, dear. It would just raise a fuss." She was trying to outwit the heat by stirring the lifeless air with a cardboard fan that must have dated from some faraway episode in her life. It had a picture of three black babies on one side: you might have thought she would have called them pickaninnies, if you didn't know she had been arrested twice for civil rights marches, the last time twelve years ago when she was seventy. The other side of the fan bore the legend LET IT BE JEST A LITTLE BIT COOLER. LAURENCE RIVERS, INC., PRESENTS *Green Pastures* BY MARC CONNELLY, COLONIAL THEATER, BOSTON.

"Why not just refuse to lend our pictures," someone said

reasonably. I think it was the general but I'm not sure—he rarely spoke of anything more current than World War II.

There was an instant well-bred outcry.

"At this stage? We couldn't."

"There's too much committed already. Ringwell would go to town on us."

"Make us look terrible—guaranteed to make him popular. Nothing like an attack on the rich."

"Anyway, he could just call another museum and borrow enough pictures for a show." Willem de Groot spoke up for the first time. "Not the quality of ours, but decent enough."

"What about old Jacob Waldheim's grandson—Jason? Why not recruit him to help?" The general again.

"Not a chance. He has no authority over the museum—the mansion belongs to the county now," Richardson replied. "And you can bet Ringwell has no intention of sharing the spotlight with a Waldheim. Anyway, Jason doesn't care a rap about us or our bridge. He's a New Yorker." The fatal term of opprobrium from a Long Islander.

There was a gloomy pause while they considered the situation. The only sound was the soft swish of Mrs. Sandringham's fan.

I'm terrible at meetings. The droning of the voices almost puts me to sleep. I realize that they are a necessity from time to time, but a necessity for other people, not for me. I'm an artist, and I'd rather draw people than listen to them.

Right then, for example, I began to daydream. They were going on and on, and in spite of myself I stopped paying attention to the words and began to imagine how I would draw the seven people sitting with me in the sweltering room.

"If we can stop Ringwell from becoming governor . . . ," Lawless was saying. "The legal ramifications . . ." I drifted away.

Belle Sandringham—she was a great subject—a girdle-encrusted primeval force with a Comanche's gaze and iron gray curls in battleship order. At eighty she didn't look a day over sixty. Belle had inherited a giant pharmaceuticals conglomerate from the late Colonel Sandringham and ran it with an iron fist, and had only taken to her wheelchair, she said, in order to get around faster.

She'd been overseas in both World Wars as a nurse. "Brave enough to have been in the Commandos," the general once said. I would draw her like a warlord, I decided.

Rosemary Craig-Mitchell—Rubens would have gone mad over her beauty, just as every man who saw her went mad over her. She must be approaching her late forties now, but she had only grown riper, juicier, more delectable with age. There was just the tiniest hint of the high living, the many husbands. But it was an alluring hint, one that stirred every man, promising generosity and fire. Rosi would never demand accountings when an affair was over: Rosi would kiss and laugh and stay a friend. No black and white drawing for Rosi. I would do her in rich colors with sumptuous highlights.

Diantha Lord—now there was a strange girl. I'd often wondered how stable she was. True, she'd survived the obligatory full Gull Harbor education—Greenvalley, Foxcroft, and that Swiss school they all went to. She'd also survived the obligatory two marriages. And she seemed to have come out of it all with a need to "find" herself. People said, "How nice that Diantha's taken up art. So good for her." The dazzling collection she'd inherited didn't hurt either.

Earlier that evening she'd collared me for a rambling discussion about modern art, followed with another about astrology, one of her earlier enthusiasms. "You're Aries, Persis? The most honest sign in the zodiac. *Comme moi—je suis née sous le signe des Poissons. Je n'ai guère de confiance en moi-même.*"

No confidence in herself—did that explain her? Anyway, Picasso would have liked her angularity and her unadorned Gull Harbor good looks. Or Henri Laurens. I would use a sweeping line drawing for her.

Lawyer Lawless? A Byzantine figure, surely. Here was a man who, in another time and place, might have leaped out at one from a dark corner. I realized this image was inspired by my prejudice against lawyers: my late husband had been one, although he seldom practiced—he was too busy drinking his way through my money before he finally died. I suppose I was unfair to David

Lawless: certainly Rosemary Craig-Mitchell found him more than acceptable, and he was unquestionably handsome by Gull Harbor's standards of tallness, leanness, and boring regularity of features.

Yet there was definitely a dark side to him. I had heard that some exotic people were his clients . . . fallen despots, Greek tycoons, dethroned kings . . . rulers of dark and bloody empires. Lawless would know and use all sides of the law, which is exactly why everyone retained him.

He would be an ink wash, in black and white—with vastly more black than white.

Then there was Willem de Groot. He was a beauty, that one, and he knew it. The knowledge was in the languor with which he now lounged on the hard library chair. It was in the indolence of his glance, the indifference with which he treated everyone who swam into his orbit. I suppose it wasn't entirely his fault— to be that beautiful had to be a burden to a man. Men aren't supposed to have a cap of golden curls, or Delft blue eyes, or a profile Praxiteles would have envied.

As if that weren't enough, de Groot was a straight-line descendant of two of the most distinguished of the early Dutch families to settle New Amsterdam and he'd never been allowed to forget it. His family had drilled into him that such unsullied lineage made him special even in Gull Harbor, which was a veritable forest of distinguished family trees.

Would he ever find a lady exceptional enough to serve as his mate? We all wondered. As he would never see forty-five again and no one had yet measured up, the prospect was not promising. "A good thing he has all those racehorses to occupy him," my Aunt Lydie once remarked. "And there are all those pretty young ladies he employs as grooms. . . ." I would draw de Groot on a rearing horse, like a Renaissance prince.

General Robert Lee Scott? He was a darling, that man, still as straight and spare as he must have been when he was a young man. His clothes, in fact, rather hung on him, as if either his servants neglected him or he forgot a meal now and then. We all kept inviting him to dinner to be sure that he was properly fed.

And nobody minded too much the endless war reminiscences, even though there appeared to be no starting point to them, no finishing point and, in fact, very little point at all.

Despite his baggy clothes, he was a very rich man. Some uncharitable people whispered that his great resources came from war booty in the distant and not so distant past, but I didn't believe it. Neither did I believe the gossip that Rosi had pried the fingers of her third husband off the gunwales of the Shields during a race at the yacht club when the boom hit him or that, by her indiscretions, she had driven her fifth husband, the French baron, to blow out his brains. People will embroider.

What was it the general had done in the war? We never knew, exactly: despite his ramblings he never really talked about himself. Aunt Lydie, who had once been mildly in love with him, said he had probably been a spy. But I didn't believe it—spies don't become generals, do they?

A single line would do the general, I decided. A very straight line.

Pierre Richardson—there was an enigma. I simply could not make him out—had never been able to make him out, although I'd known him most of my life, as I'd known all the rest. Pierre seemed a simple enough soul, saying very little and smiling gently now and then. Did it mean he had nothing to say, or that he was actually very complex and was clever enough to conceal it? The fact that he owned a great international banking empire proved nothing—he had inherited it, as he had inherited the bulk of his collection of great Impressionist paintings.

I studied him, exasperated. No, except for his love of vintage sports cars, everything else was standard Gull Harbor: big house in Gull Harbor, big house in Hobe Sound, big house in Maine, big house in the south of France, big apartment in Paris. Usual charities. Usual boards of directors. As for his looks—a finely shaped head, strong nose, sensual mouth . . .

The pale blue eyes were looking at me now with an expression I could not read. I would not, I decided, attempt to draw Pierre Richardson until I understood him . . . and that might be never.

The general was saying my name gently, forcing me back to the meeting room.

"Persis. Mrs. Willum. You do agree with us, don't you? The rest of us are unanimous."

Agree? Unanimous? What had they been up to?

Mrs. Sandringham broke in.

"If we are absolutely determined to go through with this thing of lending our collections to the museum, I shall still have to withdraw my Rubens. It was promised to the Rubens anniversary show in Antwerp long before this show came up. Too bad, in a way. It's my best picture, and every show needs a star."

So that was it. They must have decided to go ahead with the exhibition.

Diantha confirmed it. "We're keeping the pictures in. However," and here her voice dropped in disappointment—she had obviously been looking forward to the excitement of it all—"we are going to resign *in toto* as a board of directors. Do you agree, Persis?" I think she was hoping I wouldn't.

But I nodded enthusiastically. I'd never wanted to be the token artist on the board in the first place. I had more than I could handle already, between working as director for Gregor Olitsky's North Shore Galleries and trying to keep up with my painting career at the same time. As it was, I was practically a pauper, hobbling along financially on what Gregor paid me and by the sale of an occasional Persis Willum oil. The last thing I needed was something else to take up my already short supply of time.

"Oh, I agree," I said . "Indeed I do."

"And you also agree about the other?" The general spoke very softly. I had the odd impression that he was embarrassed.

"What other?" They were all staring at me.

Pierre Richardson took over smoothly. "We all feel that it would be very important, if we are to go on with this thing. You know our opinion of Ringwell and that man of his, Brown. To say that we have very little faith in them is to vastly understate the case." He smiled.

I nodded dumbly, smiling back.

Lawless leaned over and squeezed my arm reassuringly. "It's a matter of needing someone both knowledgeable and trustworthy on the spot. Like you, Persis. None of us can spare the time—we're all off all over the world all the time. Business—and pleasure, too, of course. But after the way he's behaved, it's imperative that we have a friend in his camp, as it were. Need to be sure the bastard—oh, excuse me," he turned to Mrs. Sandringham.

She raised her eyebrows and smiled.

He continued. "We need to make sure that someone keeps an eye on them, that our names . . ."

Rosemary Craig-Mitchell couldn't stand it.

"Oh, David," she cried impatiently, "why don't you say what you mean, for God's sakes? Just spit it out!" She turned to me. "What he's getting around to saying, Persis, is that we want to make sure the shifty dime-store Machiavelli doesn't take advantage of us—set us up somehow—God knows what. I mean, he's capable of anything, isn't he?"

"Exactly what I was saying," Lawless said evenly. He was not about to let her trample all over him. Maybe that was why she found him so refreshing.

I didn't know what they were getting at. In fact, I was almost positively certain that I did not wish to know what they were getting at. Call it instinct.

The Gull Harbor librarian walked in on us just then. She was wheeling a cart covered with all the odds and ends required for a coffee break. Hot coffee. Paper cups and paper envelopes of revolting sugar substitutes and a big jar of some powdered white stuff. In deference to the librarian, who was gallant and gothic and quite a proper reliquary for obscure titles and overlooked tomes, every one of us accepted a steaming beaker. How could we refuse?

The whole room was steaming now . . . and they were all looking at me through the vapors rising from their cups.

"You *do* agree, Persis?" Mrs. Sandringham's eyes were quite piercing when you really looked at them.

"Do I?" Why hadn't I paid attention?

The general took pity on me, thank heaven. "As Diantha said, we will self-destruct the board. But we would be very grateful to you if you would consent to represent us at the museum for the duration of the exhibition. We realize that it is an imposition—we know how busy you are—but you would be doing us the greatest kindness. Of course, we cannot expect you to be responsible for the protection of our pictures: security will attend to that. It is the other less tangible things that worry us."

I was stunned. "But I have a job. Gregor Olitsky. And my own work."

"I think Gregor will spare you. And we would insist that you have an office at the museum with enough room and light for you to paint."

Of course Gregor would spare me. They were all his best customers at the gallery.

"But, General . . . everyone . . ." I felt like crying. I didn't want the responsibility of their reputations, nor of their paintings, for I would feel responsible, in spite of anything they said. I didn't want to defend their reputations against Ringwell and Brown. For one thing, I wasn't smart enough, and for another, I like to keep a low profile. When you're dealing with artistic geniuses and high-powered collectors as I do in the gallery, a low profile is *de rigueur*. It is, as the general might say, a good idea not to put your head up above the trenches. Especially if you're an artist yourself, reasonably good, reasonably well put together, and under a thousand years old.

So I kept trying. "I have some commissions to do and—"

"I positively know your aunt would be pleased to hear you were helping us out." Mrs. Sandringham was hitting below the belt. She knew perfectly well that Aunt Lydie would think it a splendid idea: she was always urging me to get out of the gallery—do things—paint more. And they knew I knew they were all her friends.

I could see it coming like the express train to Amiens. I would say yes, probably smiling celestially. And I did.

"Yes." So much for Persis Willum's low profile.

"Lydia will be so pleased," Mrs. Sandringham said, her curls vibrating with self-satisfaction. These people gave no quarter.

Now that it was settled, they all began to leave in a rush, eager to be home in their air-conditioned mansions as fast as their air-conditioned Bentleys and Porsches and Rolls-Royces would carry them, leaving me to contemplate the honor they had bestowed upon me—a close association with a devious county executive and his hatchet man and a museum director none of us had even met.

Miss Dorothy Cornford, the librarian, was neatening up after the Great Hot Coffee Orgy, dabbing furiously at potential rings on the scarred and pitted table. When I was a little girl I remember that she had been young and pretty. Now she was old. But never mind—she had acquired wisdom.

I stood up to go. "Never put your head up above the trenches," I told her.

That's when I found out she had become wise. Without missing a beat, she said, "That's right. They might be using real bullets out there."

Real bullets? In Gull Harbor? The idea was laughable.

Five months later I wasn't laughing any more.

2

It was time. The Jetstream NC495WG taxied to its designated station at exactly 1:29 P.M., its tardy arrival unexplained. There was a heightening of noise and activity around us, and in spite of myself I felt a rush of excitement. Persis Willum, who ought to know better, was as turned on by the drama de Groot was orchestrating as any little country bumpkin. And there he was, making his scheduled appearance at the door of his private plane, with a comely stewardess holding the wrapped Rembrandt beside him as the cameras recorded the moment. This, in effect, marked the first step in the opening of Gull Harbor's new museum. The arrival of the Rembrandt, a first-rate one at that, automatically established the credentials of the Waldheim. The publicity wasn't going to hurt the value of the painting, either.

Someone shepherded the rest of the September Seven out of their warm cars and over to the foot of the landing steps where they were joined by Ringwell to be photographed greeting de Groot and his painting as they descended from the aircraft. There were more photographs of de Groot handing his priceless masterpiece into the armored truck as police and security men hovered over the proceedings with nervous eyes and guns at the ready. Suddenly it was over. The van whirled around with a squeal of tires and took off for Gull Harbor, flanked by police cars and outriding officers on motorcycles. My little Mustang joined the procession but the rest took off in other directions. The unwrapping of the Rembrandt at the museum would be covered only by a few reporters: the majority preferred to photograph the painting when they did their big story on the night of the opening.

17

As far as they were concerned, the main event of the day was over.

The twenty-minute trip to Gull Harbor was uneventful except for the people in other cars who gawked at us and wondered what celebrity or dangerous criminal was being transported in the windowless van. They would find out in the next edition of their newspapers.

It was 2:27 P.M. when we roared between the stone gates that marked the entrance to the Waldheim and flew up the long drive, bluestone pebbles scattering from under our wheels. There were no potholes in the drive now.

Two museum guards ran down the marble steps to receive the painting, which was handed over to them without ceremony. Then the escort group climbed onto their motorcycles and into their cars and took off, careening back down the lonely driveway like fighter planes on their way to combat. The guards carried the Rembrandt into the main gallery, formerly the ballroom, and began to unwrap it. First the quilted green covering was carefully removed, then the rolls of transparent tape stripped away to loosen the two wooden panels that bracketed the painting front and back. Last to come off was the plastic that encased the Rembrandt, and the painting was revealed in all its breathtaking beauty.

All along de Groot had been promising us a "little-known Rembrandt that would stun the art world." Well, he had not exaggerated: it *would* stun the art world. Nothing had prepared us for the true impact of the painting. This was Rembrandt's bride, painted in the tenderness and passion of new love, a Saskia van Uylenburgh as beautiful as the day she was painted, who spoke to us from the canvas on behalf of all Youth and said what the young always believe: "I will never grow old."

We prepared to hang the painting immediately: it was safer on the wall than on the floor. A bored *Newsday* photographer lounged around, watching us and waiting for his cohorts to arrive. The *Times*'s critic, David Shirey, would be along later, as would *Newsday*'s Malcolm Preston.

There were two armed guards present, one of them stationed at the entrance door. A third had just stepped out for a coffee break, which didn't help my peace of mind: why couldn't he stay inside and drink from a paper cup? It was just one of the battles lost to Ringwell's newly created culture czar, William C. Brown, the county executive's perfectly groomed, perfectly barbered, perfectly self-possessed alter ego. How I'd like to ruffle that man! My fingers itched to light up a cigarette, but I willed them to be still. Two weeks since I'd given up smoking. And counting.

A few unofficial types wandered in and out. Two electricians from Amber Electric checked the spots and floods. Somebody arrived from Gull Harbor Florists about flowers and greenery for the preview night. A harassed secretary from the county pool ran around with a clipboard trying to make sure the labels for the paintings were correct. Somebody from the liquor store inquired about delivering champagne for the opening. Somebody else was putting the finishing touches on the newly installed alarm system. There was, in short, a great deal of general confusion. Too much. I made a note to speak to Brown about our security.

He was no doubt upstairs now with Ringwell. Ringwell already had a perfectly good office at the county seat, but he had one here, too, side by side with Brown's. Ringwell would come down, I knew from experience, just in time to get into the photographs. God knows what mysterious signal activated him, but it always did. He would be out of breath, but present. Otherwise he remained in his lair, crouched behind a desk full of telephones and administered to by a battery of young and attentive secretaries, all of them civil service. Bill Brown did likewise. The only difference was that his secretaries were not only attentive but adoring: he was not, actually, bad-looking. The door between the two offices was always open.

While Ringwell would not be seen until the last moment, the new museum director was, on the other hand, definitely visible, a light-footed figure in pinstripes, run up, he confided to one and all, by his bespoke tailor in London. "Still expensive," he said, twirling, "but who could resist." The *Newsday* photographer looked as if he'd had a sudden attack of indigestion, but said nothing.

I had thought I would detest Winkworth Gay Gaud. First, there was his name. "Call me Wink," he said instantly to anyone upon being introduced. "My entire name is Winkworth Gay

Gaud, isn't that frightening? But my grandmother was an extravagant admirer of an artist named Winkworth Gay when she lived in Boston—a lovely artist. But you can't call anyone 'gay' today, so Wink it is." Then he would give a little smile and dart off.

I happen to be an admirer of Winkworth Gay's landscapes, and was sure that Gaud had simply appropriated the name, but as soon as I became convinced that his name really was Winkworth Gay, I started to like him a little bit. Before long it grew to be a large bit. I suppose he was a lightweight—I think he went out of his way to give that impression. He seemed almost a caricature of a type of museum person. Certainly his credentials were impressive —a tour in the museums of Rennes, Nice, and Pau as curator and a fistful of enthusiastic references. I could see why Ringwell had hired him—he looked fantastic on paper. If we expected the new director to have clout, however, we were disappointed. He never forced his opinion on us, never took the front of the stage, never crossed Ringwell or Brown—or anyone else, for that matter. He seemed mostly to smile and listen and watch and say a lot without ever saying anything.

I didn't care; I liked him. Was it because it was the two of us against the politicians? Because he called me "Beauty" and brought me flowers, expecting nothing in return? Because I longed for and needed a friend in my life just then? I don't know. All I know is I had grown very fond of him in the short time we'd been working together. For all his affectations, he was someone you could rely on.

Right now he was offering everyone a glass of white wine, including the electricians.

"We all have to celebrate a little," he was telling them. "We've been working on this show for what seems like forever. We never could have done it without this darling girl, Persis."

While I was making embarrassed noises, he came over to me. "Persis, have you seen Jason Waldheim yet? Has he come?"

"No, Wink. He said he wasn't sure he could make it up from Washington in time, not with that advisory committee that's been taking up all his time."

"I know." Wink looked disappointed. "Do you realize I still haven't even met the man yet? I mean, this *is* the Waldheim—excuse me." The other photographers had arrived and begun doing whatever it is they always do to get their equipment ready. "Hello, I'm Winkworth Gaud. Named after an American artist . . ."

At which exact moment, with his usual uncanny timing, H. Caldwell Ringwell walked in. And he had a girl with him. She was young, palely blonde, round-faced, with a milk-white skin, and I had never seen her before. The photographers perked up at once.

H. Caldwell knew them all by name; it was the sort of thing he always knew. He began at once to shake hands, his entire frame shaking with the enthusiasm of this activity. "George—you're sure lookin' great. Hiya, Ed, how's that ulcer doin'? Aaron—long time no see—how's the kid? Listen now, when you've wrapped it up down here, you come on up to my office upstairs and I'll give you a real drink. Got some special stuff up there. Right?"

"Right," they chorused. "We getting a shot of you today?" As if they couldn't guess.

The county executive waved at Wink Gaud: he was too smart to order his own picture taken. There were, after all, the niceties and Wink was one of the people paid to perform them.

"O.K., fellows," Wink obliged, "Mr. Ringwell first, so we don't waste his valuable time—you know his tight schedule." Ringwell beamed and succeeded in looking busy, but not too busy for the press. "How about one of him alone with the painting?"

It was done in a second. H. Caldwell Ringwell knew from long experience how to pose. He faced the cameras head-on.

"Now one with Mr. Ringwell and the young lady and the Rembrandt," Wink said.

This one took longer because the county exec had to jockey the girl around so that he could present himself at his best. Then their smiles had to be coordinated. All the while the newsmen were calling, "Who's the girl? What's she doing here, Mr. Ringwell?"

Ringwell ignored them until the last picture was taken. I've never seen a man so concerned with his camera image. Then he patted her on the shoulder and said, "It took me months of hard detective work to find this little girl. Don't think it was easy. I wasn't even sure until the last minute I'd get her. Never said a word to anyone, even Wink and Persis here."

It was true. I hadn't known until a few minutes ago that a girl was going to be added to the scenario.

"So what's the story?"

Ringwell always played his exits to perfection. "Wink will fill you in, fellows—don't want to sound like I'm bragging. Besides, I have got to get back to my desk. See you later."

Wink got the signal. "Gentlemen, it gives me great pleasure to announce that the young lady with us today is none other than Saskia van Uylenburgh, a direct descendant of the woman whose portrait hangs before you now." There was a slight buzz. The girl dimpled. "Three months ago, County Executive Ringwell spotted a clipping in a Paris newspaper that noted she would be in the United States at this time, studying modeling in New York City. Well, you know Mr. Ringwell, fellows: he's a tiger when it comes to his museum and his county. He combed New York, checking every modeling school and everyone in them until he found her. Then he sent his car in for her and he's arranged for her to be put up at the Peter Stuyvesant Club after the preview. So how about a couple of pictures of this lovely girl looking at this lovely painting?"

"What about the owner? Shouldn't he be in this, too?"

Wink explained that de Groot was supposed to have been at this photography session, but had been forced to rush back to his racing affairs in Florida: the Rembrandt had come from his home there. He'd be back in Gull Harbor for the opening. Like all the September Seven, he commuted endlessly between a roster of houses scattered throughout the world, wherever business or pleasure dictated.

They looked cheered at the prospect of photographing the pretty girl again. "Who did you say she was, exactly? Descendant of Rembrandt?"

"Nearly right. . . . Rembrandt's wife, whose name was Saskia van Uylenburgh, too."

"Descendant of Rembrandt—got it." So much for literal truths. "Spell, please?"

"S-A-S—" Wink began, then gave an expressive shrug. "Ask Persis Willum. It's the kind of thing she not only knows but can spell." Wink was being silly—he knew it as well as I did. I spelled it, frowning at him. Flashbulbs went off. The girl looked bemused until the last second, then smiled prettily. Very professional, I thought. She hadn't said a word so far—not that she'd had a chance.

"This the only portrait of the wifie?"

Wink rolled his eyes. The ball was definitely in my court.

"There were a lot of portraits. This is considered one of the earliest. Perhaps it was even painted before their marriage—no one is sure." I glanced at the release that had come with the picture: they all had one, too—but you couldn't count on their ever reading them. "This painting has been in an unbroken series of private collections in the Netherlands and France until Mr. de Groot acquired it recently. It has never, to anyone's knowledge, been exhibited to the public before."

"Year?" They were starting to look bored again.

"1634, more or less. We date it by certain characteristics of Rembrandt's work. The porcelainlike finish, for instance—see it? And the perfection of the work on the lady's features." I kept staring at the painting, drinking it in. I happen to be a Rembrandt freak, among other things. "Look at this," I went on, unable to contain my enthusiasm. "You can see the spotlight effect on this part of the figure. Melodramatic. Theatrical. Typical of the early work."

I stopped suddenly. I knew better than to go on like that. Most people were interested in only one aspect of art: how much did it cost?

And sure enough. "What's it worth?"

I braced myself. "Money couldn't buy it."

"Come on, Mrs. Willum. How much? Even Rembrandts have

a price, you know." Very sarcastic. No wonder Wink had passed the buck to me. This was bad business. Bandying numbers around in the newspaper was asking for trouble. Criminals can read.

"Impossible to say, really. Couldn't you simply say it was priceless?" It was priceless, in truth: there would never be another like it. I didn't know how much Willem de Groot had paid for it and I was sure he wouldn't say—$3 or $4 million was my guess—but placing dollar values on masterpieces like this was a silly exercise.

They weren't buying. "Two million? Three? Four?"

Oh, what's the use, I thought. If I don't answer them, they'll just go to the telephone and call a different museum or Parke-Bernet and come back with some ridiculous figure. I looked desperately at Wink. He was studying the hand-carved cornices over the doorway and windows with ruthless concentration. No help there.

"Come on, Mrs. Willum. How much?"

But I never had to answer. While all this discussion was going on with the concentration inherent in any talk involving enormous sums of money, two nuns in black habits had entered the room. The nuns were black as well and one of them was holding a sign and showing it to people as she passed. The second had a contribution box. They headed straight toward us, smiling. WE ARE DEAF MUTES, the sign said in neat letters.

Wink Gaud and the rest of the men started automatically to rifle their pockets in quest of suitable coins. I opened my bag and began to dig around in a similar search, but I was seething: how dare the guards let unauthorized persons into the museum during a photography session? What did the guards think they were hired for, anyway?

The nun with the sign paused and seemed to back up against the wall. The second one swept forward, black skirts swirling around her legs. The men got their money out, ready to drop it in her box. They kept their eyes down, too polite to stare. The nun kept going, right on past them . . . then, quite calmly and unbelievably, she was taking the Rembrandt off the wall.

"Wait a minute," I cried, not comprehending the situation. "You mustn't touch that picture!"

She paid no attention, and I remembered she was deaf.

I screamed at the guard. "Stop her . . . can't you see what she's doing?" She now had the painting off the wall, nestled against the skirt of her habit, holding it painted side in.

I still didn't understand what was happening. Why was she hanging on to the blonde girl, pushing her in front of her? What was this all about? I lunged, intent on only one thing—I had to take the Rembrandt away from her. It was *my* responsibility.

"No, Persis, don't. They're armed . . . guns." That was Wink.

But he was too late. I almost had the painting when I saw what was in her other hand—when I understood why no one was doing anything to save the Rembrandt and the girl. It was a gun—they both had guns. And one of them was swinging toward me. All I had time to do was to throw up my hands.

There was an explosion of light and a feeling of being perfectly conscious while falling a very long way down a tunnel into darkness. No pain, just an explosion in my head.

And somewhere during that long effortless descent, I thought I heard a gun go off.

But I wasn't sure. Maybe, I thought, I'm dreaming.

3

I was making coulibiac and it was going marvelously: coulibiac, dream of my life since that first lyrical taste at Restaurant Flavio in Le Touquet a couple of years ago with my aunt Lydia.

Craig Claiborne was watching. He wasn't watching me eat coulibiac, but watching me make it, which was twice as terrifying. His friend, Pierre Franey, was beside him.

"A celestial creation," Claiborne commented. "That's what Czar Nicholas II called coulibiac when he was served it at the Kremlin Palace. I certainly hope this measures up, Pierre."

Franey murmured and cocked an eye at me.

I had progressed to velouté sauce, my wire whisk flying. I scraped the sauce over the salmon in an even layer, and took my brioche dough out of the refrigerator, praying that it would have just the right airy texture.

Suddenly someone else pushed into the room—a weird old gentleman with jaded eyes and a turban of some exotic cloth wrapped around his head as if he had just shampooed his hair.

"Sir?" inquired Claiborne.

"I want my wife," stated the old party, pushing right up to the table where I was finishing my masterpiece.

"This, sir, is a private cooking lesson," I told him crossly.

He began to pound on the table. "I'm Rembrandt van Rijn and you've let someone kidnap my wife and I *want her back*."

He gave a huge bang to the table and I lunged to keep my masterpiece from being swept onto the floor. The ensuing clatter was deafening. . . .

"Mrs. Willum . . . hey, Mrs. Willum. It's all right. Relax."

New faces were hanging over me, peering down. Either the bodies they were attached to were grotesquely tall or I was lying down. They looked like butchers in white coats. But we were doing salmon, not meat. . . .

"Persis, it's me—Edgar Hutton."

Hutton? Once upon a time he'd been one of Rosemary Craig-Mitchell's husbands. In those days he'd been a doctor.

"Doctors?" I ventured tentatively.

"Booth and Mason and Hutton," they answered, smiling. "At your service."

From somewhere below my horizontal level, a starchy presence rose with knees creaking and glared at me. Her arms were full of hospital-style paraphernalia I'd knocked off the table.

Now I recognized the unique stillness. "Hospital?" What a letdown after Claiborne and Franey. "Why?"

"We had to do a little hemstitching on the side of your head," Hutton said. "Your face is quite all right, but you're going to have a headache for a couple of days." Doctors are always so cheery while dispensing bad news.

I thought for a minute. "What happened?" I began to remember the scene. Nuns.

"You took a nasty blow on the side of the head—really laid you open. Head trauma. Loss of consciousness. Retrograde amnesia." Whatever that was.

"When?"

"Yesterday." Out of it for a whole day?

"There was a gun," I said, remembering more.

"That's what you were hit with. Nasty blow . . . but the stitches won't show—we did a nice job. The scar will be O.K. when your hair grows back."

I put a hand up to the side of my head and felt the bandage lightly with my fingertips. I was beginning to sense the headache now, faintly, somewhere beneath the layers of medication.

"Was anyone shot?" There had been shots, I thought.

No one answered because someone else had entered the room and was asking permission to speak to me. I turned my head to see who it might be. The small motion made me aware that I was now the proud owner of the world's biggest headache. I frowned. Frowning hurt. I tried to raise my head to get away from the pain, and that hurt even more.

"Who is it?"

"Lieutenant Johnson, police. Could you answer a few questions for us, Mrs. Willum?"

Muscle-bound blacksmiths were beating a tattoo on my brain, and I suddenly felt all alone. Where was everyone? Where was Aunt Lydie? If she knew I was injured she surely would have come . . . she'd always come. And Gregor—why wasn't he here? He had always—well, almost always—stood by me in the five years I'd worked for him. And Oliver, who was forever saying he wanted to marry me and couldn't live without me—if he loved me, why wasn't he here now?

Then I remembered. It was February, get-out-of-town month. They were all away. Gregor had gone off on a cruise and was right this minute floating insouciantly off the coast of Central or South America. Aunt Lydie? She'd just bought another house, in Hobe Sound this time, and she was trying it out for ambience. "If I don't like it, I shall go straight on to Paris." She always went to Paris when things didn't go her way.

Oliver Reynolds, my sometime-maybe-husband: in California, covering an important exhibition of Chinese art. He'd asked me to come, could not believe I'd never been to California. I wasn't against going to California, I'd told him: it was just that I preferred going in the other direction, like my aunt. France was the place for me.

So everyone was gone and I was alone. Well, it wasn't the end of the world. I'd survived a rotten marriage. I was a pretty fair painter. I could take care of myself.

The doctors stepped back and a new face took their place above me. It was one of those anonymous faces that must be helpful in police work. "Now . . . , Mrs. Willum. Anything you can remember about the perpetrators . . . Height? Weight?"

I tried to recreate the picture in my mind. "There were photographers . . . guards . . . museum director . . . girl. We were all gathered at the end of the room where the Rembrandt was hanging."

"And then?"

I continued to sketch it out in my mind. "All of a sudden these two nuns were sweeping toward us, all in black . . . black faces, too. The guard let them pass. I remember that I was angry. Maybe I shouldn't have blamed him. . . . Nuns, after all."

I was remembering it all now. Their march across the room . . . our embarrassment and sympathy . . . our guilty haste to find money . . . our not meeting their eyes.

"Just as we were getting out our change, one of them started taking the Rembrandt off the wall. I told her to stop . . . shouted . . . she didn't stop, just took the girl and started pushing her in front of her. The painting was in her other hand. I lunged. Then I saw the guns . . . too late."

The girl—I suppose she had had a gun in her back. "What happened to the girl?"

Lieutenant Johnson's mouth tightened. "Used her as a shield to keep the guards from firing. They took her with them when they escaped. There was a car waiting outside."

It had all happened so fast. Poor girl. She had only come to have her picture taken for an art exhibition. And what about the shots? "Was anyone hurt?"

"They scattered some shots around to show they meant business after you tried to stop them."

"But . . . I'm not sure I understand." I was still groggy. "Nuns . . ."

"They weren't nuns, Mrs. Willum. They weren't even women. After they hit you, they took the time to smash the photographers' cameras before they left. It was clear from the way they moved they were men."

"Men." I tried to digest it. I rearranged the picture in my mind. Of course. Men.

"Was someone shot?"

"Not then—afterward. When they were already in the car and almost safely gone. Funny thing . . ." I thought I saw a look of puzzlement. "Seemed so useless a thing to do."

"Who was shot?"

"The director." He glanced at his notebook. "A Mr. Gaud. Tore up his insides pretty good. Now, Mrs. Willum, how about a detail or two about those 'nuns'—anything you can remember. You're an artist, I understand. You may have noticed something."

But my head felt as if a series of explosions was taking place inside it, making my entire body rattle from head to toe. Winkworth Gaud, who always called me "Beauty" . . . my friend . . . my very special friend. He'd tried to warn me. "Don't," he'd shouted. "They're armed."

I couldn't even talk to the no-face man any more.

"I want to see Dr. Hutton. Please. Right now." I was suddenly sniffling and sobbing and generally falling to pieces in front of the poor lieutenant, who wasted no time getting out. If I could have given him my head to take along, I would have done so gladly.

Edgar came galloping in so fast he must have thought I was dying. I stopped crying long enough to ask him the question, even though I dreaded hearing the answer. "Winkworth Gaud—will he be all right, Edgar?"

Edgar picked up one of my hands and patted it briskly. "You must stop this crying, Persis. It will make your head hurt."

"I'm not crying—I'm sniffling. And my head *does* hurt, Edgar. It hurts like crazy. Will Wink be *all right?*"

"You're so dramatic, Persis. Of course he'll be all right. It'll take a while, but things look very good."

My tears dried up instantly as a great surge of relief swept through me. "Tell me about it. Please."

Edgar went on patting my hand in an avuncular way. He had always been a darling: no one ever understood why Rosi had thrown him out. "Gaud was very lucky. His stomach was badly shot up, but fortunately a top urologist was at a conference right here at Harbor House and we were able to get him right away. It was a ten-hour operation. They changed teams of O.R. nurses three times." He said it with pride.

"Then he'll make it?"

"Condition stable. It looks very good."

Edgar said more things, mostly about me and how I should rest and how I could probably go home tomorrow. I didn't really listen to him. I'd heard the one thing I really wanted to hear. I tried to turn my face to the wall because my head was hurting so much, but that was the side with the stitches, so I pulled the sheet up over my face and lay as still as I could, hoping the pain would go away and leave me alone.

Edgar was very nice. He stood right there, talking away in a soothing voice that was meant to relax me. He probably had about a thousand other patients clamoring for his attention, but he stuck beside me, like a true friend.

To distract my mind from the pain, I began to think about other things. A woman had been abducted. A $4 million painting had been stolen—a painting seven people had asked me to be responsible for, no matter how much they might deny it.

Unbidden, the two "nuns" came sweeping back into the landscape of my mind, their skirts swirling against their legs, their movements quick . . . strong . . . definite. Over and over again I watched them make their entrance in my mind, trying to freeze-frame their swift progress across the room so that I could examine them in my mind's eye.

"Stop," I told myself.

Edgar interrupted his monologue. "What?"

"Talking to myself," I said.

"Oh." And he went on talking softly.

Here they came again . . . of course, men. It was the way they walked, sweeping across the gallery. Women didn't move like that. I should have known—I was supposed to be an artist.

And there was something else. I concentrated fiercely, willing myself to think through the waves of pain.

It was the eyes—that was it: black, black faces . . . but a flash of blue when the "nun" with the girl in front of her lunged at me. Men . . . blue eyes . . . black makeup . . .

"Edgar." My voice sounded far away to me, because of the sheet, but he heard me. "What is it, Persis? Pain?"

"Yes, but that's not it. They weren't black, Edgar. I'm sure of it." I pulled the sheet away and stared up at him.

I took him by surprise. "What?"

"The thieves . . . they weren't women, they weren't mute—and they weren't black. It was only makeup."

"Are you sure, Persis?"

"Artist's eye. You'll tell that detective or whatever he was?"

He nodded. "I will. Now don't you worry about it. Worry about getting well." He leaned down and kissed me on the forehead. That's the kind of doctor to have. "Get some sleep now. I'll be by first thing in the morning. I called your aunt, by the way—told her it wasn't necessary to come rushing back from Florida. Here's the button to ring for the nurse . . . and be sure that you do ring her if you need anything—that's what the nurses are here for. Good night now." And he was gone.

I pulled the sheet back up over my face, hoping it would serve as a buffer between me and the pain. The tempo of the blows on to my head was increasing. Bang-bang-bang. The two musclebound blacksmiths had gone and the hammers were being wielded by two black nuns.

Only they weren't nuns and they weren't black.

"Then who are you?" I cried out. The room was empty now. Naturally, no one answered.

4

Most of the uproar that followed immediately upon the double kidnapping at the Waldheim Museum bypassed me. I received special consideration because of my injured head. There was talk of a possible concussion, and Edgar decreed peace and quiet. Even I, though, could not avoid the Roman circus two days later that was the opening night of the new museum.

The newspapers had been having a field day, of course. $4 MILLION PAINTING STOLEN . . . DOUBLE KIDNAPPING . . . WOMAN AND PAINTING ABDUCTED IN MUSEUM HOLDUP . . . TWO WOUNDED IN BIZARRE ART HEIST . . . and, inevitably, "NUNS" NAB MASTERPIECE.

"In a daring daylight robbery today, two pistol-wielding bandits dressed as nuns stole a $4 million Rembrandt portrait and abducted the namesake and descendant of the portrait's subject from the main gallery of the new Waldheim Museum in Long Island, due to open its doors to the public next week.

"A museum adviser was injured by a blow to the head from a pistol and the museum director wounded by gunfire when the fleeing thieves fired three shots as they forced the hostage into a waiting car parked outside the main entrance to the museum. The museum is located on the isolated former Waldheim estate in the environs of Gull Harbor, Long Island. Before fleeing, the thieves smashed the cameras of news photographers who had been photographing the Rembrandt when they were interrupted.

"The bandits, wearing black habits, carried signs identifying themselves as belonging to an order of deaf mutes. Authorities said they knew of no such order. In addition to smashing the photographers' cameras, the thieves confiscated their film before fleeing.

"Speaking on behalf of County Executive H. Caldwell Ringwell, County Arts and Culture Chairman William C. Brown said that the painting was entitled *Saskia van Uylenburgh* and that the painting's namesake, a direct descendant of Rembrandt's wife, had been at the museum as a special guest of the county executive, who had discovered her presence at a modeling school in New York and arranged for her to be included among the many art world celebrities invited to be his guests at the opening. A special reception in her honor was scheduled for later in the week.

"The painting, an early portrait, was dated . . ." Etc., etc.

I arrived at the museum very early. The September Seven asked me to join them, but I couldn't possibly. With the county arts and culture chairman certain to be dancing attendance on Ringwell, and Winkworth Gaud gasping away in the Intensive Care Unit of the Gull Harbor hospital, somebody had to be there to greet the first arrivals, and I didn't think it should be the cleaning woman.

It was just before 9:00 P.M. when I made my dash up the broad front steps of the museum, pausing panic-stricken at the spot where Wink had taken his three bullets in the abdomen.

Once past that trauma, I had to admit that the Waldheim mansion had made a splendid transition to the Waldheim Museum. Great tubs of boxwood accented the porch that led to the imposing front door. Inside, the parquet floors gleamed with many coats of wax. The high, arching windows, the richly ornamented pilasters, the fine moldings, and the elaborate crystal chandeliers were as beautiful as when old Jacob Waldheim had first built the house as a modified version of Versailles.

I had never known Mr. Waldheim: he died long before my time—well before World War II, I believe, in the thirties. He lived to be a very old man. I did know, however—everyone knew—that he had once competed lustily with the likes of such formidable collectors as Isabella Stewart Gardner, J. P. Morgan, Henry Clay Frick, Benjamin Altman, Henry E. Huntington, and John D. Rockefeller, Jr., in the fevered acquisition of great works of art, a pastime that had brought out the fiercely acquisitive spirit in all of them and coincidentally great wealth to their favorite art dealers, such as Joseph (eventually Lord) Duveen.

From the time New Yorker James Jackson Jarvis noted in the 1860s that "it has become the mode to have taste," Old Masters poured into America in wave after costly wave. By the turn of the century, many of Europe's greatest masterpieces had crossed the Atlantic and come to rest on the brocade-covered walls of America's super rich, men like Jacob Waldheim. His masterpieces were the equal of anyone's—and he had the bills to prove it. He was, in other words, the archetypal Great American Collector.

What he wanted next, like all the tycoons, was social acceptance: to be a "financier" was not enough. With that in mind, he built himself a splendid town house and a handsome country house, and then sat back and waited for the invitations to pour in. They didn't.

So he decided to become a board member of the Metropolitan Museum of New York, a guaranteed door-opener. They turned him down cold even after he finally offered them his whole collection together with supporting funds.

No one knew how it happened. "God knows, his paintings were first class," said my aunt Lydia, who is on the board today and whose father was on the board before her and in Waldheim's time. The story she'd always heard was that Jacob Waldheim wasn't quite a gentleman, which was idiotic as most of those old boys weren't exactly gentlemen either. "They were *all* pirates," she said. "But if he'd been born in Gull Harbor, it might have been different. He would have had automatic cachet."

Gregor Olitsky had another version. "They say he had an affair with the wife of the wrong man."

In any case, I thought, as I paused to admire Pierre Richardson's big Renoir *Baigneuse* in the entrance hall, Jacob Waldheim had his revenge now: every social type that could walk or crawl would be on its way to the old man's house tonight. Invitations to the bash were as sought-after as invitations to a first-class bacchanal. I'd heard that even the Museum of Modern Art crowd, accustomed to turning up in "fanciful dress," was scurrying around trying to rent conventional evening dress for this occasion.

I'd been against what seemed like 99 percent of what was happening tonight and been firmly overruled by Brown and Ringwell every time. I had objected to having a band scheduled to play in the Great Hall, to the hors d'oeuvres being served with the champagne (I detest finger food in the presence of great art. It's aesthetically insulting, and besides, things drop all over floors), and to the hard liquor I knew would be served *sub rosa* to anyone who asked for it. Wink had not taken sides.

And there was another thing—for the sake of security I had tried to keep the guest list within reasonable bounds, but this was to be Ringwell's big triumph and he seemed to be inviting everyone in the world to see it. There was only one ray of sunshine. Because of the theft, the place was teeming with security tonight: police, detectives, insurance investigators, guards, and heaven knew who else. Curiously, their presence added to the excitement: people love to be where the action is and if there's a scent of danger, so much the better.

I was not looking great—who could, with a head full of stitches?—but I'd done the best I could with what I had, namely, a skinny Empire dress of pale peach silk with matching stole cut up to make a tight turban to hide the wounded head. The effect was oddly Ingres.

I barely had time to check the flowers, the bars with their nappery, and the placement of the guards when the first guest arrived.

The first guest turned out to be the exec himself, H. Caldwell Ringwell. He must have left his dinner guests finishing their coffee and liqueurs and rushed over. I should have guessed he'd be first: he hadn't racked up a record of 5¾ years in office by bringing up the rear of any procession.

His entrance now was that of an emperor of the Holy Roman Empire, preceded by standard-bearers, flanked by satellites, and smothered in sycophants. It's possible that, as politicians go, H. Caldwell wasn't the worst one to come along—not if you think of the Borgias as politicians. At six feet four, however, he was certainly one of the biggest. Now here he was with all his press agents, his staff, his bodyguards (a surprising affectation), and his favor-seekers.

"Where are the TV cameras," was his opening salvo; he didn't bother to say "good evening."

"Outside," I answered, not bothering to say "good evening" either. H. Caldwell and I had an understanding: we ignored each other as much as possible.

"I know that. I saw them setting up. But why not in here?" He frowned, potentate-style, and so did his entourage. I suppose I should have trembled in my Gucci boots, but I wasn't wearing them. Anyway, the media was not something I controlled.

"They *said* that's where they wished to be as people were coming in."

"O.K., O.K. But I'll want them in here as soon as most of the important people get here. Where's Bill Brown, anyway? Isn't he here yet? I need a rundown on who's important tonight." H. Caldwell wore makeup: I could see the Man Tan shining ochre brown under the bright lights, accentuating the pores of his fleshy nose. He turned from me and waved at his publicity people. "Here comes some of the press: get busy with those releases."

People were beginning to pour in now. The county executive started to limber up his smile in preparation for pressing the flesh of his constituents and reminding them that this cultural triumph was his doing and his alone. He gave his thinning hair practiced strokes with both hands—it was combed from below his left ear up over the top of his head in a last effort to forestall the inevitable—and waded in.

The band had begun to play. They were, as I had anticipated, much too loud and they made the dignified Great Hall shake. The entire place was jammed with people. No one could possibly see the paintings after the first few dozen arrivals. You could not get within two feet of the walls, and there were instant double lines at every bar. It seemed to me that everyone I'd ever known in my life was present, plus a million more I'd never met.

Had all of these people come to see the paintings tonight? Almost certainly not—they had come to see one another and to be seen. There was a feeling of having been trapped in a

Fellini film, an extravagant make-believe spectacle. The elaborately gowned guests could have been actors.

The September Seven arrived together, glittering like the Aurora Borealis. Rosemary Craig-Mitchell was the showstopper in a yellow dress and a long string of pearls that hung down to her kneecaps. The pearls had a gigantic ruby clasp and they swung in a most suggestive way with her every step. Had she copied the idea from the famous portrait of Isabella Stewart Gardner? Probably—it would be just like Rosi.

Mrs. Sandringham, calm and regal in her wheelchair, had stuck two white ostrich feathers on her head in honor of the occasion, and they made her look like a volcano about to erupt. A heterogeneous collection of priceless jewelry gleamed all over her person—bracelets, necklaces, rings, earrings, breast pins, and a tiara—all clinging to her at random as if her maid had stood off, dipped into the jewel safe, and flung things at her, and what had stuck, had stayed. She was nothing less than sensational.

The same could not be said for Diantha Lord. True, she had the ubiquitous Gull Harbor straight teeth and WASP coloring, but now that she was in her Art Stage, she had dressed herself up in a baggy skirt that ended just above the ankle (an impossible length for anyone) and a shapeless blouse and shoes that must have come from Goodwill. She had made one concession to the occasion, however: she wore rings on all ten fingers, every ring a priceless heirloom. Her paternal grandmother had been the Grand Duchess Tania, whose jewels were the pride of czarist Russia, so you can see that Diantha was doing her part to add to the glamour of the evening.

The four September Seven men looked gorgeous. Men in black tie always look gorgeous, just as men in uniform in wartime do. Gregor, who hates black tie and always looks better than anyone, says there's a parallel between men's evening dress and wartime uniforms—both are a form of penance. Richardson, de Groot, Lawless, and General Scott didn't look as if they were doing penance, however. On the contrary, they seemed to be having a splendid time, as were the September Seven ladies—and why not? With the exception of Diantha, who was merely separated from her second husband, they were all either widows (Mrs. Sandringham), between marriages (Rosi), widowers (General Scott), unwed (de Groot), or divorced (Richardson and Lawless). It is typical of Gull Haborites to be divorced or about to be. Gull Harbor has often, I'm sorry to say, been called "the women's exchange."

In any case, they seemed to be enjoying themselves, sticking close together and tossing back the champagne with gusto. To look at them you would never guess they had been blackmailed into lending their collections.

Flashbulbs were popping in unison with the champagne corks. Everyone was being interviewed, even Blossom Rugge, the very intellectual lady who turned up on every art occasion and whose life work it was to organize all artists into a union. I saw Mrs. Sandringham signal to Rosi to wheel her into another room to avoid a certain woman's page reporter who would, we all knew, write something catty about "Gull Harbor socialities."

People were shoving and bumping in an effort to get to the various bars and dropping their disgusting hors d'oeuvres all over the parquet floors, after which other people stepped on them. To make it perfect, Ringwell was plowing his way through the crowd to me.

"Where the hell is Brown?" he demanded when he got to me. "He's supposed to be here helping me. He's got to get that crazy Rugge woman off my neck. Why aren't we showing living artists, she's yelling. Jesus! And the newspapers—how the hell do I know where the girl is or why we haven't received a ransom note yet? Why don't they ask the police?"

The minions fluttered about making pacifying noises, but H. Caldwell was having none of it. His beefy Teutonic face was reddening visibly.

"Listen, missy," he told me evenly, "you just get your little can upstairs to Brown's office and see if he's there, and if he's not, get to a telephone and call around until you find him. Got it?"

I blinked about two thousand times and tried to think of some reply that was both dignified and devastating, but everything I thought of was either not cutting enough or just too plain rude, which was not my style. At this point, Bill Brown finally made his entrance. It was not his usual one. He normally maintained a facade of youthful vigor, but the facade had disappeared. The man standing before us looked weary and grim.

"H. Caldwell . . . trouble. We have a bomb threat."

"What?"

"It came on the phone a half hour ago. I got the call just as I was starting down from my office. An anonymous tip."

Ringwell had turned pale. "A bomb?"

"Said there is a bomb in the museum, set to go off at 11:00 P.M."

H. Caldwell took a quick look at his watch. "My God . . . it's 10:25."

"I called the police at once. The bomb squad already searched the upstairs and the basement. Nothing. A hoax, maybe. Still . . ."

Ringwell was no coward, I'll give him that, and he could make decisions when he had to. "For Christ's sake, Brown, we've got no time to lose. Get these people out of here right now."

Brown didn't move fast enough, however. Before he could act, Ringwell dispatched one of his men to throttle the orchestra, then strode to the middle of the room, stood on a bench, and shouted for silence in his moose-call voice.

"Ladies and gentlemen, we have an unexpected development." He was very calm. "Part of a very exciting evening. We've been informed that there may be a bomb in this building—probably the work of somebody who couldn't get an invitation tonight." There was some laughter. "It's probably a hoax, but as a precaution, we will ask you to go outside quickly and quietly. No time for coats. Sorry. You'll all be back in a minute or two, so don't go away. Let's move quickly."

Some people took their champagne with them. A few refused to budge and had to be nudged out by the security people. There was some confusion to start with, then most people seemed to turn obediently and head for the door. Within minutes the museum was cleared of everyone except the bomb squad. Even so, getting them out was a little like urging a cattle drive through a frothing river.

The paintings could not possibly be removed from the museum in time if there really was a bomb, but if it was truly a hoax, someone should stay behind to guard them, I thought. I tried. They wouldn't let me. They took me firmly by the arms and hustled me out with everyone else, and I had to console myself with the fact that I couldn't have been in two rooms at once in any case. Furthermore, everyone was out here with me, which was comforting.

The crisis was over in just a few minutes, during which we all kept warm by sitting in the cars in the parking lot and sipping the champagne still being passed by the waiters, each of whom had fled the mansion with several bottles, on my orders. No bombs were found, and we all went back.

The drinks flowed like an unending river. The tidbits rained on the parquet floor. The county executive explained to anyone who would listen how the museum was all his doing. The orchestra pulled itself together and proved it knew more than contemporary noise by launching into an appropriate medley of standards such as "Just One of Those Things," "Is That All There Is?" and "You Took Advantage of Me." Apparently the band had a sense of the fitness of things.

Jason Waldheim, finally back from Washington, swam out of the crowd and headed straight for me, moving like some graceful ocean deity. A beautiful, blonde, international-type lady paddled along on his starboard. I couldn't say what it was about Jason Waldheim, but I had always found him dazzling. As a young girl I had watched adoringly as he had progressed across the horizon of the world I lived in. He was always glamorous, always accompanied by some beauty—and always nice to me, even when I was at my youngest and most obnoxious.

It was the same tonight. "Persis Willum! What do you think of all this? It's quite a night, isn't it?" He introduced me to the lady, who smiled tightly and looked off into the distance.

He was standing in front of me with his feet slightly spread, leaning backward a bit, like a man on a tilting deck. Well, it wasn't surprising: he was a yachtsman of note. "We had a little more excitement than I care for a few minutes ago," I said.

"And the other day, I hear. How is your head? That was a near thing. You look wonderful, but are you all right?"

Before I could answer, someone came up and claimed his attention, several someones. He took time, though, to smile back at me before they swept him away. As I said, always nice.

The party had really gotten quite noisy. I suppose it was at least partly due to relief after the tense time of the bomb scare. The September Seven had long since gone home, but I couldn't leave—I had work to do. While the festivities continued, I began my rounds.

First, the main gallery: the Goya . . . the El Greco . . . the Raphael . . . the Gauguin . . . the Manet . . . the Matisse . . . the Picasso . . . all safe.

Then the second gallery where the smaller drawings, watercolors, and oils were hung: the Winslow Homer . . . the little Renoir . . . the Seurat . . .

And here my heart almost stopped. There were two small empty spaces on the wall where earlier there had been a Degas pastel of a dancer and a Whistler oil of fireworks in Venice.

Like the Rembrandt earlier, they were gone. This time they had disappeared when the museum was swarming with security—but also swarming with people and confusion and the frantic activity of evacuating a crowd during a bomb threat.

Three paintings now stolen from the Waldheim.

It was going to be an endless night.

5

Endless wasn't the word for it. It wasn't until very early morning that I stumbled home, exhausted from hours of interviews with the police, the press, the Seven—who appeared to be on some sort of instant grapevine—and God knows who else. And then I'd barely closed my eyes, it seemed, when the phone rang. It was the Gull Harbor Community Hospital.

"Mrs. Willum? This is Nurse Abrams in the Intensive Care Unit. Your cousin Wink Gaud is very anxious to see you. He can't understand why you haven't been to visit him before."

I hadn't been to see Wink for the very simple reason that the I.C.U. allowed no visitors except relatives, and I wasn't one. Cousin? After a first second of astonishment, I played the game. "I wasn't too well myself. But I most certainly am anxious to see him. When can I come?"

"Visiting hours begin at noon." She hung up. Rubbing my eyes, I saw it was already 10:30, and hauled myself out of bed. I'd better call the museum too, I thought.

The Intensive Care Unit of the Gull Harbor Community Hospital is a world within a world. I suppose they all are, in hospitals everywhere. An invisible moat separates those without from those inside, where death is the enemy to be held at bay. Visitors are allowed inside for a maximum of fifteen minutes at set hours of the day. At these given hours anxious relatives, plus a few pseudo-relatives like me, gather in drab little clusters in the hall and stare hopefully at the forbidding door, like nervous pets who have been locked out of the master's house.

We were waiting this way now, about ten of us, with more people coming off the elevator each time it stopped. We all watched the big door or the clock above it, studying the minute hand with grave concern. A few people spoke to one another. They were the elite—relatives who had made this pilgrimage often enough to know one another by sight, often enough to have some hope that their patients inside might survive. . . .

When the minute hand had finally moved to exactly cover the gold numeral 12, a stately nurse appeared in the doorway and motioned to us silently, like some mysterious Muse. Everyone surged forward.

Winkworth Gay Gaud was in the second cubicle to the left as you entered, practically in the doorway. He was separated from his fellow sufferers by what looked like a plastic shower curtain. All of the patients were arranged in a neat square surrounding a bank of desks and equipment from which the nursing staff monitored all beds with maximum efficiency. The head nurse, majestic with authority, challenged any visitor she didn't recognize. When she came to me, I had only to say my name.

"Persis Willum."

"Of course. Mr. Gaud's cousin. He asked me to call you. I'm glad you came. We're very fond of him here. He's been such a good patient. Remember, you must not tire him—he's been a very sick man."

A kindly head nurse. How lucky for Wink.

The room was terrifying. There were no sounds of human voices—these had been hushed to sibilant whispers. The other noises were what unnerved me. From each patient's compartment came sounds alarming by reason of their unfamiliarity—mysterious bleeps, drips, and hums. They were like science fiction noises. And the people in the beds were science fiction people, adorned with an inhuman collection of jars, tubes, bags, and needles.

Wink was no exeception. As I took off my heavy sheepskin coat (last year's extravagance) and dropped it on the single small chair next to his bed, I saw that he, too, had things poked into every available opening and a maze of tubing everywhere, through which liquids burbled and dripped.

"Hello, Beauty." Winkworth Gay Gaud did not look grand. One could scarcely expect him to. His face was a sort of overall gray mud color, like potter's clay. It wasn't easy to smile blithely and tell him he looked good, but it was protocol and so I did.

He smiled back at me crookedly, as if his face hurt him. "I suppose I could be worse, considering. How is everything at the museum?" His voice was weak.

He already knew, of course, about the Rembrandt and the girl being kidnapped and I brought him up to date on the activities since then: the intense police investigation, the FBI interest, the press reports. But I didn't say a word about last night's bomb threat and thefts. Wink had enough trouble—let it wait until he was stronger. Instead, I chattered away gaily about every trivial detail I could recall about the party, hoping to cheer him up and make him smile a little.

"You should have seen Rosi—she was so gorgeous she had the newsmen falling all over themselves trying to get pictures of her. And Mrs. Sandringham almost ran her wheelchair over Ringwell when they came face to face—it was a near thing. Not near enough, unfortunately. Did you ever meet Blossom Rugge? She used to live with that artist, Buffalo Horowitz. Well, she was there, and so was he—only he seemed to be with Diantha, of all people. And . . ."

Suddenly I was aware that Wink had made a slight motion with his hand. He wanted me to stop speaking.

"Beauty," he said, "listen to me. I need your help."

"Of course, Wink. Anything you say."

"It might not be so easy," he said.

I couldn't imagine what was coming. "Just ask me, Wink, that's all."

He paused. I had the impression that we were coming to the reason why he had requested my visit. But what could it be?

"They tell me they'll be letting me out of Intensive Care pretty soon, Beauty." He looked up at me.

I was delighted. "That's wonderful news, Wink."

"*No.*" I was startled by the vehemence with which he spoke. "It won't do at all. That's why I asked the nurse to call you. You must help me, Persis."

Did my face show my astonishment? I suppose so. I won-

45

dered if he was irrational, his mind drugged and wandering. "But Wink, I don't—"

"Don't try to understand." Now he sounded impatient. "Just promise me."

"But, Wink, you don't just get out of bed and walk out of I.C.U. You'll go to another wing and convalesce."

"Exactly. Probably a private room. Mrs. Sandringham and everyone will insist. It's what I don't want, Beauty. You must see that it doesn't happen."

The whole idea was absurd. "Really, Wink, in your condition, you can't just leave."

"I must. I'm sorry, Persis, I can't explain any more than that right now, but it's terribly important. You know everyone here—the board members—"

"But your health, Wink. You still need nurses. . . ."

"Fine. Hire them, as many as I'll need. I'll pay. But arrange for me to be brought home to convalesce as soon as I'm well enough to leave this unit. Arrange for round-the-clock nurses if you insist, but I must *not* stay here. All right, Beauty?"

The pottery gray color had drained from his skin, leaving it transparent and waxy like paraffin. It frightened me. "Nurse!" She was there in an instant.

"Now, now, Mrs. Willum," she scolded, "we mustn't tire him."

"I'm terribly sorry." I reached for my coat.

Wink's voice came thinly from the bed once more. "Persis? Promise me?"

I managed somehow to get past the nurse and lean over and kiss him. "I promise. I'll go see Dr. Hutton right this minute," I whispered. I squeezed his hand and I felt him return the pressure. More than that, he had pressed something into my hand.

The head nurse then proceeded to kick me out. She was polite about it, but firm. "He has to rest, you know. I only let you come because he was so worried about details at the museum . . . always calling for paper to make notes . . . always wanting to telephone. I thought seeing you would ease his mind."

I thanked her and left. Outside the I.C.U. door, I stopped and unfolded the piece of paper Wink had given me.

He'd written down the names of a few people he wanted me to phone. "Call Anderson *re* summer show. Call Blake *re* sculptor in residence." That sort of thing. Nothing I wouldn't have done anyway . . . trivial details. It was surprising: Wink had never been one to worry about trivial details. I studied the paper, frowning.

The edges of the paper were covered with doodles. Like the writing, which was as nearly illegible as one would expect when the writer is in a prone position, the doodles were mostly vague scribbles. There was one that caught my attention, however, because it was so unexpected. It looked to me like a drawing of a bishop in robes and a tall miter. He was seated in the back of a car. In one hand was a gun.

What could it mean? I shook my head and stuffed the paper into the nearest trash basket. Nothing—just doodles. I would remember to make the calls he'd mentioned. Right this moment, the important thing was to find Hutton.

It took me about ten minutes to track him down. Luckily he was in the hospital, seeing patients. The interview was not a success.

"He certainly can *not* go directly from Intensive Care to his home. Are you mad?" Edgar Hutton was scandalized. "It is absolutely out of the question, Persis. It would be medically ill-advised and professionally idiotic. The answer is a definite, unequivocal 'no'."

"But, Edgar, not so long ago no one even went to hospitals at all. People were born at home. Aunt Lydie's parents took an entire floor at the Hotel Belmont in New York for her to have her appendectomy. One of her friends had her babies on the kitchen table. Granted, it cost a bundle to have everything sterilized and equipment moved in and everything, but they all lived. It wasn't such a big deal. So why can't Wink go home? He's European . . . they don't go to the hospital every single second the way we do. You know it can be done. The hospital is for *your* convenience. Look, I'll make you a bargain—if you'll let him leave, I'll take him to my house. That way he'll not only have as many nurses as you want, he'll also have Mrs. Howard, my housekeeper. You remember her? The only thing she likes better than a good wake is a sick patient. She won't leave him alone for a second: she adores illness. Wink's really serious about this, Edgar. He insists on leaving."

Edgar wouldn't budge. "You wouldn't believe the aberrations patients get, Persis, especially healthy men who have never been sick a day in their lives. Any excuse to get out. They even try to jump out windows. Wink's anxiety is not unusual. They all think we're killing them—or are about to."

Luckily he had a call right that minute or I might have lost my temper, and I was much too fond of Edgar to want to be cross with him. While I was waiting for him to finish with the call, a little nurse with black bangs appeared and beckoned to me like the Lorelei.

"I have a message for you to call Mr. Waldheim. If you'll just follow me." She started down the corridor at a rapid pace. Nurses have no time to waste on the healthy.

"How did you know it was for me? The message, I mean?" I was running to keep up with her, the soles of my high-heeled boots skidding on the slippery floor.

"Because the message is for Mrs. Willum and I was on duty the night you came in. I knew Mrs. Willum was the lady with the stitches in the head." She had dashed off to the left and into another wing of the hospital. I caught a glimpse of a sign bearing the words JACOB WALDHEIM WING FOR SPECIAL SURGERY. I wondered if a lot of the special surgery was used to patch up people who fell down and smashed their bones on the hospital floors.

My fleet-footed leader finally stopped at a nurses' station placed strategically at the junction of three corridors. A doctor and a nurse were at one desk, poring over records and consulting in low voices. A second nurse looked up as we approached, smiled, and quickly dialed a number. Then she handed me the telephone. "Mr. Waldheim," she said reverently. I suppose the reverence was fitting for everyone who toiled in the Waldheim Wing, even if the Waldheim at the other end of the line was only a descendant.

"Persis, Jason Waldheim here. The museum said you would be at the hospital. I hope you don't mind my calling. Bill Brown wasn't sure when you'd be in."

"Of course I don't mind." I was surprised, but I certainly did not mind.

"Good. Because I was wondering if we could have a drink together later this afternoon. I was hoping to catch you for lunch, but by the time I tracked you down I was too late. The thing is, I want to talk to you. I could come out from town. . . ."

I thought quickly, reviewing my schedule. Wink? . . . No, he wouldn't be out of the I.C.U. for at least a few days. Tomorrow would be time enough. "No, no—I have to be in New York for dinner tonight anyway. I could just come in a little earlier."

"You're sure it's no trouble? I wouldn't want to inconvenience you."

There was a large mirror on the wall behind the nurses' desk. I stole a quick glance to be sure everything was still in the proper proportions and somewhat presentable. That's what comes of being 36½ years old. It was all right . . . everything was pretty much all there and where it belonged.

"No trouble at all," I assured Jason Waldheim.

"Good. Five-ish? I'll wait for you in my office." He gave me the address on Fifth Avenue.

Oliver Reynolds, the art critic who loves me and worries about my human frailties, says I could be talked into flying in a plane with no wings if the right tone of voice were used. Jason Waldheim had a very nice voice and a very good tone. With no trouble at all he had persuaded me to drop everything I'd planned and drive to New York two hours early for a drink.

What would he persuade me into when I got there?

6

I detest driving to New York—not New York itself, just the drive. The first part of the trip is pleasant enough—sometimes there are horses grazing in the fields along the road and at Roslyn you pass the memorial park dedicated to Christopher Morley (an old friend of Aunt Lydie's, by the way). After that things are pretty grim and I always have to put my mind firmly on outside matters to keep from noticing the combat zone that is the Long Island Expressway, with its cannibalized wrecks of automobiles and its car-struck dead animals, left to rot where they fall. What must visitors think of this nightmare alley?

I thought of Wink instead. I wanted to erase the image of the battered man I had just left. As I whirled along the expressway service road, congratulating myself on having had the wit not to plunge immediately into the bumper-to-bumper expressway on my left, I tried to remember Winkworth Gaud as he'd been when I'd first met him. . . .

It had been the day I first went to the Waldheim to fulfill my promise to the September Seven. Rosi and Diantha had come with me, as eager as I was to meet and assess the new director Ringwell and Brown had hired without consulting anyone in Gull Harbor. It was early November, and Rosi had been at some big ball in town the night before. She had dark shadows underneath her eyes and kept screaming that she was going to die if she didn't get a Bloody Mary *immediately. The* Princess Margaret had been there, she said, and Elizabeth Taylor Warner. They were both very good-looking, she told us generously . . . in fact, really handsome. All of this between moans.

Diantha wasn't amused by Rosi's drama. She was hurrying

to get to the Brooklyn Museum to see an exhibition of women artists and all that moaning was taking up the time she needed to get her directions straight . . . she wasn't exactly sure how to get to Brooklyn and secretly feared getting lost in Bedford-Stuyvesant, although, being Liberal, she was ashamed to admit it. She was fretting and Rosi was moaning as we climbed the twenty-two marble steps to the museum. When Winkworth Gay Gaud opened the front door and stepped out to greet us, they both shut up as if they had been shot.

"W-e-e-e-e-e-l-l," Rosi said, stopping dead in her tracks and letting the word out slowly in one great sigh of appreciation.

There are a lot of attractive museum people around today—Tom Hoving and Carter Brown, to name two—but Winkworth Gaud was the best. For one thing, he had a whole lot of pewter-colored hair, very thick and wavy at the back and nothing less than sensational against his very tan skin. For another, he was beautifully constructed: not terribly tall but, like a Frenchman, just tall enough. Beautifully cut clothes, too.

Rosi got her self together in a hurry. When we arrived, her hair had been twisted in a careless coil on top of her head and the jeans and georgette blouse from Givenchy she had been wearing looked very offhand. Suddenly, in the space of a deep breath, her hair was tumbling fetchingly over one eye and the blouse was unbuttoned another three or four inches. We hadn't seen her make a move.

"I'm Rosemary Craig-Mitchell," she was saying, holding out her hand and shaking her head just enough to make her long hair flow out in a frame around her face. If ever she cared to give lessons on seduction, I decided, I would fight for the right to enroll.

"And I'm Diantha Lord," said the Grand Duchess Tania's granddaughter, springing to the fore gamely. She was, after all, from stock that had crossed Siberia in the dead of winter just two jumps ahead of the Red Army—without losing a single jewel.

And Winkworth Gaud stepped forward. He didn't exactly *step* forward—he more . . . minced up. Then he puckered up his mouth and trilled, "I'm Winkworth Gay Gaud. The Winkworth

Gay is after a wonderful Boston artist my grandmother admired extravagantly. But everyone calls me Wink. You too, please. We mustn't stand on ceremony, must we?"

I thought the ladies were going to faint—from disappointment, you understand. An attractive new male is hailed with cries of joy in Gull Harbor: the ladies do everything short of firing off the cannon at the yacht club to celebrate a new arrival. There can never be too many attractive male prospects to satisfy the divorced or about-to-be-divorced Gull Harbor belles. But Winkworth Gay Gaud—oh, cruel fate. It was immediately all too apparent that, while he would doubtless make a delightful friend and confidant, he would never become the woman's home companion of the sort that would satisfy the needs of our local ladies.

I must say that once Rosi and Diantha recovered, they took it well enough. In a very short time they actually grew fond of him and traded gossip and confidences with him freely, as did we all. He was often at Mrs. Sandringham's, chatting with her about her greenhouses and helping in the potting shed. He got along famously with the general, who was charmed to discover that Wink was a war buff—the two were always off in a corner arguing about lost battles and failed campaigns. He could discuss international golf with Pierre Richardson and flying with David Lawless, who had his own small plane. Willem de Groot was delighted to find that Wink knew a considerable bit about horse racing around the world. "There was a time when if it twitched, I bet on it," Wink confessed. "That was before art became my real passion. But I still keep up with racing—once bitten, never cured." Even Ringwell and Brown seemed to like him, although they gave him very little authority.

I must admit, though, that Wink was not generous with information about himself. We did find out that his mother had left Boston before he was born to marry a Belgian painter who had died in the late twenties. Wink had grown up in Antwerp, he said, where his mother had made a genteel living by giving English lessons and occasionally selling a painting by her late husband. Other than that, he had little to say about himself.

He had a good touch when it came to the museum. He was

efficient, gentle, considerate. He did not mind having to attend to the most humble and boring details, nor the facts that Ringwell was obviously going to take credit for anything he did and that Bill Brown was usurping authority that should have been his. In the end, he was accepted by everyone because he posed a threat to no one, either as a person or as a man.

And now he was in trouble and needed my help. I made a note to make some phone calls tomorrow.

I had negotiated the expressway and was on the approach to the Triborough Bridge now, the monumental towers of Manhattan lined up along the East River on my left like a mountain range of steel and glass. Then I was fishing out my seventy-five cents for the tollbooth and noting the hour on the clock above the attendant. By the time I got downtown and found a parking place for my car and arrived, out of breath from hurrying, I was going to be late for my appointment with Jason Waldheim, but not by much.

What did Jason want with me?

7

Jason Waldheim's office was something from a 1930s movie, all glass and mirrored tables and fat, squatty, pure white upholstered furniture with a white rug to match. There was a single enormous Biedermeier desk . . . tall lamps with twisting fruitwood stems, one or two with naked Tiffany ladies dancing . . . two walls of floor-to-ceiling windows framed in heavy white satin. Roz Russell and Cary Grant never had a better set to play in. There was even a white bar along one wall, heavily mirrored. It was amusing: as if Jason Waldheim were putting everyone on.

But as he rose and walked across the deep white carpet to greet me, I saw that the office was the perfect setting for the man —he strode toward me with the ease and elegance of a tuxedoed second-story man picking up the Hope diamond while the ball went on downstairs.

"You were a good sport to come on such late notice," he said. Taken inch for inch, Jason was not good-looking—his face was too long and so was his nose—but the sum total was devastating. Maybe it was the aura of power that surrounded him and all that money: the Waldheim Fund . . . the Waldheim Foundation. . . . He must have been in his late fifties, but he looked easily ten years younger.

"I have one of the best views in town—why don't we have our drinks here?" He was already taking my coat—obviously we were staying. "What will you have?"

"White wine?" His bar looked up to it.

"Of course. I have a nice Graves chilling. A Château Olivier, 1971, if you'd care for it. Or would you prefer a Blanc Fumé de Pouilly?"

I wasn't going to let him get the best of me. "The Pouilly Fumé, please. The Graves is almost too special. A Château du Nozet? Fabulous."

I wasn't Lydia Wentworth's niece for nothing. Her table glorified the good wines. Jason Waldheim was amused. He looked at me for a second with raised eyebrows, then turned without comment and began to open the wine expertly. I heard the musical clink of very good crystal.

While Waldheim played sommelier, I studied the room again. Lights were coming on all over New York now as darkness descended, and his view *was* breathtaking. I could see the East River and the arching lights of the 59th Street Bridge looking like an angel's necklace. Now I understood why the room was all in white—nothing must be allowed to compete with the view outside . . . no disharmonies permitted. There weren't even any paintings to distract the eye—photographs, but no paintings. The photographs were perfect for the room. I wandered around looking at them. Some were hung right over mirrored sections of wall, creating an interesting, disembodied effect of pictures floating in free air. Everyone was there who should have been there to establish a thirties mood: George Hoyningen-Huhne, Man Ray, Brassai, Edward Steichen, even a couple of early Louise Dahl Wolfs.

"The photographs are perfect in this room," I said. "Perfect with all this white."

"I'm glad you approve." Jason handed me my wine. "Come and sit down."

The soft glow of a lamp reflected on the mirrored coffee table and cast slivers of icy white against the crystal glasses. A secretary appeared with a silver tray covered with assorted cheeses and Bremner Wafers and Carr's Craquelins.

"From Tony's around the corner," Waldheim said, thanking the girl, who smiled meltingly at him and left, closing the door carefully behind her. I realized suddenly that I was hungry. I had given up eating lunch the year I turned twenty-six on the theory that since everything was supposed to be downhill from then on, one needn't add to the precipitous slide in any way. Every now and then, however, the abstinence backfired. Like now—I was starved. I dove into the cheeses with enthusiasm and took a healthy sip of the wine. Waldheim watched me, smiling.

"Don't you ever eat before five?" he asked.

"Not when I'm in complete control. I'm trying to wean myself away from three meals a day: one is enough to sustain life."

"Well." He grinned and crossed one elegantly tailored leg over the other. "You certainly aren't the typical museum lady."

"No? What's typical?" I went on eating and drinking, but slower.

"Someone a little frightening, I suppose. Firm jaw and all that."

It was impossible to imagine Jason Waldheim being frightened of anything, including a woman. "I *do* have a firm jaw." I stuck it out to show him.

He laughed. "I might add that you also have 'all that.' Indeed, you've turned out rather well."

"For example?" We were being playful, what I call cocktail sparring.

He considered me carefully, cheese, crackers, and all. "Not too bad, considering all the years you spent in braces—yes, I remember those braces. Svelte, I'd say. Slim. *Soignée.*"

If I couldn't be six feet tall, seventeen years old, and cadaverously thin, then slim, svelte, and *soignée* would do just fine. It was a great line. He'd probably been using it for years.

"Thank you very much. You have just acquired a slave for life. Now—what did you want to see me about?" It was time to stop fooling around: compliment time was over.

He was ready, too. "As you know, I have very little to do with the Waldheim Museum. My interests are here in New York City, not on the island, although I do still have a house there for occasional weekends. When my grandfather left his house for a museum, we—the family—all understood that our involvement was to be minimal, if any. He gave the house to the county free of nearly all strings."

I nodded.

"Nonetheless," he continued, "I still have to be concerned

with what goes on at that damn museum. The place was named after my grandfather, after all, so to a certain extent *his* image is connected with whatever image the museum projects. And the image they're projecting is lousy."

I couldn't disagree. "What's happened there is a nightmare."

"I keep hearing these rumors that Ringwell would like to change the name to the Ringwell Museum—and, do you know, I'm not at all sure that I'd be against it. On the other hand, the mansion was left with the specific codicil that the museum would bear grandfather's name in perpetuity, so *I* can't very well initiate a change without ending up in some kind of a messy lawsuit. The whole situation is a pain in the ass—excuse me, but it's true." He got up nervously and brought a silver bucket of ice over from the bar and poured some more of the wine that was cooling in it.

"Furthermore," he went on, "I don't trust those two politicians, Ringwell and Brown. They want to use that museum for their own purposes and the farther away I stay, the happier they'll be. I can expect nothing from them. They'd like to forget that there's still a Waldheim alive." He plunged the bottle back into the ice bucket with a force that made the glasses rattle on the table.

"I understand," I said. "You have a responsibility to your grandfather's name."

"Exactly. The poor old bastard wanted his name to mean something good in the art world: and a screwed-up museum isn't exactly what he had in mind." His intense eyes searched my face. "What's going on out there? Three paintings stolen, the director shot, a girl kidnapped, a bomb threat. You've been there the whole time. What the hell's going on?"

"I don't know."

"Well, it strikes me as very odd. So many things happening in such a short span of time—how much bad luck can a new institution have? I'm very concerned."

"I know. We all are."

"I know that you're there to represent the interests of the collectors who lent their paintings for the opening exhibition.

Personally, I think that they're all absolutely mad . . . anyone doing that sort of thing today is mad, with all the art thieves around. Look how it all turned out. What a disaster."

"Aunt Lydie is like you—she doesn't believe in lending her paintings for any cause, however good."

"Intelligent woman. Now this is my question: do you think you could include me in your list of responsibilities? Along with protecting the interests of the collectors, would you accept the protection of my grandfather's name? Just keep your eyes and ears open . . . let me know if you sense anything odd . . . I don't know how to put it. Just stay on the *qui vive*, I guess. I realize it's a most ambiguous request, but *I* can't be there—you *are*. And I'd take it as the most tremendous favor. Let me know if you find anything unusual, anything at all."

I couldn't help laughing. "You sound like a man expecting to uncover sabotage."

He did not find it funny. "Sabotage? Would anyone do that?"

"Not unless it was Blossom Rugge and her gang—they're the Art Underground, against the Establishment and all that. But I can't imagine them stealing Rembrandts and shooting off guns . . . a bomb, maybe. But no guns." I wasn't being serious. I couldn't imagine Blossom Rugge's group doing anything more dangerous than talking.

"Artists . . . hmmm. Hardly likely. What about those collectors?"

The very idea astonished me. "Mrs. Sandringham and the general and everybody? You must be joking! With all the money they have, they can buy Rembrandts—they don't have to steal them. And can you imagine any of them shooting Wink Gaud or hurting the girl?"

"We don't know that the girl's hurt." He got up, put his glass down carefully on the table, and walked over with his stride that was like springs uncoiling to stand in front of the east window, hands clasped behind his back. "I lunched with someone in the FBI in Washington" (probably the director himself, I thought) "and he tells me he doubts very much it's the Art

Mafia. No word has been received from the kidnappers yet, no ransom demand . . . they'd have talked money by now. It doesn't seem to be any extremist group, either."

"What about a couple of crazies—amateurs who did it just for kicks or because they like paintings or hate museums?"

He turned to me with a grim face. "I hope not. The amateurs are the really dangerous ones."

"More dangerous than the professionals or extremists?"

"Yes. Because when things go wrong, and something always does, they blow up . . . fall apart. People die."

I felt a chill. "What about the girl?" She was the one who haunted me.

Waldheim shrugged. "According to my contact, everything's being done that can be done. Every law enforcement agency is on it, I assure you."

"I know." Gull Harbor was inundated with them. "But why did they take her? It wasn't necessary, was it?"

"Of course—they needed cover. After all, the guards were armed. Look, Persis, they're making every effort to find her. You can take my word: they're all out there looking."

"But what if they don't find her . . ."

His voice was brusque—businesslike. In a strange way, I found it comforting. "Look, Persis, everybody's being kidnapped today. Read the papers. Argentina, Italy, Brazil, Ireland, West Germany, France. Ransom is paid and that's that—most of them come home safe and sound. Look at this." He reached over to his desk and handed me the *New York Post*: GERMAN INDUSTRIALIST KIDNAPPED the headline blared. "This guy will be sent home as good as new the minute his company gets up 6 million or so in ransom." So why hadn't *we* received a ransom note yet?

He must have seen that it wasn't working because he moved away from me to open the newspaper, folding it back to page 5 to show a police artist's drawing of the kidnapped girl. Was it possible, I thought, that in this short time she was already no better than page 5 news? I looked at the sketch—it was not very good. Well, how could it be, after all? The artist had never laid eyes on the girl . . . I had.

"That's a poor likeness," I said.

"But, as you see, the newspapers and police aren't letting anyone forget about her."

"True—but they'll never find her if that's all they have to go on." I put my wineglass down and glanced at my watch. Nearly time to go on to dinner. "Look, Jason, I'll be glad to keep you abreast of anything that happens out at the museum . . . not that I think anything more is going to happen—what's left? But I'll keep my eyes open. And now I must go."

We stood up. "Wonderful," he said.

He leaned down to give me one of those brother-sister kisses everyone gives everyone else in Gull Harbor . . . but something went wrong. His hands tipped my head back and my arms went up around his neck. There was nothing brotherly or sisterly about the kiss that followed. It was great. It explained all those beautiful women who adored him.

"I've been wanting to do that ever since you got rid of your braces," he murmured.

He had taken me totally by surprise. I should have been angry, except that I'm not a little debutante: I'm a woman. And what happened was what happens between a man and a woman. I liked being in his arms, I felt at home there . . . and yet . . . why would he want *me*?

He answered before I could ask. "You're a very attractive lady, Persis Willum, you know that, don't you?—and you've got more courage than half an army. When I heard what happened to you, and then saw you at the museum last night, I realized I'd forgotten how . . . fond I've always been of you. Even with those braces." He grinned. "I realized too how much I wanted to know you better—and I *don't* mean because of the museum. What do you think, Persis? No strings. I promise." And he made it sound like a promise. But how could I have an affair without becoming involved—especially with a man like Jason Waldheim? Could I escape unscarred?

"I don't know." I drew away from him. Then I ran my finger down the seven beautiful buttons of his shirt. "I have to think."

I walked across the white room and picked up my coat. "I

usually fall in love in April." It was a silly thing to say, but it happened to be true.

"It's almost April now," he answered.

I left before either of us could say more. I would have to think about this. . . .

8

Mrs. Howard, my devoted but domineering "houseworker" (her term), was long gone by the time I got home: she had finished her cleaning chores, drawn the curtains, and put last night's chicken with orange and pecans in a casserole ready for the oven. Mrs. Howard was no cook, but she was perfecting the art of recycling leftovers. Her other culinary virtue was that she was expert at preparing salad greens . . . they would be crisping in the refrigerator right now. I had forgotten to tell her I was dining in town.

Mrs. Howard may not have been waiting for me, but her cat was. Maybe she was actually my cat, although I hadn't planned it that way and wasn't ready to admit it. Mrs. Howard had found her . . . Mrs. Howard had invited her in . . . Mrs. Howard had even named her.

"Her name is going to be Isadore Duncan because she's always jumping around," she had told me.

"Isador*a*, Mrs. Howard."

"That's what I said, Isadore Duncan. I seen the movie."

So Isadore the name remained. I continued to nurse the fantasy that Isadore was only visiting me until Mrs. Howard found a landlady that accepted pets, but in my heart I feared the worst.

In fact, I had a peculiar feeling that from the beginning the cat was meant to be mine. "A house without no pets and no men ain't no good," my housekeeper had said often enough. She quite openly preferred "misters" to women, and as I showed no signs of producing a "mister" for her, she'd produced a pet for me. Mrs. Howard and my Aunt Lydie were both determined that

I should marry again, which was totally unfair, as neither one of *them* was willing to take the matrimonial plunge.

To date, Isadore Duncan and I had one thing in common: we both detested the ringing of the telephone. The way the cat greeted me now—tail lashing and forehead frowning—advised me instantly that the instrument had been annoying her again and that I'd better do something about it, like yank it out of the wall—permanently.

"Sorry, Isadore," I apologized, rushing to the hall phone before I even removed my coat. I saw at once that she had already taken her usual steps . . . the receiver lay on the floor, buzzing angrily. I picked it up and replaced it.

"Apologies," I mumbled. The cat meowed and took off around the room at about a hundred miles an hour, a streak of orange marmalade skimming across the tops of chairs and tables, and sailing, finally, onto the mantelpiece.

"Simmer down, please," I begged. "I suppose the phone's been ringing since Mrs. Howard left and I'm sorry. Silence will now reign."

I was wrong. At that very instant the telephone rang again, deafeningly.

It was Oliver calling from California—Oliver Reynolds whom Mrs. Howard considered the most promising candidate for my live-in pet. "Persis—you all right? Your phone's been out of order, I think. I was worried."

Worrying about me was a disease with Oliver. He must have called fifty times since the theft of the Rembrandt.

"I'm fine, Oliver. Really."

"When I heard two more paintings had been stolen . . . listen, Persis, why not catch a plane and come out here? I don't like the sound of what's going on. I think you should get out of there."

"Don't be silly, Oliver. Whoever's doing all this isn't interested in me. They're interested in paintings, and they must have stolen enough from us by now. It's all over, I'm sure."

Oliver was an art critic and inclined to be ponderous at times.

Being a big-time critic makes people that way. He was also convinced that I was giddy, heedless, and even downright facetious. In the short time before he spoke again, I could imagine him reviewing all of these things about me in his mind and counseling himself to be patient with me.

"Please be serious, Persis. You must realize that what's happening out there is not a matter for levity."

I was instantly contrite. "I know. I'm sorry. Tonight I'm going to stay right here with my doors locked and do a portrait sketch of the girl who was kidnapped." I'd gotten the idea at Jason's that night—it had to be better than the one the newspapers were using now. "Maybe if the police give it a lot of distribution, it will help. The sketch they're using now is no good at all."

"Sounds like a good idea. Have you talked to Ed Simms at the FBI?" Simms was the Art Squad's top man and was always called in on major thefts.

"You know Ed, Oliver . . . he's like the grave. Never tells you anything. Actually, I've talked to so many people, police and FBI both, that I can't sort them out. It's been nonstop question time every day, as you can imagine."

"What does Ed have to say about it all?"

"I just told you—nothing. I'll bet those FBI types don't even tell their wives their right names, they're so secretive. Mrs. Simms probably thinks her name is Mrs. Rumplemeyer or something."

"Please be fair, Persis. They have to be discreet, you know that perfectly well."

"Then why are you asking me what he said?" I demanded, reasonably enough. "You know they won't say anything until the case is closed, and even then they'll never tell the whole story."

That Rembrandt theft in Boston last year, for instance . . . so many questions still remaining. It had been stolen in broad daylight from Boston's Museum of Fine Arts. In due time it was recovered. But who was the man in the ski mask who negotiated the return? Why was there a rendezvous in a parking lot? And why was the painting returned if no money changed hands, as the authorities insisted?

For some reason I was neglecting to tell Oliver about what Jason's Washington FBI contact had said. For some reason I was neglecting to tell Oliver about Jason

Oliver had been thinking about the Boston theft, too. "Could there be some connection with the Rembrandt stolen in Boston? What do you think, Persis?"

"I don't think so, Oliver. Everyone's always trying to steal Rembrandts. He's extremely popular on the heist front."

It was a fact. First of all, Rembrandts are often a convenient size to carry—not too large. Also, Rembrandt is famous and therefore easily recognized by potential thieves as being valuable. Lastly, Rembrandt is eminently available . . . almost every museum of any stature has at least one.

Oliver was inclined to agree with me. "You're probably right . . . those Boston thieves got down to business with the police and the insurance people very quickly. There's something else going on here, I think."

Oliver was no dummy. He often worked with the FBI on the recovery and identification of stolen art.

"Still," he went on, "these people, whoever they are, are dangerous and I want you to remember that fact." (I was likely to. I had a hemstitched head as a reminder.) "So if you won't come out here, I could try to change my schedule and come out to be with you. I'm supposed to go to Spokane and then Minneapolis and eventually Austria, but I'll come right now if . . ."

"What for? What else could possibly happen? We've had everything: armed robbery, bomb scares, a kidnapping . . . we're *swarming* with security."

"Well . . . I don't like the sound of the whole thing. I want you to stay out of trouble."

I didn't see any point in telling him I'd practically gone to work for Jason Waldheim as a spy, so I changed the subject. "Are you eating, Oliver? You're so thin. Promise you won't skip meals." Oliver was so preoccupied he sometimes went all day without eating. "Now, don't worry . . . I'll be careful. Love and kisses." I hung up, feeling vaguely guilty. Oliver was so *nice*—why couldn't I be breathless over him?

The telephone rang again. Isadore protested. I picked up the receiver while she glared at me. "Yes?"

"Mrs. Willum?" I did not recognize the voice.

"Who is it?"

"Bill Brown. Where have you been? I've been calling for hours and the line's been busy."

Between Isadore and Oliver, it was no wonder. It was now 11:40. "I'm sorry. What is it?"

"You ought to have a second phone if you're going to keep one line tied up all the time."

I blanched at the thought of Isadore and a second phone. "Gregor Olitsky says one's quite enough. I work for him, you know."

"That's why I'm calling. You *used* to work for Gregor Olitsky. You've been promoted. My boss got in touch with your boss on the *Gripsholme*. . . ."

"S.S. *Statendam*," I interjected automatically.

". . . and your boss has agreed to lend you to us for the duration of this museum crisis to serve as interim director."

"What?" He must be a raving lunatic. I tried to be reasonable. "Mr. Brown, what you're saying just doesn't make sense. You don't need a director over there—you already have one, even if he happens to be in the hospital. He's going to recover."

William C. Brown seemed to pick his words with care. "No, he's not at the hospital. And he isn't the director."

"But I saw him there just this morning." Could they have moved him somewhere so soon? "Is he out of I.C.U.?"

"I'm so awfully sorry to have to tell you this, Mrs. Willum, but he's in the morgue. He's been there since 10:00 P.M. Winkworth Gaud is dead."

9

"Everything considered," Mrs. Sandringham was saying sadly over the soup course (avocado with sherry), "it seems we should have followed our original instincts and had nothing whatever to do with that museum. Poor Winkworth—it's appalling."

Complications, the hospital had said . . . Wink had died of complications. A heavy scent hung in the air, like death. It could have been my imagination—we had all been to Wink's funeral earlier in the day. Or it could have been Mrs. Sandringham's cymbidiums which were everywhere, drenching the room in their languid beauty. She was famous for her greenhouses full of orchids. As they bloomed they were brought into the house, and were replaced by fresh plants when they faded.

We were nine for dinner—a dinner that was really, I suppose, a sort of high-class wake. Our spirits were low, and by an unspoken common consent we were trying not to discuss Winkworth to keep our spirits from plunging even lower—or had been until Mrs. Sandringham introduced his name. All of the September Seven were present, and Mrs. Sandringham presided in splendor at the head of the table.

I had the impression that tonight, in honor of Wink, she had swathed herself in yards and yards of mournful lilac tulle beneath which an assortment of jeweled pins gleamed dimly on her chest like an old campaigner's ribbons and medals.

She had placed Diantha Lord's brand new live-in man on her right, a gesture that might have qualified her for canonization. Diantha's man—formerly Blossom Rugge's—was Buffalo Horowitz who looked and smelled like a buffalo, probably on purpose:

there appeared to be no inch of him that wasn't both hairy and rank.

I'd known him years ago as plain Harry Horowitz, a typical New York artist-illustrator fighting a losing battle to make ends meet. When the craze for Western art developed, Harry had spotted the pot of gold in the old corral and become a "cowboy artist" overnight. The fact that there was already a perfectly good Western artist named Buffalo painting away out there hadn't bothered Harry, he simply appropriated the name along with all the rest of the cowboy paraphernalia—boots, ten-gallon hat, Remington mustache, high rancid smell, and all.

Next to Buffalo sat Diantha, barely able to keep her hands, let alone her eyes, off him. He was no beauty, but Diantha was new to the liberated life-style and maybe—who knows?—he looked good to her after the pruned and barbered, yellow-, green-, and red-corduroy Gull Harborites she'd grown up with.

The rest of us were scattered around the big dining table at the prescribed intervals. I had hoped I would draw de Groot as a partner because I was dying to ask him a few discreet questions about the history of his Rembrandt. It bothered me that I couldn't place it. But Willem de Groot was across the table and one simply did not shout loudly across the centerpiece that there did not seem to be a record of his Rembrandt in the most recent collection he had listed in his provenance for the press release. True, the collectors, a wealthy old merchant prince and his wife, were long dead and their paintings had been sold at various times at auction. However, there was no record of the Rembrandt ever having been sold. I could not even find it listed as having been in their collection, although that was not too odd—many collectors kept very quiet about their best pictures for fear of having them stolen. Still, it was a puzzle. . . .

The Rembrandt was another subject we were not talking about tonight. And the girl was yet another.

Rosi Craig-Mitchell sat at the foot of the table where we could all get the full benefit of her dazzling beauty. I was almost 100 percent sure that David Lawless was holding her hand under the table. Why did she have to pick a man like Lawless? She was so warm and careless—he was so cold and careful. Maybe that was the reason she liked him . . . the old saw about "opposites attract." Was it just his legal mind that made him seem so cold? I had the feeling he could stand by and watch someone cut out your still-beating heart without lifting a finger to stop it. The Seven all worshiped him, of course, because their whole lives were run by lawyers to some degree, and Rosi was no exception. Still, I worried. She had not been notoriously lucky in her choice of men.

Now, General Scott and Pierre Richardson, they were something else. I had one seated on either side of me, and I was glad. I was depressed, and they were just right for me—low-key and undemanding. I was just turning to the general when the conversation, which had been rather sedate until now, suddenly took a strident turn.

"They ought to turn all the museums over to the people." When she was being earnest, which was most of the time these days, Diantha could be a real pain. Levity and Godlessness had always, in fact, been one and the same thing to her, beginning with our schooldays together at Greenvalley. She had always been the one to tattle.

"The *People*," she was saying, looking at Buffalo Horowitz for approval, "are the only ones who can make a museum valid."

"Gracious," said Mrs. Sandringham, eyes widening.

"Yes, the *People* must lead."

"What people, Diantha?" Pierre asked.

"*The* People. Mankind. Natural *Man*, pure and good."

Lights went on in three of our heads simultaneously.

"Jean Jacques Rousseau," I said.

"*Confessions*," the general chimed in.

"*La Nouvelle Hèloïse*," Mrs. Sandringham cried, delighted to have solved the mystery.

We all exchanged glances. Now we understood the phenomenon of Buffalo Horowitz in Diantha's life—she was adventuring into eighteenth-century philosophy in her search for Meaning and she had stumbled on Rousseau, the father of Romantic Sensibility, the advocate of closeness to Nature and the Natural Man.

Diantha was trying out what she considered a contemporary version of Natural Man . . . Buffalo Horowitz.

"Well, well," said the general, pleased, "I didn't know the modern generation read Rousseau."

Rosi, at the far end of the table, was feeling left out. "Whom are you talking about? Do we know anyone named Rousseau?"

Leaning back in her wheelchair, in which she'd come to dinner, Mrs. Sandringham began to explain, but Rosi wasn't listening . . . she appeared distracted. "I thought we were talking about someone we knew," she said.

They began serving the main course just then, so all conversation was suspended while the waitresses served the ham in a sauce of Dijon and Gruyère. It occurred to me that Diantha would probably object to eating red meat, as she was now an advocate of Nature and thus probably also a vegetarian, but a quick look confirmed that her Romanticism hadn't affected her appetite. She was attacking her food with the gusto of a dockworker. So was her roommate of the hour.

The conversation resumed. It wandered amiably along through the main course and the salad course, never getting into difficulties. At the head of the table our hostess struggled valiantly with the cowboy artist (or Natural Man) and I vaguely heard Buffalo tell her that, no, he had never been on a horse and, no, he didn't plan ever to be on one—he didn't think they could be trusted.

Mrs. Sandringham, obviously desperate for harmless conversation, wondered if it might be difficult to paint horses if you didn't ride them and Diantha rushed to point out a list of horse painters through history who, she insisted, had never ridden. Trying gamely to be agreeable, Mrs. Sandringham said she understood: you didn't have to be hanged to paint a hanging.

Then it slipped out—or be murdered, she said, to paint a murderer.

The word *murdered* must have triggered it.

"What do you think? Was Wink Gaud murdered?" It was Rosi. She wasn't smiling and she wasn't joking.

The shocked silence around the table lasted through the fruit and the cheese. We were astonished. But Rosi wasn't going to let it go. When the dessert of Poires Josephine had been served and the two waitresses had withdrawn she asked it again, challengingly. "Well, *was* Winkworth Gaud murdered? Come on, all of you? I want to know what you think."

David Lawless recovered first. I suppose it was his legal training. "Why on earth would you suspect such a thing, Rosi?" He sounded horrified.

"Well, it's not so crazy when you think about it, and I've *been* thinking about it. Complications, the hospital said—that could mean anything. There are lots of things that could have killed him . . . tranquilizers that disappear in the bloodstream, for example, muscle relaxants. I wasn't married to Edgar for three years without learning something. After three or four hours even an autopsy wouldn't show them. All you need is a needle. He was sedated, sleeping a lot . . . the nurses wouldn't have noticed."

"Rosemary, *what* are you saying?" Mrs. Sandringham's voice was so angry that I jumped in my chair.

Rosi was defensive. "He was supposed to be getting *better*, wasn't he? What happened then?"

"It's absurd. Damned nonsense." This was de Groot. "He just died, that's all. The hospital said it could happen like that—suddenly—with somebody as badly hurt as he'd been. Not that unusual. All that trauma, after all."

"But they *said* he was improving. They were confident. Edgar said so."

Pierre took over. "Doctors are fallible. They're not gods, Rosi. You know that."

"It couldn't happen," I said. "That Intensive Care Unit is like a fortress. The head nurse wouldn't let anyone near Wink unless he specifically asked to see them." As he'd asked to see me . . . and I remembered the urgency . . . the insistence in his voice as Wink had said, "I must *not* stay here." Was *this* what he had been afraid of? . . . No, it was absurd.

Rosi held up her hand. "I know. But the head nurse went home early. Edgar let the cat out of the bag without meaning to. He told me everyone in that place has the flu and she was coming down with it, too. Running all through the hospital, it is. The nursing staff is decimated, according to Edgar. He was here looking for one of those gigantic checks he always hits me for—the building fund, you know—so I asked some questions without his knowing what I was after. Half the nursing staff is out. They wouldn't have been paying as much attention to Wink as to the other patients: he was being moved out of I.C.U. soon. Now, suppose he was sleeping . . . suppose someone injected him . . . *pow*—respiratory arrest. It would be unexpected, but normal. It wouldn't be the first time. Suppose someone dressed like staff comes in, pulls the curtain, fixes a hypodermic—and that's that."

We all stared at her.

"Great, merciful God," said the general. "What an imagination."

"I won't buy it," Pierre said, after a pause. "I'm on the board of that hospital and I don't believe it could happen."

"Certainly not, Rosi," said Lawless, frowning at her.

"Patients *do* die," Rosi cried.

Poor Wink, I was thinking . . . a human porcupine of needles and tubes when I had last seen him. Of course, he could have died. Rosi was mad.

Mrs. Sandringham was having none of it. "It is sheer nonsense, Rosi," she said firmly. "I'm surprised at you. I thought you had better judgment. Winkworth Gaud had been severely wounded. He underwent a ten-hour operation. His condition may have been considered stable, but that doesn't mean things can't go wrong. Believe me, I saw enough of it in France during both wars to know what I'm talking about." When Mrs. Sandringham wanted to make a point, she could be intimidating in her absolute authority.

"And," she went on, "I've done plenty of volunteer work in the Gull Harbor hospital since. I know enough about illness to know that what happened to Winkworth Gaud isn't that unusual. The least little thing that goes wrong can do it. So—I want this dangerous and irresponsible speculation to stop right here in this room at this very instant."

When a genuine, grade-A grande dame makes a speech like that even the planets stop spinning and stand still and listen.

"Good show." The general raised his wineglass to her.

"Right on, lady," said Buffalo Horowitz, finally putting down his dessert spoon and fork and proving that he had not been oblivious to the scene after all.

"We must never think such a terrible thing again," said Diantha piously, forgetting for once to speak in capital letters because of the gravity of the subject.

Rosi presented us with her first smile of the evening, but she said nothing. Her face was flushed.

"Yes, Rosi," Lawless told her, "it is best not to speculate irresponsibly." But I noted that he gave her hand a consoling pat to soften the implication that he was criticizing her.

Mrs. Sandringham rolled back her wheelchair. "Shall we go into the drawing room for coffee? Any of you gentlemen who insist on cigars may join us later."

After that remark, any gentleman who had been thinking about a cigar abandoned the thought instantly and joined everyone else as we trooped out of the big dining room after our nonsmoking hostess. The orchids and their scent were in the drawing room, too, their exoticism very much at home with the English furniture and the solemn portraits temporarily hanging where the masterpieces now at the Waldheim usually reposed.

But that wasn't quite the last of Winkworth Gay Gaud.

Pierre Richardson had come to sit next to me while the butler, Winston, made the rounds with a great Georgian silver tray groaning beneath an elaborate coffee service. All evening long I'd been admiring the studs on the front of Pierre's dress shirt. Now that he was very close to me, I couldn't help seeing how special they were.

"Those studs are beautiful," I told him. "Did you steal them from some museum?" It was a joke in the worst of taste and I had the impression that everyone in the room stopped talking. I could have bitten my tongue.

Pierre didn't appear to notice. "Not stolen, Persis. A fantastic goldsmith named Ho Ching made them; he worked in Canton in the 1850s."

As the chatter in the room resumed, Pierre leaned closer and said softly, "There's one thing that troubles me, Persis. About Wink Gaud . . . would you say he had a scholar's education in art?"

I'd thought about it a lot, as a matter of fact, so I answered honestly. "I loved him, he was a wonderful person—but, no, I wouldn't say he had a scholar's background. He was much more the typical director—good at fund raising, great with people and the press, marvelous at getting things done . . . exactly what one would expect from his background. But there was something else about him, too . . . something I could never put my finger on."

Pierre nodded. "Precisely. But listen to this: I was wearing these same studs at one of those big pre-Preview affairs . . . and Wink Gaud walked past and said 'Ho Ching'—just like that."

I was surprised. Even *I* hadn't known what they were, and I was supposed to be more knowledgeable than most. I couldn't think of anything to say. We sipped our coffee and looked at one another. After a moment or two, I excused myself and went off in search of a bathroom mirror: I'm always convinced that hot coffee melts my lipstick and makes it run down to my chin, although it never turns out to be so.

I wandered upstairs and into the first bedroom with an open door. That's when I discovered the stolen Degas. It was hanging right there on the wall. Mrs. Sandringham might say it was a copy of the original . . . they were always having their important paintings copied and the copies were usually fabulous. But I knew better. I had studied the original at the Waldheim.

And this was it.

I was astonished—this seemed to be a night for it—and also in somewhat of a quandary. What was I to do now? I couldn't just march up to Belle Sandringham and say, "Pardon me, lady, but do you know you have a stolen painting on your wall?"

Unthinkable. On the other hand, who could I tell without making Mrs. Sandringham look like a thief?

I stood for a moment, thinking, then left the room and quietly closed the door. No, I'd have to look into this myself.

10

My portrait of Saskia van Uylenburgh came out in all the newspapers the next day, although I didn't see it—I was over at Wink's small gatehouse on the Waldheim grounds packing his belongings in case anyone turned up to claim them. I was glad to do it for Wink's sake, although it was a heart-rending business at best. There was frighteningly little of him left behind: a collection of suits without labels (was it because we might find out they weren't bespoke, I wondered?), brand-new American underwear, socks, handkerchiefs, shoes and ties, and no more of anything else than one might expect to find in a traveler's motel room. Nothing that contained the particular essence of Gaud . . . nothing reminiscent or expressive of any particular person. It was depressing. I left with the feeling that I was departing from a house where the tenant expected to be in residence for only a very short time, which was exactly how it had been. Poor Wink.

Mrs. Howard was waiting when I finally stumbled home, tired and tearful. She was wild with excitement.

"I waited to tell you. You was on the six o'clock news."

Mrs. Howard is an insatiable television viewer, and I knew that being on television ranked in her order of importance only lower than quitting this moral realm and getting through the Pearly Gates. I tried to look suitably impressed.

"They said your name—right out on the TV—Jim Jensen, it was. Mrs. Persis Willum. Well, maybe he didn't say 'Mrs.,' I'm not sure—but, anyway, your name, and about how you was one of them victims of the crime and how you done this sketch from memory of the girl that's missing. About how you was an artist.

And your stitches. And being Miss Wentworth's niece." (Naturally, they would drag Aunt Lydie into it somehow. They always did: she was just too rich for them to resist.)

"I'm going to watch the ten o'clock news, too," Mrs. Howard went on, blissful at the prospect. "They'll show the drawing you done. Say you're a well-known artist."

I groaned. My stock might be soaring with my faithful "houseworker," but I knew there was bound to be trouble in other quarters if my name was too heavily emphasized, other quarters being H. Caldwell Ringwell and his culture czar. They had made it amply clear that the only name they wanted coupled with the museum was H. Caldwell's. He would stand for no competition, however trivial. There would be trouble.

There was.

At 9:37 A.M. the next morning, I was invited to appear before H. Caldwell in his museum office down the hall. He didn't even pretend that he was glad to see me.

"Sit down," he ordered, his rear firmly glued to his chair. At least he didn't plan to keep me standing like a chastised schoolgirl.

I sat.

"Quite the publicity seeker, aren't you?"

"No. Why?" I knew perfectly well, but I wanted to hear him say it himself.

"Those drawings in the newspapers and on the TV. We didn't ask you to do them. Took it on yourself, didn't you? You should have let us release them, but I suppose you were anxious to see your name in the paper, right?"

"No, Mr. Ringwell. I just wanted to help—"

"The only thing you're supposed to help is this museum and you'd better keep it in mind. Why, you didn't even know that girl. Or did you?"

I said I hadn't seen her before that day.

"Well, there you are," he said triumphantly. "If you never saw her before, how come you were able to draw a picture of her, anyway?"

I explained that I had a trained eye, like any portrait painter, and a good memory for faces and that I'd only thought the sketch might help find her. Had *he* known her? I asked, just to change the subject.

"Never saw her before that day, either." There was the least little change of tone—the smallest hint of defensiveness—and my antennae quivered, sensing something.

"If you never saw her before, how did she get there?"

He hesitated. "Someone sent me a clipping in the mail. Got another one from my clipping service saying the girl was here in New York. Put my staff on it right away. Great public relations scoop to have her here for the show. Finally found her at a modeling school registered under 'Saskia Van'."

"Did you double-check her identity?"

He helped himself to a cigar from the humidor on his desk and made a big production of lighting it and getting it going with puffs in my direction while I tried to calm my breakfastless stomach.

"Certainly," he said, finally. "De Groot said she was OK—and he'd know. He even arranged for her to stay at that fancy club, the Sons of Peter Stuyvesant. And I had my office check, too. Although de Groot's word should have been good enough."

I wasn't so sure, although I couldn't exactly have explained why. First the Rembrandt, then this girl . . . we were taking an awful lot on de Groot's word. . . .

"How did you check her out, then?" Odd, I thought . . . at first Ringwell had been attacking me, now he was on the defensive. I have pressed a nerve somewhere.

"Oh, there's some sort of Dutch historical society in the city —de Groot mentioned it to me—they keep track of this sort of thing. We just called them up and they confirmed her identity. Simple as that."

De Groot again . . . "Do you have the number?"

"Should be around somewhere . . ." He rummaged half-heartedly in his desk, then called in one of his secretaries and asked her for the number. The girl appeared not to have the foggiest notion of what he was talking about. As I mentioned before, his staff would hardly set the world afire.

There followed a nasty little contretemps in which Ringwell (who had probably been dying to do it anyway) lost his temper and shouted at the secretary. She, in turn, said a number of quite rude things about him under her breath, not loud enough for him to hear but just sufficient to demonstrate her independence.

I stayed very quiet, not caring to draw any of the fire, but it did no good. When the girl finally stamped out of his office, he turned to me furiously and, blowing a big cloud of nauseating smoke my way, demanded, "Why are you asking all these damned questions anyway? It's none of your business where that woman came from and it wasn't your place to give her picture to the press. Just remember, Mrs. Willum, the next time you get an uncontrollable urge to see your name in print, check with this office *first*. Good day."

He didn't bother to get out of his chair this time, either. As I was leaving, however, a remarkable transformation took place. I turned in the doorway for one last look at his lovely face and found his scowl had been replaced by the famous Ringwell Public Smile, as if our contretemps had never taken place. He obviously believed in taking no chances politically. Ringwell's mouth was stretched wide—just like a shark with a million teeth.

11

Winkworth Gaud's office was as impersonal and unrevealing as his living quarters had been. It was to be my office until a new director was found and to me, again, had fallen the task of cleaning out Wink's few possessions. It was an exercise in heartbreak because his presence was everywhere, not so much in objects as in atmosphere.

Once again there was very little to clean out, except the usual yards and yards of art books and periodicals: *Art News*, *Art in America*, *American Art Review*, *Art Voices*, the lot. There was correspondence from artists and art foundations. Organizations had sent letters hoping to be accorded a Benefit. Schools wrote about tours. Other schools and women's groups wrote asking Wink to address them. There were clippings he'd saved, perhaps with ideas for future Waldheim exhibitions in mind, and notes in his scrawling, near-illegible handwriting.

It was while cleaning out the bookcase that I found the folder. It was jammed casually into a large volume on the Hudson River School, as if Wink hadn't cared who found it, but I quickly saw it was something special.

The first thing inside was a yellowed plastic case. Someone had once used it to preserve a clipping, and it looked, in fact, as if it might have been around the world several times. Either its contents had finally disintegrated with age, however, or there had never been more, because it was now empty except for a torn fragment of yellowed newsprint that read 20 TRUCK.

Beneath it was a page torn from *Antique Monthly*, January, 1977. Next to an item headed "Fake Rembrandts," Wink had placed a very nearly invisible pencil mark—at least, I suppose it was Wink. I read the item that followed.

The Rembrandt Research Project, composed of a team of Dutch experts based in Amsterdam and headed by the distinguished scholar, Dr. Hans van der Donck, is causing shudders in the art world with a revelation that a number of paintings in leading collections are fakes.

Over the last few years the team has used X-ray techniques on known Rembrandts to reveal the original brushwork. The results have brought forth several surprises, including challenges of the authenticity of four Rembrandts in London's National Gallery and another in the Wallace Collection. Rembrandt collectors everywhere are said to be trembling.

American museum directors, asked if they were worried about the attributions of Rembrandts in their collections, all denied any concern. Several American experts expressed concern that the Amsterdam team was relying too heavily on science and not enough on careful use of the eye. London's *Sunday Times* quoted Professor Swelton Fleet of the Albright-Knox Museum in Buffalo as saying, "Let's hope they don't throw out the baby with the bath water."

It went on, with more details. There was another clipping too, from *International Museum News*. It was a two-page spread chronicling the foundation of the new Waldheim Museum, complete with pictures of old Jacob Waldheim, his grandson, the seven collectors whose paintings would comprise the opening exhibition, and the two county officials responsible for the whole affair. It was quite a story: I remember how pleased Ringwell had been when it came out. Had Wink seen this before he applied for the job?

A third clipping, this time in French, could have come from either *Figaro* or *Paris Soir*—I couldn't tell, for it was neither identified nor dated. Loosely translated in my generally trustworthy

French, it noted that a truckload of Haylon gas had been apprehended at le Treport when the truck, heading northeast on route Nationale 40, was involved in a chain accident in some night fog. The driver of the vehicle had disappeared in the commotion and the truck turned out to have been stolen several days earlier in Paris. The canisters of gas had not, fortunately, broken open in the accident and it was assumed that the gas, like the truck, had been stolen. The police were investigating.

With the clipping there was a letter, also in French. It was from Jacques-Paul Mathen. I recognized the name at once: Mathen was the head of the famous Paris Art Squad, a special police unit formed in 1970 to deal primarily with art thefts. Ed Simms had spoken of Mathen often—he respected the Frenchman enormously. And now he had written to Winkworth Gaud.

I translated quickly, consumed with curiosity. Mathen's letter was simple and direct. It assured Gaud that there was no sign of activity in any of the ports along the route of N. 40 and that police theorized the probable destiny of the gas was Antwerp, thence by Russian ship to the Soviet Union for purposes unknown. He also confirmed that a set of plans was indeed missing from the files at Sogegarde, but whether they had been stolen or not, nobody knew. A search was being conducted now. They had no reason at present to presume a connection.

I knew route Nationale 40 from past trips to the Pas de Calais region of France: 40 was a comparatively little-traveled road that wandered along, following the shore of the channel, occasionally entangling itself with N. 25 from about Le Havre to Dunkerque and beyond. In due time it ended up in Belgium.

I knew Sogegarde, too, and a tingle went through me at its mention. It was a 240-foot-high, 180-foot-wide tower hidden off the Place du Trocadero in Paris built by the Société Géneral, one of France's big three nationalized banks, to guard the art treasures of its valued clients. The tower, hidden from view behind a conventional building, can be seen only from the Eiffel Tower. It is surrounded by a moat. There is only one entrance. The security measures are the most complex and sophisticated that the best minds of intelligence officers and art experts could conceive and though I had never been in it, Gregor Olitsky used it often.

So tight is the security there that Sogegarde will release almost no information about itself other than a very general artist's drawing of an aerial view of the building and a few facts calculated to deter prospective thieves. At night, for example, the employees leave the premises by crawling through a narrow, winding passage that is later flooded for the night—extraordinary but true. Should an intruder get in, Haylon gas, used to extinguish fires without harming the paintings, would be released to asphyxiate the prowler. It was a veritable fortress. . . .

But what did this all have to do with Winkworth Gaud?

More mysteries. I thumbed through the papers again, my head buzzing with questions. First Belle Sandringham and her painting, now Wink Gaud and these cryptic clippings . . . what did it mean?

It was getting dark in the room. I reached up and turned on the light. I ought to go home; it was late. But I couldn't move. The presence of Winkworth Gaud seemed to hang in the room like a great cloud . . . and gradually I was haunted by another presence as well—the spectacle of a man with a big nose who loved to dress up and paint himself decked out in rich robes and exotic turbans. All day long he had seemed to hover in the air, complaining about the boredom of having to paint portraits of the new bourgeoisie, complaining about not being able to marry the new woman in his life, Hendrickje Stoffele, for fear of losing his first wife Saskia's dowry, complaining that he might have to sell his own considerable art collection to satisfy his many creditors. He was a man I had obviously never known except through his paintings . . . yet tonight I felt I knew him far better than I had known Winkworth Gaud, a man I found I'd really never understood at all. . . .

Perhaps there was a message in it. Maybe it was time to visit de Groot and find out about *his* Rembrandt.

12

Willem de Groot looked very classy. I suppose anyone would, surrounded by a couple of million dollars' worth of thoroughbred horseflesh belonging to one of the greatest racing stables in the world, Amsterdam Stables. This was the American division. There was also a European division, based largely at Chantilly outside of Paris.

Normally de Groot would never have been on Long Island at this time of year. No one in his right mind was on Long Island at this time of year unless he was too poor to get away, like me. Even Ringwell and Brown had managed to schedule flying trips to the Bahamas and Bermuda, respectively, albeit only for weekends when they assumed the electorate wasn't looking.

De Groot was here, however, as were the rest of the September Seven, thanks first to the opening of the museum, and then to Wink's death. Now I supposed they would be departing for more attractive climates at any minute.

De Groot had obviously been riding, probably to watch the morning workouts. He exuded a cashmere-Vuitton-leathery elegance in whipcord jodhpurs, yellow turtleneck, beige pullover, and a perfectly aged tweed hacking jacket. The shine on his boots almost put my eye out. He was too dazzling to face before lunch, especially for a lady in a going-to-see-the-horses outfit of dingy blue jeans, fatigued sneakers, and a salt-stained L. L. Bean shirt left over from a mildly diverting Maine sailing trip.

"I didn't mean to interrupt your morning schedule," I said, snatching dark glasses out of my bag and clapping them on my nose to tone down the dazzle. I noticed with envy that de Groot's hair, unlike my perfectly ordinary medium-blonde mop, fitted the million-dollar atmosphere to perfection. It was pure gold, every perfect golden wave fitting with tongue-and-groove neatness into every other perfect golden wave.

"It's all right. We're largely finished for the day," he said.

I looked around at the acres of millionaire's landscape: barns, paddocks, stallion walks, training tracks, and a collection of beautiful white horse vans with AMSTERDAM STABLES, GULL HARBOR, LONG ISLAND lettered very small in gold on the sides. There were acres of people, too . . . painting things, scrubbing things, airing things, shoveling things. De Groot may have been finished for the day, but the peons were just getting started.

"Care to join me for a picnic lunch?" He snapped his fingers and there was the rustling of unseen minions. "I hope it's not too early for you. I've been up since 4:00 A.M."

I'd only been up since nine and it was now eleven, but I didn't quibble. Picnics with de Groot weren't everyday fare for me.

"Good," he said. "I'm famished." He ushered me into what I suppose was meant to be his office. You could have put my whole house into it twice and had room left over for a ball. I stopped in my tracks and stared—I couldn't help it. Before me was a big Tudor fireplace, a beamed ceiling . . . and paintings. What paintings. Naturally they were of horses, but who cared? I could see a Delacroix of the Moroccan period . . . a Fernley of brood mares in Melton Mowbray . . . a Stubbs portrait of a woman on her favorite hack with a Jack Daniels terrier trotting behind . . . a Munnings of de Groot's grandmother riding sidesaddle with the Meadowbrook Hunt . . . . There were other paintings, too—lots of them—mostly of Victorian dogs in gold frames hanging in vertical rows in front of the tall bookcases that lined the room. Plants and fresh-cut flowers were everywhere.

"Your *office?*" I managed to say.

"Do all my paperwork and record keeping right here. Convenient."

"I'd never want to work. It's too beautiful."

"Friend of mine, Mario Buatta, pulled it together. He's got flair. I don't notice it much, to tell you the truth, but I like the pictures. Some are family. We raided Christie's and Sotheby's for the rest. It was fun." He spoke languidly, as if it hadn't been fun at all but boring.

A bottle of champagne had appeared while he was speaking and was now cooling in a bucket on the table between us. The wine cooler was a simple little George III affair with horses rampant. The champagne was Taittinger.

A manservant in a cream-colored coat cleared the *Blood Horse* and *Classic* magazines from the table and began to serve the picnic. I had never before had a picnic at a stable and I was pleased to learn what one had on such an occasion: crab quiche, a cold salmon mousse, salad *au riz*, and a chicken roulade stuffed with eggplant, mushrooms, and herbs drenched in cognac. There were also cheeses and fruit.

De Groot began to eat everything in sight, as would I if I'd been up since 4:00 A.M. All I could manage to do was pick at this and that while sipping my champagne and studying the lord of Amsterdam Stables. He had an air about him, as if he didn't really belong with the rest of us mere mortals.

"I suppose you've come to report to me on how things are going at the museum and what they've heard about my Rembrandt," he said. "Go on."

"Well, not exactly," I said, uneasily. "There's nothing new there . . . but it is about your Rembrandt." I took the plunge. "You see, I've been trying to research its provenance. I try to keep track of every great painting on Long Island, both for the gallery and the museum, and I'd love to know exactly when you acquired it. Gregor asks me to keep records." All of that was true, but it was far from the only reason I wanted to know about his painting.

His chilly, Delft blue eyes looked at me and he said nothing.

I plowed on regardless. "And I'm puzzled about something else . . . I'm not having much luck on the provenance itself. There don't seem to be any records of your Rembrandt in the previous collections listed in its provenance. Do you know why that is?"

"Naturally," he replied. "Previous owners didn't want to advertise owning such a picture for fear of its being stolen. I thought I was safe, showing it at a museum with new security systems and guards. And look what happened." He cast a baleful look at me.

This was not moving at all well. The only thing keeping me going was the chicken roulade, which was meltingly delicious, and as I swallowed another mouthful I said, "There is a reward, I suppose?"

"Certainly we've offered a reward." De Groot did not go on. Getting information from him was like interrogating a stone. Obviously he'd been advised not to discuss it by his insurance people, but it did mean that if the Art Mafia were involved, there was room for negotiation. If they were involved. I decided to try another tack.

"I understand you knew Saskia?"

He was momentarily confounded. "Saskia? The painting? Or the girl?"

"The girl. Ringwell told me you vouched for her and that you arranged for her to stay at the Peter Stuyvesant Club."

He poured us each the remains of the bottle of Taittinger. "I'm not really interested in that Saskia. My painting is what interests me."

"Maybe their welfares go together," I said. "How did you first meet the girl?"

"I never laid eyes on her in my life."

"But Ringwell said—"

"I don't care *what* Ringwell said. He's an ass. I never laid eyes on the girl."

"Then how—"

"Look, this is how it happened, once and for all. Ringwell called me, said he had this girl, a descendant of Rembrandt's wife. Very exciting to have her on hand at the same time as my Rembrandt portrait, right? Ringwell wanted to put her up at the Stuyvesant club and he needed a sponsor. Said she knew some good friends of mine who race horses in Europe. So naturally that was all I needed to know."

"Did you check with your friends?"

"Listen, I was just boarding my plane for Florida. I didn't have time to phone all over Europe tracking down my friends. Just the fact that she knew them was enough. We all know one another, you realize. Like a special community. Ordinary people wouldn't even know my friends' names."

I didn't bother to ask the names he was talking about—as an ordinary person I was certain not to recognize them. And yet rich people who race horses in Europe are known to the European press. Anyone doing a little checking could come up with names de Groot would know, in spite of his wishful thinking about exclusiveness.

I didn't belabor the point, however. Instead, "Is there a service in New York that keeps records on distinguished persons of Dutch descent?"

"Other than the Peter Stuyvesant club? Not that I know of."

The houseman came in and began to clear away the so-called picnic. I realized that I had been doing away with my share without even knowing it. Oh, well—it certainly beat whatever offering Mrs. Howard would leave at home for me tonight.

Now the houseman was murmuring something to his master about a call and de Groot was waving him aside impatiently. "Yes, it's always the same people one knows all over the world—no need to check on her. Believe me, the people I'm talking about are a more exclusive group than the descendants of the British rabble who hopped aboard this country at Plymouth Rock and think they're so blue-blooded. Compared to the European elite and the Dutch, they're scum, most of them. Nobodies."

As a descendant of one of those very same nobodies, I suppose I ought to have protested. But it was all so very long ago. Who cared, really?

What interested me more was that de Groot had not actually checked out Saskia van Uylenburgh and that there was no service that kept records on persons like her. And then there was the Rembrandt. I tried once more. "What about your Rembrandt?"

The temperature in the room dropped about sixty degrees. "What about it?"

"I—" But I got no farther. There was a knock at the door, and a girl burst into the room. She looked frantic. "You *must* come, Mr. de Groot. It's Theseus."

De Groot leaped to his feet instantly. "What's wrong?"

I suppose she was one of those young college girls you see around every stable these days, beautiful to look at, with shining hair, million-dollar teeth, and eyes for nothing but horses.

"They sent me to get you. We think it may be colic. The horse is going crazy."

De Groot recoiled as if she had physically struck him. I knew how he felt. I grew up around horses, one of the benefits of having been brought up by an aunt who is at least 50 percent thoroughbred racehorse herself. I knew perfectly well that, short of breaking a leg, a bad case of colic is the most final thing that can happen to a horse—and a hideous way to die. The animal literally dies in agony of a stomachache.

"Theseus?" I asked, already pitying the creature and recognizing that it had to be an important horse from the way de Groot had reacted.

"Stakes horse. Best I've ever owned." He whirled on the girl. "You called the vet?"

"On his way, Mr. de Groot. His service thought they could catch up with him and have him on his way in minutes."

"Minutes aren't good enough," de Groot said. "Get on that telephone and find me another vet. And where's my trainer?"

"On his way back from Belmont, sir."

"He'd better be." De Groot was recovering now, taking charge. He left the girl at the telephone and strode out the door. I followed. We started down the corridor to the enclosed barn area at a very fast walk, almost running. As we rounded the corner of the tack room, a groom stepped forward, carrying a rifle. He thrust it at de Groot.

"In case it's needed, sir."

De Groot took it, but he wasn't pleased. "The fool must know I can't do anything like that—the insurance." But he didn't put the rifle aside, just hurried along as if he'd forgotten he was carrying it. Insurance or no insurance, my aunt would have put down a horse that was in agony, I thought, but maybe Thesius wasn't that bad. I hoped not.

Suddenly we almost stumbled over a group of people who were bending over a form lying prone on the stable floor. "It's Wilkins, Mr. de Groot," someone said.

"What's wrong with him?" de Groot asked impatiently. "Theseus's groom," he told me. "Picked a hell of a time to be sick."

"We found him like this, sir. Can't seem to wake him up. He smells funny . . . ." It was obvious that everyone was scared to death of the master of Amsterdam Stables. They scarcely spoke above a whisper and it wouldn't have surprised me to see them tug at their forelocks.

De Groot snorted contemptuously. "Cheap wine, probably. Best excuse I've heard yet for not being on the job. He's fired." We swept on, leaving the group still bending over the prostrate form.

There was another group around Theseus's roomy box stall, and they looked frightened, too. There was no trace of color in their faces, and small wonder. Inside the box a splendid gray horse, now black with sweat, reared and plunged wildly, eyes rolling, nostrils distended. He was so lathered up the foam was dripping from his shoulders and flanks like shampoo in a shower. As he crashed forward and back in the confining space, he looked completely mad. I thought he would shatter himself against the paneled wall at any minute.

De Groot was thinking the same thing and quickly worked the latch on the stall door. "Got to get him out of there before he hurts himself. Somebody get a twitch. Maybe we can walk him out of it." He put the rifle down against the outer wall, opened the door, and started to enter the stall.

"I don't think—" I started to say, but it was too late. He was inside and striding up to the gray horse, which reared and tried to back away from the hands that reached for his halter. De Groot moved forward again, shouting at the terrified animal to be still.

As he advanced, the horse lunged aside, seeking to avoid the man, and one hoof glanced against de Groot, knocking him into the deep straw that covered the stall floor. I never stopped to think—I was inside the box in an instant, trying to soothe and gentle the animal with my voice while, at the same time, trying to drag de Groot out of danger. The horse had backed into a corner and stood there, trembling.

De Groot was on his feet before I had moved him an inch, screaming with rage. "That son of a bitch—I'll kill him. I'll murder the stupid bastard." He lurched out of the box. I knew the rifle was there. I moved right behind him.

"Willem, stop it! The horse doesn't know what he's doing."

"Well, I do! I'll kill him if I damn well want to. He's going to die, anyway."

We were struggling over the rifle now. The people who had been standing around were no help; they had drawn back and were standing there, gaping. De Groot had at least twice my strength. I hadn't much hope of hanging on very long, so I did the only thing I could think of: it wasn't sporting but it was effective —I kneed him in the groin. He dropped the rifle with a howl of pain.

"I don't think that horse is going to die if the vet gets here soon because I *don't* think he's got colic," I told de Groot while he was still doubled up. He slid down against the stall wall and sat there, clutching his groin and looking up at me. Theseus was kicking at the sides of his stall now. I prayed the vet would arrive.

"Why not?" de Groot asked, finally having gotten his breath.

"Look at him, Willem. You've seen horses with colic. They're in pain—this one's scared!"

He thought about it, his anger forgotten. Finally he dragged himself to his feet and looked in through the bars at the top of the gray's box, studying the crazed creature inside.

"I just bought him last month. I bought him especially to win the Arc de Triomphe. It would be a shame to kill him." As the horse's hooves thundered against the walnut panels, he continued, almost to himself, "We've never had a win in that one.

Sometimes if you don't have a good horse for a great race you buy one . . . like I bought Theseus . . . like I bought the Rembrandt. You get a winner any way you can—but you get one."

A tall man wearing an expression of eternal puzzlement at life's unpleasant surprises came rushing down the corridor on legs that moved swiftly, as if geared to endless running. He and de Groot went back into Theseus's stall and in due time I could hear that the vet had encountered yet another of those surprises inside. My God, I heard him saying, how did they get at him, anyway? . . . Looks like one of those hallucinogenics . . . scared out of his wits, poor bastard . . . don't blame him one bit . . . let's see if this will calm him down.

A telephone was ringing persistently nearby. At first I didn't pay any attention; I think I was in a mild state of shock after the last few minutes. Being so close to a crazy man with a gun leaves one rather unsettled. The telephone went on and on, however, and as no one appeared to be doing anything about it, I looked around, followed the buzzing to the source on the stable wall, and answered it.

"Amsterdam Stables." I sounded quavery.

"De Groot, please." The voice was faint and muffled, the way all voices in the Gull Harbor area sound when a little rain falls and the telephone system goes into deep shock. Except that it wasn't raining today.

"He's not here," I said.

"Get him."

"I can't. He's with a sick horse."

"Then give him this message." I came to attention. The voice, however faint, had an authority that leaked through the wires like distant cannon fire. "Tell him that horse is just a sample of what will happen if he forgets to protect his pedigree."

There was a click. The telephone went dead.

Pedigree? I thought wildly. Was de Groot up to something shady with his horses? But surely he wasn't likely to jeopardize his racing empire by fiddling with bloodlines, not with the penalties so severe. I couldn't believe it . . . and then the thought hit me: unless the caller meant the Rembrandt and *its* pedigree. . . .

92

I would give de Groot the message. If I didn't, Theseus or some other valuable horse might die. But I had the strong feeling that when I did, I would never hear another word about the source of that Rembrandt. Not, at least, from Willem de Groot.

13

Diantha Lord and I were staring at ourselves in the gilded mirror that hung over the fireplace in my office at the Waldheim . . . the office that had so shortly before been Winkworth Gaud's. We didn't, either of us, particularly like what we saw.

"All this natural food of Buffalo's is making a hag out of me," Diantha complained. "No more red meat, he says. If only I could have a square meal once in a while. I'm beginning to look at stray cats and dogs with murder in mind."

She did look drawn, as I'd had every reason to note: I seemed to be seeing her or some other member of the September Seven nonstop since Wink's death. Far from departing to wherever it was they all went this time of year, they had remained on Long Island and seemed to be taking turns coming every day to the museum. Either they were keeping an eye on their paintings or on me or both.

Things were slow at the museum now, at last. Everything had finally settled into an uneventful routine, broken only once by a fire scare that brought every piece of equipment for miles around clanging up to the museum's door . . . it proved to be nothing but an old World War II flare, cooking away in the museum's cavernous basement, though how that happened I don't know.

True, I'd come back to my office once or twice after a day of doing research to find my office in disarray, but I thought little of it and dismissed it as my own messiness . . . like most artists, I am not addicted to extreme neatness.

When I wasn't occupied at the museum I spent every spare minute at either the New York Public Library or at 122 East 42nd

Street in the archives of *Art News* magazine, looking for clippings about art thefts in which no ransom had been demanded and no painting recovered. An interesting pattern had begun to emerge, I thought. Interesting enough for me to keep all my notes either with me or locked up in the trunk of my car at all times.

"You're seeing a lot of Jason Waldheim, aren't you?" Diantha said suddenly just as I was about to ask her if she thought I ought to wear my hair a different way.

"I see him now and then," I admitted.

She gave me a thoughtful look in the mirror, the kind my aunt used to give me when I was up to something she disapproved of. "You had better be careful, then. He's a Scorpio and that's bad news. Oh, yes, he's sexy and smart. But watch out . . . he won't let you get too near him."

I didn't laugh at her, although I wanted to. "Jason?"

"No, Scorpios. But you can draw your own conclusions."

My conclusion was that she didn't approve of Jason Waldheim. But that was fair enough . . . I didn't approve of Buffalo Horowitz, not because of his zodiac sign but because he didn't bath often enough.

Diantha took the two sides of her cheeks just in front of her ears and pulled upward to see how she would look with a face lift. "You knew Buffalo before, didn't you? When he lived with Blossom Rugge?"

I confessed that I had.

"What is she like, this Rugge woman?"

I thought for a minute, wondering what to say. A sort of a nut? A dangerous ideologue? A woman I wouldn't want to cross? Blossom was all of those things.

"She's not too great-looking," was what I finally said, avoiding Diantha's eyes in the mirror, sure that the less she knew about her ex-rival the happier she'd be.

A secretary walked in on us then with the mail. She must have thought us mad to be standing there, staring at our reflections.

"Waldheim Pony Express," she said, tossing some letters on the desk before going off to deliver the bulk of the post to the culture czar. I left Diantha gazing dreamily at herself and went to sort through the day's delivery, hoping for something of interest.

There was something very much of interest.

The envelope was addressed to Winkworth Gaud and I opened it, as I did all mail addressed to him at the museum. Not that there was much of it. Most consisted of crank letters from artists and people trying to sell things.

This envelope was different. It was postmarked somewhere in Brazil and it was hand-addressed in that spidery European writing.

Dear Mr. Gaud: Your letter of the 19th November has just reached my hand, forwarded from Israel, where the post is no more efficient than elsewhere in the world, I regret to say.

My researches into the identity of the person in the photographs you sent me will require considerable time before I can give you a definite answer. Many years have passed since the events that concern us and appearances change. Plastic surgery is not unusual, as you yourself point out.

Nonetheless, the evidence so far justifies further research on our part. Naturally, it is of paramount importance to be completely sure of our facts before accusations are brought. Especially against the SS.

A complete investigation will require a full year at least. Witnesses must be found . . . documents assembled. Proof must be incontestable in our unceasing efforts to uncover and bring to justice those who have escaped to a good life in other countries.

The blood of the dead will not let us rest.

Sincerely,
Meyer Freudenthal

The famous Nazi hunter. I knew who he was—didn't everyone? I folded the letter up carefully and put it back in its envelope.

"I hear there's a man in Bulgaria who makes you look fabulous," Diantha was saying. I realized that she had been watching me in the mirror.

I didn't answer. I was thinking about Germany, not Bulgaria. Nazi Germany, to be exact. Dear God, what was this all about?

14

Shortly thereafter, the false calm that had reigned so blissfully was shattered not once but several times. The first event followed hotly on the arrival of the letter from South America: the trunk of my car was broken into while I was in New York. Nothing was stolen. My attaché case didn't appear to be disturbed. Still, it was disquieting.

Next came the crazy telephone call from the lady named Eloise Dallas.

I was sitting in my office, minding my own business, when it came. For about 1½ seconds I thought she was some kind of a nut, then I changed my mind. Whoever she was, I realized, she definitely had her wits about her.

"Mrs. Willum? Persis Willum?" The voice had that certain *je ne sais quoi* that instantly identifies the speaker as someone you might have gone to school with. On Long Island it is called, by people who don't have it, Locust Valley Lockjaw and it means you are probably presentable and able to make passable dinner table conversation.

This was that kind of voice.

"I'm Persis Willum." Ordinarily I would never admit it until I knew who was speaking, but this caller sounded safe.

"Marvelous. I just thought, when I saw the sketch you did of the kidnapped lady, that it would be a good idea to speak to you. A little late, I know, but I've been busy, I'm afraid. There are some things you just don't tell the police."

"Who is this speaking, please?"

"Why, it's Eloise Dallas—didn't I say? I'm a friend of your aunt's. You may have read about me in Dick Winston's column in the *Times,* among other places. Not because I'm a criminal but because, to my surprise, I seem to have turned into something of a hell-raiser."

I was instantly intrigued. "I must confess I haven't heard of you . . . what are you raising hell about, if I may ask?"

"Prostitutes," she said, a little smugly, I thought.

"Oh." Life does have its little surprises.

She laughed a rich, warm laugh. "Now bear with me, please. What I have to say is pertinent . . . but it requires a little preamble, if you don't mind."

"Preamble away, Miss Dallas. I'm fascinated."

"I live on East 30th Street between Park and Lex., 122, to be exact. It's a lovely neighborhood . . . tree-lined streets, gardens, brownstones that we've restored ourselves. Every year we have a block party to raise more money to plant more trees. It's a real neighborhood. At least, it *used* to be." Her voice altered suddenly.

"What happened?"

"Five years ago the prostitutes and the pimps took it over, like shock troops occupying a city. They even carried weapons. Every night, until seven in the morning, the streets—and our gardens and the vestibules of our buildings and the two parking lots across the way—belonged to them. We were prisoners in our own houses. Those troops of booted, satin mini-skirted harridans armed with furrier's knives and razors hidden in their boot tops or bushy wigs were programmed to attack anything that gave them grief . . . and they did. Very often they robbed their johns —you know what a john is?—after servicing them in our vestibules, and ganged up to beat them with two-by-fours. Am I offending you?"

I was beginning to wonder if, after all, the caller wasn't some kind of a nut. "I assume you're telling me all this for a reason, Miss Dallas?"

She snorted. "Of course. I warned you—be patient."

"I'm sorry. Please go on." I don't think I'd ever seen a prostitute (or what my aunt still calls "a lady of ill repute"), although I do remember seeing a lady drop a handkerchief on the street of

Fargo, North Dakota, once. But I was only seven years old and on a trip through the Black Hills with Aunt Lydie and I may have dreamed it.

"You can't imagine what it's like, living there now. Things going on in our vestibules . . . in parked cars . . . under the street lamps . . . in full view of our windows. Curses. Hurled rocks. Screams. Filth."

"And the police?"

She laughed the same throaty, warm laugh. "Hah. You may well ask. You call—no response. Or they come—and cruise right by. The police say the judges release the girls immediately. And the American Civil Liberties Union . . . whose civil liberties are they protecting, anyway? Not ours."

"Anyway, to be brief," the lady from 30th Street continued, a hint of humor in her voice as if she was aware that brief was the one thing she was not being, "we formed a block association in self-defense . . . to gather statistics and evidence so that we would have—what's that new word?—clout and get our assemblyman to endorse three new bills dealing with prostitution. Each of us had assigned nights on which to document all the goings-on and make notes and log descriptions of the participants, if possible, and write down license plates and so on and on. Anyway, you must understand that all of the prostitutes in our streets are black. So when this white girl appeared . . ."

I was beginning to get that prickly feeling . . . the one that comes just before the cyclone strikes or the bomb drops or somebody spills the soup all over you at dinner. I held my breath.

"So when this white girl appeared," she repeated, "looking, I might say, like an innocent angel, I couldn't believe it. A white man brought her . . . he waited every night parked in a car. Guarding her, I suppose, or those other whores would have cut her up and spit her out. Never seemed to have any business. Then she disappeared—after a week and a half. Never saw her again. I saw it happen . . . it was my night . . . she just got in the car and drove off and that was the last of her. I logged the license, naturally."

I was sure my heart was stopping. "And?"

"You must have guessed by now. It was the girl I saw in your drawing on television."

"Oh, no. It can't be true," I said.

"It is. I've told the police that much and they were delighted. Well, no wonder. But they don't want it spread all around until they have a chance to follow up on the lead I gave them, and they asked me not to talk. But you're Lydia Wentworth's niece and she's my good friend and you're working out there so I wanted you to know. You will know how to handle the information. And now that you know, *I* can stop worrying about it."

"Thank you," I told her weakly.

"But," she said firmly, "I did not tell them about the license. There are certain things one just does not do."

"You didn't?" Why not, I wondered? "Shouldn't you?"

"You never know what's going to turn up when you start a thing of this kind. Believe me, I know it's not wise when one of us is involved."

"Are you telling me that you checked that license number yourself?"

I heard her sigh. "Of course I checked it out, what would you expect? He will probably say the car was stolen. But suppose he hadn't reported it to the police? Then what would it look like? I knew his mother and father: both gone now. But it's the sort of thing we never let get into the papers—we protect each other. We have to—no one else will."

I was beginning to get a message. And I didn't like it one bit.

"Miss Dallas," I asked gently, "in whose name was that car registered?"

"Pierre Claude Richardson, II. And it had not been reported stolen. I checked that, too. Well, it's all yours now."

And she hung up. Leaving me with my mouth open.

15

I'd barely had time to try to figure out what in the world Eloise Dallas's information meant, when the phone rang again.

"Persis? This is Aaron."

Aaron Mellow was a cynicism-encrusted *Newsday* photographer who had been around forever. He had, in fact, been around the day the Rembrandt was stolen. Aaron said little as a rule, but saw much and drank more. I don't think he especially liked to drink, it was just that his generation of newsmen considered it part of the image. So he worked at it hard.

"Mellow. How are you?" I had a fair idea of how he was from his opening words. More mellow than sober, I told myself, in a fearsome if silent play on words. It was late in the day.

"Depends," he answered, hollowly.

Very well, I thought, I'm ready. "Depends on what?"

"A lot of things." I suppose he was emulating Edward R. Murrow or Quentin Reynolds. The Foreign Correspondent. They could get away with it, however; I doubted Mellow had ever been off Long Island.

"Did you know Gaud was carrying a camera the day he was shot?" he asked.

I tried to remember. A camera? "No—I don't think so. Why?"

But there was no rushing him. "Did you know I was the first to follow Gaud out the door?"

I hadn't known. "You saw him shot?"

"Not exactly. You know how it went, don't you? No, that's right, you couldn't . . . you were on the floor."

I certainly had been. All I knew was what had been in the papers . . . in the horror of Wink's wounding and death, details like who had followed him out the door first hadn't interested me.

"It went like this. One of them was covering the exit. None of us moved a muscle with that gun on us. They'd already sprayed a few bullets around to teach us respect, and there you were on the floor—a good example that they were in earnest. No hurry to die, any of us."

"I can't blame you," I murmured, sure that I myself would not have moved so much as an eyelash if I'd seen the gun first.

"Well, maybe that guy Gaud was in a hurry to die, because what he did was crazy. After they took off out the door he took off after them, moving fast, as if the danger never occurred to him. A few seconds later we heard the gun: he'd bought it, top of the steps . . . boom—just like that. It all happened in less than a minute."

My stomach turned. I could almost feel the impact of the bullets hitting Wink. "Please, Mellow—don't."

"Sorry. Anyway, we'd all heard this car start off, tires squealing. Some of us thought it was before the shots, some after, but we finally decided it was after, because it would have to be if they were going to hit him accurately. So, I rush out, hoping to get some kind of picture, even though my camera's smashed . . . hoping it's not too wrecked. And there's Gaud all crumpled up. But he got off one shot first."

"Shot?"

"With his camera. Still had this little Minox in his hand—so small you could hardly see it. I put it in my pocket . . . not going to let those other photographers get it, you can be sure, in case there's something in it. My first loyalty is to my paper. Not to mention it could mean money for me." He paused for dramatic effect. I could feel my Eloise Dallas tingle coming upon me.

"It wasn't a very good shot," he told me finally. "I've been working on it at odd times ever since, trying to bring it up. I have my own darkroom and good equipment, but even so it's been tough . . . hard to get anything out of it." This was said with a certain amount of professional snobbery. Was there a photographer in the world who wasn't a maniac for technical perfection? I remember one photographer—a teacher, no less—who accused Gregor of showing fake Brassais because Brassai, who was essentially a street photographer, hadn't shot the pictures under perfect studio conditions.

But I wasn't thinking of that now . . . I was trying to digest what Mellow had said. Was he saying that maybe Wink's being shot hadn't been an accident, a last-moment flurry of panic by the thieves? That maybe the picture had something to do with it? "Never mind if it was out of focus—you finally got something recognizable, didn't you? What was it?"

"That's why I'm calling you. You're an artist. I remember something you said once when we were doing that Gainsborough Brown story about the 'artist's eye' . . . you know, artists can see things even the camera can't see, and vice versa. . . ."

"What are you saying, Mellow?"

"It's like this: he got off this one shot—only one. It's a miracle he got anything at all. He was using a Minox and that's pretty sophisticated stuff for an amateur, plus he was moving. Maybe he wasn't an amateur—who knows? Anyway, I want you to have a look at this to see what you think before I show it to my editor or to the police. Maybe I'm crazy, and there's nothing too it, but I want to be sure, you know what I mean? I figure you're an artist . . . maybe you can make something of it."

I was being consumed by waves of curiosity and anxiety. "Make something of *what*, Mellow?" Edward R. Murrow wouldn't have tortured me like this.

He appeared to be studying the print, because there was a long pause. "Well, it's the damnedest thing. Now, remember, it's mostly a foggy blur and maybe I'm completely crazy . . . but the way the camera jumps up, it looks like Gaud is reacting to some physical force at the exact moment he snapped the picture. In fact, I think it was the moment he was shot. The camera records the impact."

"Then why do you need me?" I asked faintly, not wanting

ever to see the photograph Wink had taken at the moment he was shot.

"Because of the car and the people in it—I want to know if you see what I see."

"And you see . . . ?"

"The car is turning the corner at the end of the wing of the museum, almost out of accurate firing range. And everyone in it has his back turned."

"You mean—"

"I mean that if it turns out you see what I see . . . then nobody in the getaway car shot Winkworth Gaud."

16

Aaron promised faithfully to deliver the photograph personally by hand the following day and it was while I was waiting for him and wondering what I should do about it—and about Pierre Richardson and Belle Sandringham—that Blossom Rugge struck.

They were marching around and around in circles in front of the museum, their thin, querulous voices dissipating quickly in the chilly March air. By the time I got downstairs there were already two squad cars, each with its own bored officer in attendance. Both perked up when I stepped outside—we were old acquaintances from the opening night fiasco.

"Morning, Mrs. Willum! Lots of activity here this morning."

That was one way of putting it. Blossom Rugge's gang, the Art People's Union—about ten scruffy men and an equal number of just as scruffy women—were tottering wretchedly about in the cold, carrying hand-lettered signs which said things like ART FOR THE PEOPLE—NOT THE RICH, ONLY DEAD ARTISTS WELCOME AT THIS MUSEUM, AND WALDHEIM UNFAIR TO THE LIVING.

Oh, heavens, I thought, who needs this?

Evidently Blossom Rugge thought *we* needed it, because there she was in person, exhorting her troops through an old-fashioned megaphone and handing out news releases to the one local reporter who had made the scene so far. There would be more reporters later, I felt sure.

I walked up to her. "Blossom, what's going on here, anyway?"

I'd known Blossom for years, and she still scared me. Maybe it was because she was so single-minded in her devotion to her cause of unionizing artists, a task I considered unrealistic and impossible. Maybe it was because she could command respect from all these unruly creative types. Maybe it was because she was so totally lacking in female vanity: she was dark-eyed and not unattractive, but she certainly made a point of trying to look as awful as possible. She wore the kind of glasses, for example, that give the impression that the person is wearing several pairs simultaneously, pancake-style. This endowed her with an expression so inscrutable that it lent her a vaguely Oriental and mysterious . . . and alarming . . . air.

She had to be here for a reason and the reason had to spell trouble. Everything Blossom did spelled trouble for someone: it was why she had power. The thought flitted through my mind that perhaps she had unleashed her minions on us in retaliation for Diantha Lord's having made off with her Natural Man, Buffalo Horowitz, though why anyone should want to take revenge for that . . . well, love had its reasons. Whatever the cause, she was here and I didn't like it. It could only mean more bad publicity for the museum.

She was peering at me enigmatically through all those glasses. The tip of her little button nose was red and she was sniffing wretchedly. Her dark brown hair, parted approximately in the middle and hanging dispiritedly down each side of her face, looked like the tail of a badly groomed horse. I couldn't really decide what she was wearing—possibly it was uniform parts left over from the Franco-Prussian War. Well, at least she was warm.

"Oh, it's you," she said, as if I had finally come into focus. She did not sound thrilled to see me. Luckily she lowered the megaphone she was carrying, or I would have been deafened. "What are *you* doing here?"

I was momentarily taken aback. What did she think I was doing here? Then I remembered . . . it was Blossom's well-known technique to attack first with anything, even the least little nonsequitur, to keep you off balance. Never give the other guy an inch.

"Listen, Blossom," I said, "Don't you think it's pretty dumb to be marching here? The Waldheim isn't going to exclude living artists—this is only the first exhibition. They're looking for a new director now, and as soon as he's selected, they'll work out their program, which is *sure* to include exhibitions of work by living artists."

"Hah," she replied, glaring at me. "Another European director, I suppose? What's wrong with Americans?" She had leaped on that like a hungry lioness.

"Why not wait to see whom they hire before you get upset, Blossom?" I asked, trying to be reasonable.

"Down with the Rich who let the Poor Artists starve," someone shouted in my ear. Blossom led a few cheers before giving me her attention again. "What do *you* know? You're one of *them*, the Elite. You're in the Social *Register*." She said it as if being in the Social Register was akin to being on Murderer's Row.

It was perfectly idiotic: Blossom knew I didn't have a sou and that I worked as hard as anybody. What was she up to, anyway? "I *do* know that your so-called starving artists will be given a chance to show their work here, and I can't understand why you would put on this demonstration before being sure of your facts."

"Nuts," Blossom said. She had an impressive number of degrees from any number of schools, but she never admitted it. "I have it straight from the horse's mouth that you're going to shut us out, Willum."

"Come on, who gave you that information?"

Blossom was looking at her watch—it was the second time she'd done so—then favored me with her attention once more. "That's my business, but I *will* tell you it's someone on the inside, a source that's absolutely reliable, so don't think you can pull anything on me. I've been told the Waldheim's going completely noncontemporary, just another bastion of dead artists. Well, you aren't going to get away with it."

"Have you asked Ringwell or Brown?" I asked, bewildered.

"Are you kidding? Those politicians? Do you think we're dumb enough to expect a straight answer from them?"

Frankly, I had to agree with them there, but who could this mysterious source be? Buffalo? And why hadn't I heard anything about it?

"And you want to know something else, Willum?" Blossom was really getting cranked up now. "I just got some letters in the mail. Anonymous, but, boy, do they know what they're talking about. You want to know what they said? That some of your precious Waldheim dinosaurs are fake! Hah! What do you have to say about that?"

I wouldn't say anything for a moment. Fakes—from the collections of the Seven? The thought was absurd. I opened my mouth to tell her so, but Blossom was waving her arms vigorously now, commanding a livelier tempo from her troops, and I decided to forget it entirely. Her raggle-taggle band had obediently stepped up their pace and were running now, hair flying, clothes flapping. They won't be able to keep up that pace for long, I thought—they are all too out of shape from sitting at their easels, nibbling on cookies, and drinking wine.

A few onlookers had arrived and were standing around in attitudes of wonder and astonishment. Demonstrations never happen in the Gull Harbor neighborhood. The police stirred nervously. The rhythm of the demonstrators increased. I looked at them, bemused, and wondered if any of them were artists I knew . . . surely I would know someone. Then I wondered if they really were artists or if they had been recruited from the campus of a nearby college. Maybe, the way they were carrying on, they had been recruited from a madhouse.

I scanned their faces carefully. No, I did not know any of these people. There was something about one face . . . but I couldn't put it into context, unusual for me. Maybe I was just imagining it.

Several new cars drove up. I saw Blossom give her watch a triumphant look: the press, and right on schedule, it appeared. She rushed forward to greet them, dispensing releases with abandon. Now that the full complement of news people had arrived, the demonstrators really gave tongue. *Money can't buy genius,* they shouted. *Down with the Waldheim.*

I kept watching the one face I thought I knew, trying to place it. I couldn't understand the blank I was drawing. He saw me looking and traded stares briefly, then he turned and quietly melted away from the rest of the demonstrators. I tried to push through the Art People to follow, but it was hopeless—I kept getting waylaid by Blossom, who was punching and pushing and laying about with her megaphone in what I hoped was not malice toward me but merely excessive zeal for her cause, coupled with a determination to give the photographers their money's worth of action shots.

Suddenly the demonstration took an uglier turn. Some of the protesters began hurling rocks at the museum windows, fortunately missing them—artists are notoriously nonathletic. One policeman called on his radio for reinforcements and the second officer began a valorous attempt to haul away the chief demonstrator, Blossom Rugge, who immediately kicked and screamed and poured out a score of words I never thought I'd hear uttered on the grounds of any museum. Just as the officer was clamping handcuffs on her wrists and stuffing her into the back seat of the squad car, she caught sight of me through the crowd and become further enraged.

"You there, Miss Goody-Goody." She paused momentarily to deliver a beautifully directed kick at the restraining policeman's vulnerable shins. "Just wait. We aren't through with you yet—or the Waldheim!" The officer stopped being a gentleman and stuffed her into the car for good.

The Art People had finally noted the plight of their peerless leader, or maybe they'd been ordered to let her be carted away by the fuzz . . . it certainly made for a better story. In any case, they now turned their attention from ineffectual rock throwing to a sincere effort to rescue Rugge from the clutches of the law. The law, being outnumbered, very intelligently sped away, siren blaring, to the sanctuary of the Gull Harbor police station.

Reinforcements were now arriving, squad cars from as far away as Rum Island . . . a total of seven, representing almost the entire mobile police force of the immediate area. With their leader gone, the demonstrators prudently scattered across the muesum's spacious grounds, the police cars following like rodeo cowboys. The local lawmen rarely had an opportunity for such sport and they were making the most of it.

I walked slowly up the steps of the museum, my head aching. This was a public relations nightmare—a nightmare, if Blossom Rugge was to be believed—abetted at least in part by someone on the inside. But why? Was Jason right? Did someone have it in for the Waldheim? I wished that I could just sit down and cry.

Dejected, I tugged at the gleaming brass handle on the museum door. And that was when I heard Mellow's hollow voice. "Hey there, Persis . . . hold up a minute . . . I've got it for you." There he was himself, bounding up the steps after me and then stopping beside me, bent over in a convulsion of cigarette coughing. When the seizure had passed, he straightened up and handed me an envelope.

"Been carrying this around since I phoned you. Knew they'd send me this way sooner or later today, so here it is! I'm on assignment, though, can't stay . . . call you later!"

He beamed at me proudly, then bounded back down the steps. I smiled after him gratefully: I wouldn't sit down and cry just yet.

17

Photographs are funny things. The camera is the consummate liar—far more so than the artist's brush, I think, although photographers may disagree. With an artist, no matter what his technique or style of painting, his point of view toward his subject or his emotional involvement . . . no matter how he may try to disguise his subjective feeling toward what he paints . . . he never quite succeeds. The truth is revealed in some measure, however small, because the work is the creation of the artist and the artist's hand and artist's eye, and no one else's.

That, at least, is how it appears to me.

The photographer, on the other hand, is something else. No matter how much the photographer imparts, the camera has a life and a style and a will of its own. It can work as one with the photographer, or it can work independently, presenting nuances the photographer never intended, details the photographer himself never noted. It can be devious. It can be subtle. It can be outrageous.

So I approached Mellow's (really Wink's) photograph with respect and suspicion. The light on the big magnifier on my desk was lit. My special magnifying eyeglass, used in searching out vagrant signatures on paintings, was in my hand. I pulled the 8-by-10-inch glossy from its manila envelope.

It didn't look promising. As Mellow had said yesterday on the telephone, the picture was blurred, and the developing and enlarging of it to the larger 8-by-10-inch size hadn't improved the clarity. Aside from that, it was much as described—a magnified blur.

I began to move the lamp back and forth on its flexible stem, counting on the trusty Luxo lamp to resolve the image. It was a little like trying to focus a camera. Finally I began to get it. I moved the lamp another fraction of an inch.

What I was looking at was the blur of a car moving at top speed around the corner of the wing of the museum. No faces showed. No whites of eyes. No gleam of metal on gunbarrels. No one was looking back, shooting.

For a long time I sat dejectedly at my desk with the photograph in my hand, oblivious to the museum business going on around me. The photograph Wink had taken placed everything in a totally new context. The "nuns" had not shot Wink. Someone else had aimed at him and fired. Was that why Wink had begged me to get him out of the hospital, where he was vulnerable? If I'd gone back to him instead of rushing off to New York to see Jason Waldheim, would he still be alive?

I don't know exactly how long I sat there. All I know is that when a secretary came in with the mail and said, "Are you all right, Mrs. Willum?" I realized that tears were spilling over and running down my cheeks without my even being aware of them.

I had finally sat down and cried.

18

Ed Simms, thirty-seven years old and chief of the FBI's Art Recovery Squad, was one of the people who had been floating in and out of my life for years with the mystery and surprise of a marker buoy appearing and disappearing in a fog. At this moment he was extremely visible, sitting opposite me behind his desk in his New York headquarters.

Wink's photograph had finally sent me running to the law and he was the lawman I knew best.

Simms was a nice man. He had the kind of square-cut American face and ingenuous brown eyes that gave one confidence. Each time I saw him I thought, with looks like that it's a good thing he never decided to become a crook.

"How do you like your coffee?" he asked. He had a little electric burner for boiling water in his office and he was fussing over the coffee mixings now at his desk like a hostess presiding over a tea table.

"Everything, please. You?"

"Black. You learn to do without frills in this business."

I smiled nervously. "Oh, come on, Ed. You don't lead such a hard life. I associate the Art Squad more with brocade walls, marble palaces, and mad millionaires."

"Dingy warehouses and deals in dark parking lots would be more like it, Persis."

We drank our coffee, looking at one another and saying nothing. Simms was waiting.

"Did you know that the girl who went under the name of Saskia van Uylenburgh was really a prostitute?" I asked finally.

He sighed. "We know. A lady named Eloise Dallas told us.

Looks like a scam, though we don't know yet how it was all done. Apparently she was some little trollop who read all the publicity about the museum and decided to pose as Saskia long enough to get her foot in the door of Gull Harbor where all the rich folk congregate."

"Have you found out her real name?"

"Neither her real name nor anything else about her, but we will—we've just begun to investigate. It takes time. Those hookers come from all over . . . and nobody talks."

I frowned: there was something else I didn't understand. "What about those Paris press clippings Ringwell got about her? That's why he started looking for her in the first place."

"Ringwell's secretary can't put her hands on them." The winter sun was working its way cautiously into the room and shining thinly on his brown hair. The effect was that of a Byzantine halo.

"His office help is not notoriously efficient," I murmured.

"Civil service," he said. "Still, I think we can safely assume those clippings were phonies. It's not hard to get that sort of thing done. Passports . . . false documents . . . fake press clippings . . . all you have to do is pay the man. Would Ringwell call Paris and check? Hardly likely. As a matter of fact, *we* tried checking, but as Ringwell couldn't remember the date or the paper—he wasn't even 100 percent sure it was Paris—we drew a blank."

He shook his head, discouraged by the vagaries of a certain county executive. "And that man of his . . . Brown . . . he was no help either. Said he never actually saw them."

It surprised me. "He seems so coldly efficient. I'm amazed that secretaries' heads didn't roll."

"They don't roll in civil service—they just change places." He shook his head again. "We could use a break in this case."

I placed the manila envelope containing Wink's photo on the desk before him. "I think this is the break, Ed, although you may not like it. Do you have a magnifier of some kind?"

"Over here." He got up and was out from behind his desk in one swift movement. The magnifier was on a work table under

115

the window in the institutional-green room. I was pleased to see that it was a Luxo lamp like mine, but a larger version. As we waited for the lamp to heat up, I explained about the photograph and Mellow. Then I drew the 8-by-10-inch glossy out of the envelope and put it under the lamp. We both bent forward as I moved the magnifier up and down, trying to bring the photograph into focus. I fiddled. He helped. Finally the picture emerged.

Simms whistled softly. Then, after a moment of silence, quietly: "This changes everything."

"The thieves didn't shoot Wink," I said. He nodded.

"Murder?" I asked. He didn't answer. He didn't have to. We both knew.

The rest was academic. He went through his motions—I went through mine. We said the regulation things. It was obvious he couldn't wait to be rid of me: he had things to do, *new* things, dictated by the photograph I'd brought.

We said good-bye. He saw me to the door. I heard him on the telephone before I was even halfway to the elevator, his voice crisp and sharp through the closed door, barking commands.

And as I stood waiting for the elevator to arrive, I asked myself why I hadn't told Simms about Belle Sandringham's Degas and Pierre Richardson's involvement with Saskia, the prostitute. But once again it was academic. I knew.

Wink's photograph had changed everything.

I didn't want my friends involved in a case of murder.

19

In all the excitement of Wink's photograph and my visit to Ed Simms in the hallowed halls of the FBI, I almost forgot that I had sworn a solemn oath to Rosi to lend moral support in a tennis tournament she and David were in.

"You have to come," Rosi had insisted. "We're going to need all the help we can get, and you know how competitive David is. Please." I'm a terrible tennis player, but a great spectator. Rosi never took anything very seriously, including tennis, so I had promised because I knew David would expect her to perform well. Maybe a one-woman cheering section would help—and besides, there was something I wanted to ask David. Luckily I remembered the affair at what was literally the last minute.

They were playing the tournament in Mrs. Sandringham's indoor tennis courts, which could easily have doubled for somebody's palace. The architect had been the great Bradley Delahanty, whose impeccable taste was reflected in buildings all over Gull Harbor, each architectural triumph more ravishing than the last. This particular building had columns and arches and great tubs of trees, and I would have been perfectly happy to spend the rest of my life living right in the middle of the thing.

Unfortunately, they had already finished their match by the time I arrived. It must have been a lopsided score—from the look on David's face I knew instantly that the game had not been a triumph for him and Rosi. The drink already in his hand gave me the same message.

"Sorry I missed you," I said. "I came as fast as I could."

He glowered at me. "It didn't take us long to lose. I told

Rosi she should have offered her own place for this affair. She plays better on her own turf." They all had tennis courts, naturally.

"Where is Rosi?" I asked, looking around for her. There were the usual number of interested spectators, all of them wives or husbands or relatives of the players. It was a pretty chic-looking group Both the men and women had that sort of throwaway elegance that was Gull Harbor's trademark.

"She's taking a shower. Drink?"

"No, thanks."

He really didn't care. "Keep me company while I wait for Rosi." David slid slowly into the depths of an enormous chintz-covered sofa done up in a brown-and-blue floral pattern. It made a great background for David's brown eyes and dark skin. David had a fighter's body, nicely muscled and full of natural grace, like an animal.

"David," I said, trying to read his sharp, clever eyes, "have you any idea where Willem de Groot got his Rembrandt?"

He stopped sliding and held himself very still . . . then, imperceptibly, he began to draw himself upward again—a fighter getting into position. "Why do you ask?" Same old lawyer trick, answering a question with a question.

I tried to keep the tone light so that he wouldn't be alarmed: lawyers are easily alarmed, I find. "Because I take it for granted that you know everything, and I'm curious. He bought it *somewhere*. And since you're everybody's favorite lawyer I thought you just might know." Indeed you are everybody's favorite lawyer, I thought, and that's why you drive a Mercedes and a Jaguar that looks like a hornet, and why you can keep a fifty-two-foot yacht in the British Virgin Islands and a whole flock of bank accounts in Switzerland.

"You're just curious?"

"Yes, that's all. I never heard of a Rembrandt in the de Groot collection before, so I assume he just acquired it, and I wondered where."

David looked at me thoughtfully, his calculating eyes wary.

"Is that why you're spending so much time in the art libraries? Researching the Rembrandt?"

It was as good an explanation as any—furthermore, it was partly true—but what I said was, "Why would I do that?"

"Don't worry—it's all right. It's just that we all feel responsible for you, with everything that's happened, so we're kind of keeping an eye on you. You *are* researching the Rembrandt, aren't you?"

Not exactly. The research, as I mentioned earlier, had to do with every art theft in which there was neither a demand for ransom nor the recovery of the lost object. It was painstaking work, but I'd begun to spot a pattern. Prior to World War II, there was practically nothing, but after 1947 the special kinds of thefts that I was looking for had accelerated. My list was slim but growing. One thing I had noticed: it was a true connoisseur's catalog—every one of my thefts involved an absolutely first-rate picture.

A case in point was the Haarlem Rembrandt, another portrait of Saskia van Uylenburgh (which is why it particularly interested me), in fact, critics said at the time, the best: "the finest example of an early Rembrandt portrait known to exist." It had been stolen two years ago "by a team dressed in workmen's clothes. They entered the museum carrying a ladder and paint cans and left carrying the Rembrandt."

All of my research notes had been in my attaché case, but now I carried them around with me in a series of bags like a shopping bag lady. David knew I was researching Rembrandt— could he have been responsible for my car being broken into and my office rifled . . . nonsense. Why would he do a thing like that?

"Actually," I told him, "I'm researching a show for Gregor's galleries next season. We're doing 'native painters' of America and they're very poorly documented."

David probably wouldn't know what "native painters" were. His collection was Nolde and Rouault and Soutine and people like that—Europeans. Unless he'd read my notes, my explanation would satisfy him.

"So," I continued, trying to get the conversation back on the track, "what about the de Groot Rembrandt? Do you have any idea where it came from?"

"Yes, David, what about Willem's Rembrandt? Where did it come from all of a sudden?" Rosi had joined us. I hadn't seen her coming, but I ought to have smelled her perfume and known she was near—she was wearing lots of Estée this year. It was a scent you couldn't miss.

As usual, she was all sparkling and beautiful; it was enough to make you grind your teeth, if you were a woman. Tonight she was being beautiful in a white tennis skirt and white sweater with Cardin's big C on the sleeve. She made every other woman in the place look like a housemaid. "Thanks for coming, Persis. I'm sorry you missed the match. It was a classic of some kind but don't ask me what kind. David, be a darling and get me a drink . . . no ice, please."

David went off on his errand of mercy and Rosi plunked down beside me, curling one leg casually beneath her and letting the other, which was long and smooth and tan, just hang out for everyone to admire.

"Now, Persis, what I want to know before David comes back is what you've found out about Wink Gaud's death. . . . Edgar tells me you were over at the hospital asking questions."

I had indeed been at the hospital earlier in the week asking a few casual questions, not because I'd taken Rosi seriously when she said Wink might have been murdered, but just out of a general sense of wanting to know how and what had happened. Now, with the implications involved in the photograph found in Wink's camera, everything I'd learned had a different interpretation. Almost everyone had been seen in the hospital during the late afternoon or evening of the day Wink had died. There had been a board meeting at 8:00 P.M. to deal with the question of some new equipment for the physical therapy department, Pierre Richardson presiding. Ringwell and Brown had been present in the late afternoon for the unveiling of a new addition to the Children's Wing. Board members who had attended one or another of these events included Rosi, Lawless, Mrs. Sandringham, and de Groot, who was standing in for his father who was ill and a patient in the hospital. Diantha Lord had worked the late afternoon shift as a Gray Lady in the canteen. The general had been on volunteer duty at the reception desk from 7:00 until 11:00 P.M. Jason had been in and out on some Waldheim Wing business. The only persons not known positively to have been on or near the scene were Blossom Rugge, Buffalo Horowitz, Persis Willum, and—possibly—the president of the United States. And even they might have been overlooked in all the comings and goings.

Any one of the aforementioned group or their emissary could have slipped into I.C.U., wearing a hospital coat and looking very official. It wouldn't do to tell Rosi these things, however. With the latest developments she'd probably go into orbit and start announcing the murder to the world. The police would just love that.

"I didn't find out anything, Rosi."

"Oh." Her face fell. "That's what Edgar said you'd find out . . . nothing. But I tell you, Persis, I'm still convinced he was murdered—and I'll tell you something else. There was something very peculiar about Wink. . . ."

But David had returned. It was the swiftest errand of mercy on record—so quick I wondered if he was afraid of missing anything we said. And, in fact, what he said was, "Did I miss anything?"

Rosi put her pretty nose into her drink and didn't answer for a minute. Then she looked straight at him and said, "You do know something about the Rembrandt, David. I know you do. I overheard Willem asking you if you knew how to get your hands on a major one for him, and no questions asked."

David was horrified. "Rosemary!"

"But you know I always eavesdrop, David. I have absolutely no scruples, and everybody knows it, so you shouldn't have secret discussions when I'm around if you want them to stay secret."

He was nearly speechless. "Rosi . . . it's not ethical . . . ."

"Ethical? Who says I have to be ethical? You men do things every day that *I* don't consider ethical. All I do is eavesdrop.

Compared to a lot of things in your profession, eavesdropping is pretty small change."

David threw up his hands. "I surrender."

But she was just getting started. "What about all the work you did for Petroklus . . . registering his ships under all those foreign flags? And what about that man in Africa you helped supply the arms to, so your clients could get in on the copper rights when he took over the country? And. . . ."

This time David was not fooling. "*Be quiet*, Rosemary. Not another word. You don't know what you're saying."

She stopped at once. "Sorry, David, but you make me so mad sometimes . . . saying I have no ethics. I know everything you do is legal, but . . ."

"It's all right, Rosemary. I understand. Now enough."

"In that case, what about de Groot's Rembrandt? I'm just as curious as Persis to know where it came from." Rosi was like a Norwich terrier—once she had an idea by the scruff of the neck, she didn't let go.

A small clutch of tennis-watchers came by to chat with us and gave David a short reprieve, but Rosi didn't forget. The minute they left she reminded him. "The Rembrandt?"

He'd had grace time in which to think it over and he must have decided he might as well give in. "Just as you said, Rosi, he told me he wanted a Rembrandt—'the best'—in time for the museum's show. 'Get it any way you can, Lawless. I'll pay the bills and no questions asked.'" David paused and assumed an expression of bafflement. "He seemed to think I'd know how to arrange such a thing."

Of course he knew. What you do is let it be known in certain quarters that you want a particular thing and presently, presto, the desired work of art appears. Theft to order is what it's called. "Don't you know how to arrange it, David?" I asked innocently.

"Well, certainly I do, I suppose. There's one very important gallery, in fact . . . but that's neither here nor there. The point is that before I really got to thinking of doing anything about it, he called me, very elated, to say that he had a Rembrandt—a splendid one—so I was not to bother, thank you. You can imagine

I was happy to be rid of the assignment. I like money as much as the next man, but something like that—" What he was saying was that he might have ended up doing business with the underworld. It wouldn't be the first or the last time, I was sure. I wondered if Rosi was aware of it.

"So you don't know where the painting came from?" My hopes were sinking like falling soufflés.

"Not a clue. De Groot wasn't talking."

"Oh, damn," said Rosi. "I was hoping for a good scandal. David, you never have anything fascinating to tell me. It's disappointing." We fell silent for a moment. She sighed. "Well, there must be *something* you can tell us . . . what about the bridge? Are we making any progress?"

"Not really. Legal maneuverings . . . stalling tactics . . . trying to forestall the inevitable, I'm afraid. There's not much we can do now."

Rosi's eyes widened. "Oh, don't say that, David. You know, I saw that terrible man Brown at the museum the other day and he actually had the nerve to ask me where I was planning to move to after the bridge was built. Where do people like that *come* from, anyway?"

"I looked into that when the thing began," Lawless said. "Typical story. Brown got into village politics on Long Island as a volunteer fireman—you know the kind of local thing—then he hitched his star to Ringwell. Started out as his errand boy and general flunky, until Ringwell got to depend on him . . . as Ringwell rose, Brown rose, and he finally ended up as his hatchet man and adviser. Oddly enough, he seems to have some genuine interest in art—spends his vacations visiting museums in Europe . . . not completely culturally deprived like Ringwell. So I suppose it's logical that the county executive would put him into the arts and culture post."

"Culture!" Rosi snorted. "What's he like to work with, Persis?"

"I rarely see him, and I'm glad."

"I take it you're not mad for him," Rosi laughed. "Not when you have someone like Jason Waldheim pursuing you."

"Oh, Rosi—he's not pursuing me." I sincerely hoped she wouldn't say anything like that in front of Oliver Reynolds when he got back. "I'm just some kid who amuses him, that's all. And I admire him for his brains."

She gave me a wicked glance. "Well, it wouldn't be his brains that would interest me." I wondered, with a twinge of jealousy that surprised me, if she and Jason had ever been lovers.

David looked at his watch. "I don't want to break this up, ladies, but I've got a squash game in half an hour in Mill Creek."

"He's a game maniac," Rosi said, not without admiration. "Muscle happy. He jogs two miles to his office every morning. Why don't you jog off now to get the car, David, and I'll gossip with Persis until you get back."

David sprinted off and Rosi and I headed for my Mustang.

"Wouldn't it have been easier to let me drive you both to where he was parked?" I asked her.

"Oh, no. David never rides when he can walk or run. I told you, he's a fitness nut. I must say, it pays off. He could fell an ox with one blow. Isn't that the mysterious way they measure strength in books? You know, I have a *tendresse* for older men." This was indeed news. I'd always thought she had a *tendresse* for men, period.

She had scrambled into my car with me and was peering at me intently through the six o'clock dark. The gay and careless beauty was suddenly serious. "I have something to say to you, Persis, and I want to say it before David gets back. I'm crazy about him, but that doesn't mean I trust him—you understand? This is what I want to say . . ." She paused. Even her voice sounded different—much lower, almost gruff. "I don't think you should be poking around into Wink Gaud's death. It could be dangerous—don't you realize that? If anything happened, I'd feel responsible because I was the one who first suggested that it might be murder. I never dreamed, when I said it, that you'd get involved."

"I've just asked a few questions, that's all."

She didn't insist. "All right . . . I've said my piece."

"Thanks. I appreciate your concern, Rosi. You're sweet."

124

"Sweet? Well, hardly."

We sat in silence for a while, each thinking her own thoughts. They must have been similar, though, because she suddenly said the name that had been on my mind.

"Winkworth Gaud. There was something about him. . . ."

"What do you mean?"

Rosi hesitated, then she turned on all her blazing charm. "You know how I am, Persis. I'm not bright, like you . . . I don't have any real talent. You can paint—it makes you special. My only specialty is men, my only talent, you might say. I like men . . . more than that, I understand them. They've been my life's work, sort of."

I nodded. It was a fair assessment.

"All right, then this is it. Don't ask me to explain how I know because I can't tell you, but there's a certain . . . chemistry between people. I'm particularly sensitive to it, and I'd stake my reputation, if I had one, that Winkworth Gaud wasn't . . . what he pretended to be."

I didn't understand. "Pretended?"

"Yes. You know . . . flitty."

"But that's just the way he was, Rosi. We all knew that, but nobody cared. He wasn't pretending anything."

She shook her head, blonde hair flying with the vigor of her denial. "No, no, it was an act, I tell you. There isn't a man alive who can fool me when it comes to sex. Take that Bill Brown, for instance. So cool. So aloof. Well—and I haven't told this to anyone else, mind—I just thought I'd find out one day and I called his bluff . . . and I was right: he's a madman. I barely escaped with my life. I had to tell him that I wasn't accustomed to animals . . . that infuriated him, but it stopped him cold. Into kinky sex, I'll bet, our Mr. Brown. Ugh." She shuddered, then she appeared to put it out of her mind. Rosi wasn't one to bear a grudge.

"Now I only told you about Brown to prove my point. I know about men—and Gaud was something else. He was *all* man. I felt it whenever he was around me. There was an electricity, although he never touched me."

I was too astonished to do anything but stare at her dumbly. The Winkworth Gaud she was talking about was a Gaud I certainly had never known.

She began to gather up her sweater and her purse and her racket bag. David Lawless pulled up next to us and was getting out of his Jaguar. Rosi still had a couple of last words for me, though. Clutching her things, she leaned over and whispered, "Winkworth Gaud was just as much a man as that delicious bunch of muscle coming toward us right now . . . maybe even more so. I knew Brown would turn out to be a fake, that's why I tested him. Winkworth Gaud was a fake, too, although I never got to prove it. He was having us on, darling. Now why do you suppose he did that?"

She leaned over and kissed me lightly on the cheek. Then she was gone.

20

Blossom Rugge's People's Art Union demonstration at the Waldheim had occasioned the usual uproar in the press; not, to be sure, on the scale of that which had followed the original theft-kidnapping, but it was a chance to rehash everything all over again. There was something else in the news, too, which didn't help matters any. The police had discovered where the shots had come from that had hit Winkworth Gaud.

Under the terms of his agreement with the county, Jacob Waldheim had specified that his bedroom and study be preserved in order to serve as guest quarters for an artist-in-residence at the museum. Above the wood-burning fireplace in the study hung a small collection of old Jacob's favorite guns. As the rooms were having their floors refinished at the time of the opening, anyone could have walked in and helped himself to a gun. And someone apparently had. There was a beautiful view of the museum's front steps from the windows.

Reading about it all made me almost physically ill, but I knew I had to put my feelings aside for a change. I had been sadly neglecting my job at the museum for the past few days, and the paperwork had been piling up all over my desk, the stacks staring at me reproachfully. Unfortunately, my job at the moment also required listening to one very angry county executive.

"Jesus Christ, Mrs. Willum," he was shouting across my desk. "Can't you do anything about these newspapers? They're killing us!"

"I don't really think we can keep a murder investigation quiet, Mr. Ringwell," I said as calmly as I could.

"Maybe not, but at *least* we should be able to do something about this Rugge woman! Art for the people—that's all I seem to hear about."

"Why not arrange for her and some of her other members to create a board of artists to advise the museum?" suggested Bill Brown, sitting down beside me. "We don't have to listen to them—but it might placate her enough to keep her quiet."

"Hmm," said Ringwell.

I was surprised at Brown. It was actually a practical suggestion and besides, I thought to myself, maybe they'd even contribute something useful. "But how are we going to get her to accept the offer?" I asked.

"Simple," said Brown. "We get someone to go see her and charm her into it." And he looked at me.

"Oh, no," I said, backing off. "The woman can't stand me and I can't say I—" And then I broke off. An idea had just hit me. I knew just the person to do it . . . .

I put it to Jason over dinner at L'Endroit. We were having their sole with Dijon sauce and feeling gastronomically euphoric.

"Darling," I said (we'd progressed to the "darling" stage), "do you think you could possibly go to see Blossom Rugge and convince her to form a board of artists to advise the museum? Maybe over dinner?"

Jason began to choke and the waiter rushed over to us, his face full of concern. People aren't supposed to choke in three-star restaurants. Jason waved him away and pulled himself together.

"I trust you're not serious," he said, groaning. "Remember, I saw a photograph of the lady in the papers."

"But, Jason," I said, "you'd be just perfect for it. We simply *can't* afford any more bad publicity at the moment, and you can charm the birds out of the trees, as you well know." I gave him a little smile. "Besides, it is my personal belief that deep down inside her, Blossom Rugge is just as snob conscious as any of us. The magic of a Waldheim in the flesh just might help persuade her that we are decent people and not out to shoot down living artists."

He wasn't impressed. "No way."

"For me?"

He looked at me speculatively. "All right, Persis, I'll tell you what. I'll do it—if you'll come, too . . . and spend the rest of the day with me. And the night."

I laughed. The day, I told him, was one thing. The night was something else.

He gave in gracefully. The day, then. He had meetings in town. We would meet at Blossom Rugge's.

But it did not work out exactly as planned.

21

Blossom's lair wasn't too hard to get to. Her address was in an area of artists' lofts in that pie-shaped location known as Noho, just above Houston Street and bordered by the two Villages—the East Village on one side and Greenwich Village on the west. Snuggled up against it were Little Italy, the Bowery, and—three blocks away—Soho itself. A very proper People's Art-type neighborhood. The Art People's leader inhabited an ancient building that housed, in order of appearance, a tiny entry papered with notices of community meetings to combat crime, the New Style Button Company on the second floor (its name written in chalk across the door), and Blossom herself on the third floor, which was attained by a hazardous ascent on rickety stairs.

Jason and I had been scheduled to see Blossom at three, but I was actually here an hour early due to a last-minute call of distress from Diantha Lord last night.

"Persis, you must help me. Buffalo is seeing that woman again."

"What woman, Diantha?" She sounded truly distraught.

"That Rugge woman, of course. I overheard him. He's going to see her tomorrow, Persis. I can't stand it if he goes back to her again. You've got to do something."

It seemed to me that losing Buffalo wouldn't be the worst thing that could happen to someone, but then, I wasn't Diantha. "I'm seeing Blossom myself tomorrow at three. What can I do to help?" If she wanted Buffalo so much, the least I could do was offer to help keep him in the corral.

"Be there an hour earlier . . . that's when she's seeing Buffalo. Just be there. He won't dare give in to her if he knows you're listening and will tell me." She seemed to think that Blossom intended to rope and tie the hairy cowboy artist and never let him escape again.

"I'll be there," I assured her. And here I was. The Rugge door didn't have a doorbell. But it did have Buffalo Horowitz in the flesh, standing in the hallway knocking on it . . . rat-tat-tat . . . rat-tat-tat. He looked surprised to see me. I'd have thought he'd heard me coming up the stairs.

"Hi," he said, pausing in midknock. "What are you doing here?" He was in his regulation costume: Wrangler jeans, soiled Stetson, tight denim shirt, and high-heeled boots. I wondered if he dared sit down in the jeans for fear of their splitting. Looking at him standing there at Blossom Rugge's door, I found it hard to believe that he had once been Harry Horowitz with a Brooklyn accent and a New Yorker's paunch.

"Isn't Blossom in?"

He kicked at the door with the toe of his boot. I expected to see corral dust flying up. "Don't understand it—hasn't answered yet. Damn woman—told me to be here." He was laconic. He was also annoyed.

"That's odd, if she was expecting you." Which I just happened to know was true.

He shrugged. "Strange woman—always was. Probably just stepped out and expects us to wait." He leaned against the door, crossing one tightly sheathed leg in front of the other and pulling in his gut self-consciously. Despite myself, I looked at him with admiration. "Buffalo, you look marvelous." He really looked the part—bone skinny and bowlegged. How could he be bowlegged? "You must ride." He'd denied it during his dinner conversation with Mrs. Sandringham.

"You kidding?" His eyebrows shot up, then he saw where I was looking. "Oh, that. Always was bowlegged. Used to wear batwing chaps to hide it, but no more. Makes people think I'm the real thing." At least he had no illusions about it.

He was getting impatient. He banged at the door again.

"Are you still seeing Blossom?" I asked between knocks.

The idea seemed to horrify him. "You kidding?" It was his

favorite expression today. "That was over four years ago, before I went West. We split up then. Blossom doesn't approve of today's cowboy artists . . . says they're not authentic . . . compromising their art and all that silly stuff. Being head of the Art People's Union, she has very rigid standards. Has to. Only right. But me—I like to eat."

He continued his assault on the door. "Makes me laugh, though. She's always ready to take my money, even if my art isn't authentic." He grinned slyly.

"You give her money?"

"Why the hell do you suppose I'm here? Who else supports this gang? Not the people's artists, you can be sure. They wouldn't last a day without me . . . but, what the hell, I'm making all this dough, more than I can spend. Blossom supported me when I needed it. Now she says she needs it, although she doesn't seem poor to me. I'm happy to contribute if it makes her feel happy and keeps her from bothering Di—"

He stopped suddenly. He had been going to say that paying off Blossom kept her from begging Diantha for funds. And telling about her old affair with Buffalo. And who knows what else. Hush money of a sort.

I guess he felt he'd said too much. "Listen . . . I gotta get going. Can't stand here all day waiting. Silly broad wants money, least she can do is be here when I come."

"Right." I agreed, partly because he *was* right and mostly because I wanted him to leave the field to me. "I think I'll wait a minute or two—I just got here, after all."

"Up to you." He uncrossed his legs, hitched up his jeans. "Word of advice, though . . . don't stand out here—she could take forever. Go on inside."

"You mean the door's open?"

He wiggled the handle. "No, but it doesn't matter. Got a credit card? The lock on this door always was lousy."

Before I could protest he had taken out a card of his own and inserted it between the door and the frame. After a few seconds of fiddling, he turned the knob and the door opened.

He bowed and waved me toward the open door. "Don't

worry about it. Tell her I'm sorry I couldn't wait . . . I'll give her a call. Tell her next time she wants money to be home." He practically pushed me inside. I heard the clatter of his high-heeled boots as he ran down the stairs.

I should have had qualms about entering Blossom Rugge's "pad" uninvited—I was brought up to have qualms about opening other people's mail and being an uninvited guest, things like that—but I didn't hesitate. The dingy stairwell made me nervous and there really was no point in standing around outside when after all the door *was* open now. And besides, I was curious. . . .

The light inside was dim. It was shut off from the big front window by a series of cheap bamboo shades, all of them hanging at different levels. I stepped across the room and lifted one of the shades enough to glimpse a factory sign across the street. It said, astonishingly, SCREW AND SUPPLY.

I let the bamboo fall into place again as if it had burned my fingers. Good heavens . . . could the sign be real? I hadn't seen Buffalo on the street, but maybe he hadn't reached the lobby and gone out yet.

I glanced around the room. The most charitable word I could think of was *disaster*. The place was a shambles . . . papers were strewn everywhere, particularly and specifically on the floor . . . posters . . . newspapers . . . correspondence. Occasional pots of paint confirmed my earlier suspicions that the demonstration signs had been homemade, and right here.

In addition to the papers, there were plants everywhere, all of them in various stages of nongrowth. Apparently Blossom Rugge had a black thumb. I felt an unaccustomed twinge of sympathy for her . . . in today's society being a failure with plants is worse than being a failure socially.

Soiled cushions were strewn about on the floor: there were no chairs. Paperwork and addressing must have been done on the floor: there were no tables. There was, however, an abundance of cigarette butts and empty boxes of health foods, an unlikely combination. Or were the cigarette butts marijuana? I wouldn't know, I've never smoked pot . . . a true provincial. In any event, the whole place stank of a combination of dirt, food, and cigarette smoke. There was something else, too, but I didn't analyze it just then. I was too busy looking at a row of paper cartons that snaked around the room. Each had the name of a museum written on its side in Magic Marker. WALDHEIM MUSEUM one said. The box was tied shut with heavy cord: finished business. QUEENS MUSEUM said another. It was open. Inside were news clippings and tear sheets from various magazines. I glanced at them briefly. They didn't make any particular sense, except that I guessed the Queens Museum was scheduled for a demonstration in the near future.

It was while I was looking at a carton marked CHADDS FORD, BRANDYWINE MUSEUM and thinking how thrilled the Wyeth people would be to know that they might receive a visitation from Blossom and her followers that I smelled it again—and this time I knew what it was.

The recognition came too late, however . . . there was already an arm across my throat like a steel band and a pad across my face, choking me. And there was no escaping the overpowering smell I recognized from Willem de Groot's stable—chloroform.

I kicked. I clawed at the arm that held me like a vise. I tried not to breathe. But in the end, it was a waste of effort. I rolled backward through the familiar dark tunnel into big, black nothingness.

22

Somebody was strangling. Poor thing, I thought. Somebody was gasping and retching in a thoroughly revolting fashion. It was a minute or two before I realized who was producing all the unattractive sounds. Me.

"Ugh." I said. "Argh." And more noise like that. I couldn't help it. I felt awful.

"I think I'm dying," I gasped.

"No way," said a voice, a deep, reassuring, and very sexy voice. It brought me round immediately. "You're quite all right, I think."

"Jason! What happened?" Then I began to remember.

"The door was open when I got here so I walked in . . . and there you were. I thought you were dead." He was holding me in his arms. It was extremely nice. I didn't want to move. "I was late—I can't forgive myself. The meeting went on and on, then there was traffic."

"Late? Why, what time is it?" It had been early when I met Buffalo at the door and stepped into Blossom Rugge's loft. Now the light in the room was darker than before, much darker.

"A bit after five . . . the building was empty, no one around, so I just walked in. How long have you been lying here? Are you all right now—really?"

"I think so. Somebody put this smelly rag over my nose and mouth and . . ."

"I know, I can still smell it. Chloroform. Can you get up? I ought to look around, you know."

I tried to sit up. It was not a success. Jason scooped me up in his arms, the way one would carry a child. "There must be a bed

135

in this pigsty somewhere. Let me get you comfortable, then I'll call a doctor."

"No doctor. Not necessary. I'll settle down in a minute."

He was walking with me toward the back of the loft. I had my arms around his neck and my eyes tight shut. I heard him pull back what sounded like a beaded curtain . . . then he stopped and stood very still.

"Keep your eyes shut, Persis. Don't look." He had begun to back up slowly.

Naturally, I did just the opposite. My eyes flew open and I turned my head. I was sorry I did.

She was lying on her back on a dingy sofa bed. It wasn't half nice enough for her. Part of her hair covered her face completely. She could have been sleeping, and for an instant I thought she was, but she wasn't quite entirely on the bed . . . the arm and the leg that hung down to the floor were swollen . . . there were purple marks like bracelets above her elbow and her knee . . . and her head . . . .

"Oh," I said.

"Oh, damn," said Jason.

It was the girl we had all been looking for. She wasn't on 30th Street. She wasn't on Eighth Avenue or Broadway. She was here.

And she was dead.

23

It was like the Policeman's Ball, except that no one was having fun. The law was all over the place, uniformed and in civilian clothes: patrolmen, detectives, forensics people, Art Squad, FBI, Long Island detectives, and so on and so on.

Jason and I were in the middle of it all. He had tried to protect me, but it was no use. I had to answer questions, thousands of them. I was sick once or twice and they gave me a respite, but only for a moment. I had to tell it over and over, from a dozen different starting points, until I was exhausted.

"If your appointment was at the same time as Mr. Waldheim's, why were you here so early?"

"Why did you force your way into the apartment?"

"Why didn't you leave when Mr. Horowitz left?"

The terrible thing was that all my reasons sounded so feeble and unconvincing. A friend had asked me to be present when Blossom Rugge met Buffalo Horowitz. "What friend?" That was confidential (Diantha would surely deny it anyway). It was a strange neighborhood . . . I didn't want to wait for Blossom outside on her doorstep. "Why? Who would see you there? You were inside the building." True. But still . . .

And so it went. It was terrifying. Especially when they got to the questions about the girl.

No, I'd only seen her once before, the day of the kidnapping. "Then how were you able to draw a picture of her?" From memory. It's my profession. "After seeing her just once?" Yes. I'm a professional. "Did you know she was going to be here? Is that why you came early and without Mr. Waldheim? Is that why

137

you 'loided' the door?" Certainly not. How could I have known. . . .

Jason put a stop to it, finally, by saying something about a lawyer and they said they were just asking questions as they would of any witness and after that they eased up. And then I was sick again. And then Ed Simms turned up. I told him the story over again and he told me to go home. "You've had quite enough for one day," he said. "Get her out of here, Mr. Waldheim."

"About time," Jason said.

As he hustled me down the stairs, they were just coming up in the opposite direction with a stretcher to take Saskia away. I tried not to look.

"Jason, they didn't seem to believe that you found me on the floor . . . that I didn't know poor Saskia was there . . . if she *was* there at the time."

"I know."

"But *why* didn't they believe?"

He didn't answer. He'd managed to squeeze his Mercedes into a small space in front of the Screw and Supply factory across the street and was unlocking the door.

"Did they think I made it up?"

He had the door open and helped me in. It closed with a satisfying *thunk*.

"Do they think I gave myself a dose of chloroform?"

He was next to me, concentrating on putting the ignition key in the lock. "You could have."

I thought that one over. Yes, I suppose I could have. So what did it mean?

I looked at Jason out of the corner of my eye. He was still busy fiddling with his keys.

"Jason, pay attention to me. Look at me. I want to know what you think. Do *you* think *they* think I was lying?"

He looked at me, finally. The blue eyes were sad. "Persis, when I asked you to keep me informed, I didn't mean for you to get into trouble."

"Meaning?"

"Meaning somebody's not playing games. This is all for real . . . dangerously real." It sounded like Oliver. I couldn't believe it.

"Keep out of it, Persis." He was looking right at me.

But I persisted. "Do you think they think—"

He didn't wait for me to finish. "Yes, I do. At least, they're probably not sure. You keep turning up. . . ."

"Well, I can't believe it. It's stupid. How could they? What about Blossom Rugge? Why aren't they worrying about her?"

"She left a note. Off to organize a march against the Chadd's Ford Museum. They'll check it out."

"So you think—"

He eased the Mercedes into the first of its forward gears and the beautiful mechanical creature purred into motion. "What I think, my dear, is that you had better stick to your museum and your gallery business and leave the investigations to the professionals . . . because, as of this moment—since you ask me—you could be in danger. There's a murderer somewhere. Look at what he did to that girl in there. And he doesn't know how much you know. . . ."

He was right. I'd heard the policeman talking about how "Saskia" had died. The bracelets were rope marks. The swelling was edema from lack of circulation. She'd been tied up for days . . . roped in a crouching position so that she would be dependent on her jailers for everything.

And, finally, executed by a single bullet in the back of the head.

But could any of us, anyone I knew, have taken part in such a horror? No, no. No one in Gull Harbor could have done such a thing. It was out of the question. No. I said it over and over again to myself.

It was a little like whistling in the dark. In my heart I knew perfectly well that the murderer could be any one of us.

24

Word of "Saskia's" death ("The identity of the murdered girl is under investigation by the police") had finally filtered through to the rest of the world. It had even penetrated the sanctum sanctorum of Hobe Sound, Florida, because there were three telegrams from my aunt the next morning. I wasn't at my best due to a chloroform hangover. My aunt's preemptory telegrams didn't make me feel any better. They all said pretty much the same thing in pretty much the same tone of voice: YOU MUST LEAVE LONG ISLAND AT ONCE COME HERE . . . SITUATION LONG ISLAND DANGEROUS COME HERE AT ONCE . . . IMPERATIVE YOU LEAVE MUSEUM SCENE COME FLORIDA INSTANT. My aunt considered the long-distance phone an extravagance. She didn't need it—her tone of command came through loud and clear via Western Union.

As soon as my head felt better, I would sit myself down and compose a long telegram in reply, assuring her that all was well (I hoped), and I would add her to the growing list of those who were warning me to be careful: Oliver, Rosi, Jason, now Aunt Lydie.

Gregor surfaced, too—by telephone from France. "I've been in Cannes on the Princess Trouminsky's yacht. I don't like the sound of all this," said Gregor, who adored the long-distance telephone. "For the love of heaven, Persis, don't get arrested for murder."

I assured him that I wasn't planning to. "I won't mention the North Shore Galleries if I am."

I was being silly—it was my hangover—but he took it seriously. "Well, dammit, Persis, I'd appreciate it if you wouldn't *get* arrested. It's bad for business, no matter what they say about any publicity being better than no publicity. I'm sorry I let you get mixed up in that museum. Maybe it would be better if you left town, for a while at least."

Another worrier. I didn't know I knew so many.

"Maybe they won't let me leave town."

Gregor snorted elegantly. I heard him calling to some servant for a Kir. "Of course they'll let you leave town. You're not charged with anything, are you? So don't be silly."

They couldn't understand, any of them. I didn't *want* to leave town. It was like a love-hate relationship . . . I'd love to leave but I hated to go. As for being charged with anything, well, I didn't think so. . . .

And then the barrage of calls continued. Diantha Lord phoned me in a state of high ecstasy to thank me for sending Buffalo back to her in one piece, although I really hadn't had anything to do with it. Others in the September Seven called, worried about my welfare. And when I finally dragged myself to the office I had a visitation from H. Caldwell Ringwell and William C. Brown. They were so anxious to see me that they were actually waiting in my office for me to appear—Ringwell in my chair behind my desk and Brown in the one reserved for visitors. That left me standing. They were not there out of concern for my well-being, however.

"Well, well, well," said Ringwell, after a perfunctory inquiry as to how I was, "and what was all that about yesterday?"

I told the whole story to them as best I could, but it didn't really seem to satisfy them.

"This is going to be hell on the museum," Ringwell said fiercely. "And you didn't even see Rugge, then? Didn't get her to call off the demonstrations?"

"She wasn't there. I never saw her." She could have come and gone several times after I was chloroformed, of course. So could H. Caldwell Ringwell, William C. Brown, and half the voters in Gull County.

"Damn!"

Brown got into the act then. "Are you sure you're telling

us everything about yesterday?" Brown's tone was as emotionless as ever, but he had risen from his chair and taken me by the arm. His grip was so tight it felt like another ounce of pressure would send his fingernails through to the bone. The suddenness and ferocity of it scared me.

"You're hurting my arm," I told him, gasping. He didn't say anything and he didn't let go.

Ringwell looked up. "No, let's go, Brown. I think that's all." Ringwell began to heave his body out of my chair. Brown did not make a move. I could feel my face contorting with pain, and it made me furious.

"Come *on*," Ringwell ordered.

This time Brown let go. My arm was throbbing; there would be bruises. Speechless, I watched them go out the door. I had seen the two of them in a whole new light. There was no question that H. Caldwell Ringwell was the leader . . . but there was also no question that there was another William C. Brown beneath the smooth facade I knew. And the second Brown frightened me.

Oliver, predictably, was the worst fussbudget of all. "I'm coming straight back, Persis. No, don't try to stop me . . . I'm flying in from Chicago this afternoon. Someone has to be there to look out for you."

"Oh, Oliver. No."

"No, don't argue with me. I'm coming."

"I forbid it." Of course I couldn't let him come. "I'll be furious. It would disrupt your whole schedule. I'm going to practically lock myself in my room and keep out of trouble—I promise. Besides, Ed Simms says there's nothing to worry about." It was a lie. He had said no such thing.

"He did? Tell me exactly what he said."

"I don't remember exactly, but he told me I was in no danger at all . . . made a point of it. So you see?"

Oliver thought it over. "He wouldn't say that if it weren't true. All right . . . I have to go with his word—but I'll call tomorrow. And I'm ready to come in an instant."

Beloved Oliver . . . so protective, generous, kind. Why didn't I just give up and make Mrs. Howard and Aunt Lydie happy by marrying him? "I *will* stay out of trouble, Oliver."

"All right." A faint doubt must have lingered in his mind, though. "What are you doing today, for instance?"

"Today?" I said. "Oh, nothing. Just working around the museum."

Which was not exactly true, either. What I was actually about to do was to go to New York to see Ed Simms at the FBI.

I wanted to ask him if I was a suspect for murder.

25

It was a gray day. The dim light that filtered through Ed Simms's office window cast an institutional-green pallor over his normally healthy-looking face. I suppose it made me look as if I'd just emerged from under a rock, too.

"Nice to see you," he said.

I took a deep breath and plunged ahead. "Ed, I've come to ask if I'm a suspect in the murder of . . . that girl," I said, wasting no time.

He looked at me for a long moment . . . then smiled. "No, Mrs. Willum . . . why do you ask?" He was formal today.

"Because the police gave me such a hard time at Blossom's loft."

"Oh, that. They *were* hard on you, weren't they? But you have to think of it in context."

"What context?" I asked, remembering with resentment the grilling I'd been subjected to.

"Big case for them, remember. And they're very nervous, jumpy . . . edgy. You know. Not too proud of their record to date, either."

I didn't care about the police and their nerves. All I cared about was what they thought of me. Apparently they had believed me. It was nice to know. "Thanks. I thought I was headed for the pokey or whatever you call it these days."

He shook his head. "No . . . mind you, they *were* suspicious for a little while, but," and he smiled again, "you just don't make a very likely murderess, ma'am. It also helped that Diantha Lord called us on her own and confirmed your story."

Bless Diantha. I gave a shaky sigh. "Good. Then maybe you'll be interested in making a deal with me?"

"You want to make a deal with the FBI?" He was looking at me with barely concealed amusement.

"I might. It depends."

He was frankly entertained now. "I must say, you brighten my day. You do have nerve, marching in here and offering to trade with the bureau. What do you have to trade?"

"You tell me about 'Saskia' and I'll tell you about the Rembrandt."

"It's your duty to tell what you know, in any case." The smile was gone.

"But this isn't anything I *know*. It's theory, based on solid research. Speculation. I'm under no obligation to discuss it with anyone."

He thought it over. Finally he smiled again. "O.K. You first. Shoot."

I drew a deep breath. "I've been doing a lot of research since de Groot's Rembrandt was stolen. I think I've stumbled upon a pattern, Ed."

I stopped to see how he would react. He didn't. All he did was light a cigarette, making a big business of it and blowing a beautiful, fragrant cloud of smoke my way. I loved it. They ought to have an AA for smokers . . . I would never stop wanting a cigarette.

"From the beginning," I continued, delirious with the second-hand smoke, "I had a hunch about the de Groot theft. Teamwork . . . precision . . . perfect disguises . . . timing: these people were skilled professionals and this was by no means their first caper. So I started to dig into past thefts, going back to the Punic Wars."

He put down his cigarette and stared at me.

"Not literally," I assured him. "I always exaggerate."

I had to remember that he was a literal person.

"The pattern," I continued, "began to emerge after World War II. There were always two or three robbers, always in a variety of disguises. There was always a brand-new museum just getting its act together or an old one that hadn't yet moved into the modern world of sophisticated museum security. And there was always a prime masterpiece, the best—worthy of the greatest museum in the world."

"Interesting. Go on."

"I have six cases I'm pretty sure about, counting ours. The disguises—painters, electricians, moving men, firemen, policemen . . . and nuns. The paintings—Vermeer, Memling, da Vinci, de la Tour, Rubens . . . and Rembrandt. I should say 'another Rembrandt.' " I frowned.

"Why do you say 'another Rembrandt'? There've been a lot of Rembrandts stolen. That's not news."

"What I mean is that there was another Rembradt theft that fit the pattern perfectly; and what puzzles me is that it was a portrait of Saskia van Uylenburgh, too—an early one." I couldn't get it out of my mind. Why would such aesthetically selective thieves steal *two* portraits of the same woman, two portraits from the same period?

He was silent for a while. "What started you on all this?"

"No ransom demand and no return. I began to wonder if there were other cases like that. And there were."

It was impossible to know his thoughts. His eyes had taken on a hooded, secret look. "Interesting. Thanks."

"You're welcome. Now it's your turn."

"I guess I owe you one for your research—and for the drawing you did of the girl . . . it may help us to identify her one day soon."

"I hope so. It was awful that she lost her life because of an art exhibition."

"She lost her life, Mrs. Willum, because someone wanted a Rembrandt, and she happened to get caught in the middle . . . an innocent bystander. It happens. Incidentally, we're circulating your drawing of her in every acting school in the United States."

I was astonished. "Why acting schools? I thought she was a prostitute."

"Ah ha, so there *is* something you don't know." He looked

wearily amused. "Acting schools because we got a letter. Some student-actress responded to a blind ad in a Minneapolis paper calling for a blonde girl, Nordic or Dutch ancestry, able to speak with an accent and pose as a modeling student for several weeks, New York area. Interesting, hmm? She didn't get the job, but when she read about the Saskia murder she wrote us. A long shot, but we're pursuing it. So far we've found ads in papers all through the Middle West: St. Paul, Duluth, Superior, Sault Ste. Marie, Cincinnati, Escanaba—the works. Your sketch will help."

"Do you think the girl was kept in Blossom's loft the whole time she was kidnapped?"

"Do you?"

"No." I'd thought about it a lot. "Why would the door be left open? Why would I be able to walk in like that? No, I think they killed her and dumped her there to be found. I think they were bringing her upstairs and found me there and had to knock me out. The people in the building and on the street were probably so accustomed to seeing queer people coming and going at Blossom's that they paid no attention to two men supporting a girl who looked spaced out on drugs. Maybe they even killed her in Blossom's loft." I shuddered.

"You'd make an excellent detective. That's exactly the theory we're going on. Well . . . it's been good talking with you, Mrs. Willum. Do try to stay out of any trouble."

Just like Oliver. I got out of my chair in a sort of a fog. We said good-bye, shaking hands. I stumbled out of his office. The image of that dead girl in the loft room with me kept spinning through my mind. All because of a Rembrandt . . .

I thought about the theory of thieves and ransoms I'd just given Simms, and the names of the artists again marched through my mind: Vermeer, Memling, da Vinci, de la Tour, Rubens . . . Rembrandt.

And a Degas hanging on Belle Sandringham's wall . . .

26

I thought about the paintings all the way back to Long Island, and when I arrived at my office, I pulled out a new sketchbook. I was thinking about how all the thefts seemed to begin after World War II, and about Mrs. Sandringham and her Degas and wondering where she'd been during World War II. Before I knew it, I had made a quick sketch of what she may have looked like then, over thirty years ago. I wasn't exactly sure what to do with it, but I had the feeling it connected somehow. I looked at it for a while, and then put it aside. Maybe, when I had the time, I would do the rest of them as well—all the people involved with the museum and the de Groot Rembrandt who might have been around when the thefts began. Maybe there was a clue in them somewhere. . . .

Two days later my office—where I now kept everything under lock and key—was expertly broken into. My finished likeness of Belle Sandringham was missing, as was all my material relating to the thefts of the masterpieces. I had put it all neatly into an envelope, ready to send to Ed Simms.

The very next day—at 2:45 P.M. to be exact—Blossom Rugge arrived at the museum for the last time. She arrived in a large wooden crate marked ART WORK—FRAGILE on both sides. The crate was carried by two men in blue overalls who had driven up in a brown van. The guard at the door signed for the crate, which was addressed to the Waldheim Museum, Attn. County Arts and Culture Chairman. Two handymen opened the crate as a matter of routine.

Blossom Rugge had finally managed to penetrate the museum, with as much spectacle and drama as she could have dreamed of. No one had ever been more dead. It was quite a while before the police came and discovered the neat bullet hole at the base of her neck.

The receipt for her, which the guard had very properly initialed and marked "received unopened" in case the contents were found to be damaged (as indeed they were), had a very fancy letterhead done in script, with many flourishes. It read "Pei D. Sei, Art Movers, International, New York–San Francisco." It surprised no one that not the slightest trace of such a firm could be found.

The uproar occasioned by Blossom's arrival at the museum was by now almost as familiar as getting up in the morning. We went through the motions like robots, questioners and questioned alike.

By the time I staggered home, Mrs. Howard had fled for the day as usual. Also, as usual, she had left a note.

> FANCY-FISHY CASEROLE IN OV'N 35 MIN. 350 DEGREZE.
> CAT WON'T EAT NOTHING OUT OF CAN. TRY FANCY-FISHY—
> MITE LIKE. CHINA PLATE MAYBE?

Isadore was in the grip of a flaming temper tantrum when I walked in. In an earsplitting, querulous voice she immediately began to list her complaints for the day, her bad temper increasing with every breath. She had already, I noted, knocked the telephone off the table. Oliver again, no doubt.

"Let me at least get my coat off before you give me all this grief," I begged, replacing the receiver and rushing to the kitchen with the cat two jumps ahead.

A quick inspection of the "fancy-fishy" confirmed what I had feared—chunks of canned tuna fish swimming dispiritedly in a murky pool of canned mushrooms and soggy noodles.

I scooped a couple of spoonfuls onto a china plate (as per Mrs. Howard's instructions) for Isadore.

"Eat," I commanded, trying to make my tone at once official

and beguiling, "you'll love it. It's *tuna fish*."

Isadore stopped screeching, sniffed once daintily, and stalked off, mortally insulted. In two graceful springs, she soared to the sink counter and from there to the top of the refrigerator, where she crouched down haughtily inside the French bread basket, watching me scornfully from over its front rim. I decided to ignore her and busied myself with the brewing of a cup of tea. I turned the oven to 350 "degreze" and retired to the library to wait for the "fancy-fishy" to do its stuff. Isadore thumped down out of the bread basket and followed.

I sipped my tea and tried not to think about Winkworth Gay Gaud and Saskia van Uylenburgh and Blossom Rugge. Instead I rummaged around for another of my sketchbooks and began some more drawings of the September Seven. I was deeply immersed in an interpretation of a young General Robert Lee Scott when the telephone rang. I leaped so fast to get it before Isadore did that I almost knocked over my teacup.

"Persis?" It was Gregor's warm voice. "Seen any nuns lately?" Very funny, Gregor. He sounded far away, as usual.

"Where are you now?" I asked.

"It's after midnight here."

"Where?" One never knew, with Gregor.

"Paris, naturally. Don't you remember that I was going to be here?"

I didn't, because he hadn't told me. But it wasn't important.

"Don't you remember that I'm giving a party for Bunny Brayer before his show opens here? The people from Giverny will all be here. *Everyone* will be here." Giving parties keeps Gregor busy. He loves giving parties, and he gives them very well. He'd just opened a new branch in Paris, which made entertaining even more important. Sometimes I think giving parties is the only reason Gregor is in the art business.

"Lydia Wentworth says she may come over from Florida for it," he went on. Gregor had almost succeeded in marrying my aunt once and he had never given up hope. "Everyone promises to be here: Rosi Craig-Mitchell, General Scott, Belle Sandringham, Willem de Groot—everybody. You can't imagine how exciting it will be."

I knew what was coming next: he would need me. Gregor could never give a really big party without me at his side to help.

And I was right. "I want you here tomorrow, Persis," he said. "I've made reservations for you on Air France for tomorrow morning. And listen, darling, be an angel and bring my St. Laurent scarf if you have time. The gray one. Or is it Givenchy? You'll recognize it. I'm at the Vendôme again . . . everything else in Paris is full. But I like the Vendôme—it's *intimate*. And I've reserved your favorite room, number 26."

Long experience had taught me why he would need me. I would arrange the flowers, I would run all over Paris rounding up our favorite artists to be present, I would get paintings from the Paris gallery and hang them on the hotel walls, I would see to all the canapés and drinks, and I would bully the guest list into showing up, a chore that required at least three phone calls per invitee.

I realized that I was looking forward to it—it would be a needed change from my present routine. Furthermore, there were other things I could do once I was in Europe.

"I'll see you tomorr—" I started to say, but he had hung up and was doubtless already dialing another number. The greater part of Gregor's day was spent on the telephone, and the night, too. Hotel switchboard operators had been known to threaten suicide.

My mind now crunched into gear. Mrs. Howard would have to take Isadore home with her. (If I played my cards right, it could be for good.) I would call the museum from the airport—Gregor had already been in touch with Brown or the county exec if he was operating in his usual style. Pack enough clothes for a week's trip, I told myself, including the extravagant new silk de la Renta copy for the party. Money? Credit cards or a check cashed at the Vendôme. . . . Gregor would supply the rest.

The bell on my kitchen timer went off and I hurried to take the fancy-fishy out of the oven—I had a lot to do now. Isadore was again ensconced in her bread basket, and reached out and tried to bop me on the head as I went by. Would *warm* tuna fish make her happy, I wondered?

It was worth a try. I served us both and apologized for not inviting her to sit at the table. Her responding meow was not particularly gracious, but she ate. I ate. Then we each went our separate ways to bed, she to the laundry room to bed down in the dirty clothes basket and I to my bedroom with a suitcase to pack.

I was filled with a growing excitement and anticipation. Wink had come from Antwerp. And Amsterdam was the world's center for Rembrandts and Rembrandt knowledge. France was where the Haylon gas Wink had been interested in had been stolen. Maybe in one of these places I might get lucky.

I went to bed, finally, but I knew I wouldn't sleep all night. There were too many questions to let me sleep.

And not enough answers.

27

Bells were clanging somewhere. Hundreds of bells.

I groaned and tried to ignore them. They went on ringing—even louder, it seemed. I put my pillow over my ears and tried to go on sleeping. It wouldn't work. The bells joined together into one relentless sound that pierced my head like a sword. I couldn't stand it. I tried to sit up and found that I couldn't, so I fell back again. The noise went on. Let it go on, I told myself groggily. Forever. See if I care.

It did go on. Forever.

It was the telephone on my bedside table, I finally deduced. Just the telephone. So let it ring. I didn't feel like answering. I didn't feel like anything—except sleeping and never waking up again. I would not answer . . . never again. But the telephone was ringing all over the house, wherever there was an extension . . . noisy . . . insistent.

And it shouldn't be ringing. Not this long. Something was wrong—but what was it? I tried to think. It wasn't easy . . . my head hurt. But I must think. Why was the telephone not stopping?

Then I understood. Isadore Duncan . . . she should have knocked it off the hook by now. She should have silenced it. I spent my whole life trying to answer telephones before she got annoyed, yet this one had been allowed to ring interminably without any sign of protest.

I dragged myself into a sitting posture, shaking my head in an effort to clear it. Slowly, painfully, I pulled myself out of bed and to the window which I pushed open, using what felt like the last ounce of my energy and strength. Then I lay across the windowsill, gasping and struggling to draw the clear night air into my lungs. Gradually my head cleared, though the painful aching did not abate.

I forced myself to the other windows in my room, flinging them open, then to the two guest bedrooms, the unused maid's bedroom, and the three upstairs bathrooms, doing the same in each of them. Moving quickly now, I rushed downstairs and flung all the doors wide. The fumes . . . how lucky that I didn't smoke . . . that I hadn't reached automatically for a cigarette on waking, as I once would have done!

Isadore Duncan was in the basket in the laundry room: I picked her up, basket and all, and set her outside the kitchen door in the fresh air before I ran to turn off the oven. Two things registered on my subconscious, although I was not aware of either one of them until a good while later . . . the kitchen clock said 2:00 A.M. and the temperature dial on the unlighted gas oven was set for 400 degrees. What had happened? I couldn't understand it. Had I turned the oven off . . . then turned it on again, forgetting to relight it? There were no pilot lights on my enormous Roper Town and Country antique model gas stove; I had long ago had them all turned off. With eight burners and three ovens and a topside grill, the combined heat from the pilot lights alone had kept the kitchen unreasonably hot. Besides, it was energy-wasteful to keep twelve pilot lights burning around the clock.

I tried to remember what I had done earlier in the evening. *Had* I turned on the oven again? Was I, at 36½, getting senile? Would I have set the new temperature so high?

The telephone was still ringing. I became aware of it with a shock. Something important . . . it had to be. Life and death, at the least. I reached for the kitchen phone, leaning with it, and my head, out the kitchen window.

"Yes?"

It was Gregor. "What time is it there? I keep forgetting. Sorry if I disturbed you. But I wanted to tell you . . . you don't have to come tomorrow, Persis . . . I got my dates muddled. The next day will be fine. But if you're all organized, come ahead." And he hung up.

Gregor. Heedless, careless Gregor. He'd saved my life. Without Gregor's call, I would be dead—and Isadore Duncan, too. Mrs. Howard would never have forgiven me if Isadore had died.

I went outside and sat down on the kitchen stoop. I could dimly see Isadore in her basket in the light from the kitchen. Her eyes were open and she was coming around. We stared at one another like groggy survivors of a shipwreck.

"I guess I'll be needing a keeper soon, Isadore," I whispered. "Please excuse me. I nearly done you in."

"Meow," said Isadore politely.

After a while I picked up her basket and brought her back inside. It never occurred to me then that it might not have been an accident.

28

The party at the Vendôme was in full swing by 5:00 P.M. Gregor had engaged a large suite on the first floor and together we had transformed its slightly weary Second Empire elegance with the aid of monumental vases of flowers and a dozen paintings bullied out of the hands of reluctant painters we knew.

Earlier Gregor had abandoned his former favorite, the Meurice, for the Plaza-Athénée. Now he had abandoned the fashionable Plaza-Athénée for the tiny Vendôme. The Ritz had been cast aside light years ago. . . . "My dear, Mr. Ritz *liked* the Germans!" And from the frazzled air of the fragile little manager of the hotel as he stood in the suite entrance, it was apparent that he was earnestly hoping Gregor would soon abandon the Vendôme, too, for greener fields. The transfer of affection, his desperate eyes seemed to say, couldn't come a moment too soon.

Luckily I had arrived rested. Before leaving I'd called Simms with the sudden panicky thought that maybe they wouldn't let me go to Paris—material witness and all that—but he'd been surprisingly casual about it. "Quite all right," he'd said. "Go wherever you like." So I had. The flight over had been a good one. Four black-haired stewards and stewardesses had coddled and cosseted us into a state of airborne euphoria aided, in my case, by several splits of Canard-Duchêne, brut. By the time Air France 010 had landed at Charles de Gaulle I was ready for Gregor—almost. No one could ever be really ready for Gregor.

The rooms Gregor had chosen were all gold and red . . . gold leaf and red velvet. There were flowers everywhere—white, yellow, and orange tulips in one large Lalique vase . . . purple iris, white and yellow chrysanthemums mixed with roses and giant orange tiger lilies in others. There were roses everywhere of all colors, and even a splendid bouquet in each of the two bathrooms.

Three Algerian waiters dashed about serving drinks and hors d'oeuvres under the watchful eyes not only of the Vendôme manager, standing discreetly in the background, but also of the Vendôme housekeeper, *la gouvernante*, whose head kept appearing around various corners, checking her arrangements. Each time he caught sight of the housekeeper, Gregor would cry that she looked exactly like the Vicomtesse de Ribes and she would blush and disappear for a while. Two forlorn and terrified little maids in white emptied ashtrays and took coats.

Gregor was having the time of his life, waving his arms at the waiters like a mad orchestra conductor and embracing everyone he could get his arms around including, once, *la gouvernante* herself, who almost fainted. He had wanted to have a real orchestra, five pieces no less, and had only been dissuaded (reluctantly) by my telling him that in such a small hotel the noise would be so deafening the guests would probably all move out, which would upset the management. As he was an unabashed and enthusiastic lover of noise, Gregor took this very poorly and somehow got it into his head that it was all the fault of the little manager who, as a consequence, could do nothing right.

The guests were an astonishing lot, as always when Gregor entertained. There was the usual covey of artists babbling to one another in French and eyeing each other with loathing and suspicion. There was a sometime film producer and his cocaine-addicted wife . . . a French count at whose château the champagne we were drinking had been produced . . . a vicomtesse who wrote best-sellers about illicit romance, whatever that is today . . . a famous French character actor and his newest mistress . . . a designer from the Crazy Horse with two gloriously tall and beautiful chorus members—one of each sex . . . a much-divorced American beauty currently married to an Italian count . . . several just plain millionaires with nothing else to distinguish them . . . two Arabs . . . four Africans . . . a clutch of magazine and newspaper people . . . and all of the September Seven.

Rosi was there with David Lawless. ("She came up from her château at St. Georges Motel, Persis, dear . . . so nice of her," Gregor whispered. "Having a cozy little time down there with David, I understand. They're—how do you say it these days?—a 'number', I'm told.")

There was Diantha Lord—without Buffalo. ("Flew in just for this party from London where she's sitting in on some courses at the Courtauld, my dear. So flattering, don't you think?") And de Groot and Richardson and Mrs. Sandringham.

They were all huddled in a corner, drinking champagne and talking about "Saskia van Uylenburgh's" death and about how this time they really were going to withdraw their pictures from the Waldheim. This time, by God, they had all the excuses they needed without worrying how they would look in the press. The Rugge murder was the last straw. The museum was an absolute disaster.

"Bad luck you had to be there when the girl was found, Persis. Must have been a nasty shock." It was General Robert Lee Scott. I hadn't seen him come in.

"It wasn't nice," I answered, wondering whether he meant the finding of "Saskia" or Blossom.

"I can imagine. A terrible thing for a sensitive young girl like you." Young girl? Me? How sweet of him. "You must really need a change of scene after all that."

"I do, and I hope to get it. I'll be going on from here to Amsterdam and Antwerp."

The rest of the Seven had joined us. "Those places? Whatever for?" They sounded astonished at the idea of anyone leaving Paris for less sophisticated climes. As I have said, Gull Harborites always went to the same places where they always found each other. Amsterdam and Antwerp evidently didn't qualify. They didn't belabor the point, however. It wouldn't have been good manners. Instead they began to chatter of other things.

I tried to draw Pierre Richardson aside, hoping to bring up the subject of Saskia van Uylenburgh, but the general joined us. He was saying something about grouse shooting. I asked them both if the decision to withdraw the paintings from the museum was final, and they said it was. In a way, I was relieved. I could never have run away from the happenings there, but I was not unhappy to be able to retire from the field honorably, my reputation for faithful service and devotion to both friends and masterpieces intact.

Just then a chic group descended on us, jewels flashing, enthusiasm at twelve o'clock high. "We're off to the Crazy Horse. Come along. It's so divinely camp. Join us, join us!" They disappeared in a swirl of furs and velvets and joyous cries.

Gregor was in his element. "We're going later. It's so completely *crazy*, don't you think? Everyone will be there . . . we'll have one of those great, long tables . . . we'll eat and drink all night. . . ." In his enthusiasm he nearly embraced one of the Algerian waiters.

"Eat all night," the general said, ignoring everybody. He sounded bemused. "You know, in 1940 in Paris they decreed 50 grams of cheese per adult . . . 360 grams of meat or charcuterie per week. For infants alone, they allowed 100 grams of rice per month . . . no more. . . ." I recognized the signs, he would now reminisce forever. Paris had set him off.

"You were here?" But he couldn't have been. It was the Occupation.

". . . In 1941 you could get six packs of cigarettes or three packages of tobacco per month. One liter of wine a week . . ."

A new cadre of guests rushed up to us, sparkling with champagne enthusiasm. "The Lido," they cried. "We must all go to the Club Lido. It's *much* more fun than the Crazy Horse." They dashed into the next room, seeking recruits.

The general paid no attention to any of them. He was lost in his own world of the past. "And in 1942 this glorious thing happened—it wasn't to be believed. At noon a British Beaufighter flew the entire length of the Champ Elysées. It dropped a tricolor at the Arc de Triomphe . . . then, flying at the height of the rooftops, it dropped a second at the Place de la Concorde. Imagine! It only lasted two or three minutes. The plane was back in

England 150 minutes after having taken off." I could have fallen in love with him: he was so noble and brave . . . and out of step with the rest of us.

Diantha was dancing around in joyous circles. "Let's go . . . let's go . . . let's go. . . ." I had a feeling that her People's Art phase was nearly over, or would be soon.

Gregor was back. "I've reserved a table for us, a great big huge one. They say the show is fabulous . . . cowboys on real horses . . . real camels . . . and all those heavenly girls, all bare on top. . . ."

The general stared over everyone's head, not hearing them. It was as if he was cataloging the terrain of a past or future battle. "The Germans called their organization *der Einsatzstab Reichsleiter Rosenburg fur die Besetzen Gebiete* . . . the Reich Leader Rosenburg Task Force for Occupied Territories. . . ." He was looking at me now. "By 1944 it had assembled 21,902 priceless works of art. Imagine, if you can, priceless works from the collections of the great Jewish dealers and collectors . . . Wildenstein, Kahn, David-Weil, and Baron Edouard de Rothschild. The Jeu de Paume raped . . ."

"You were there, general," I said, very positive.

He shook his head. "Not many know this . . . in the beginning I was an O.S.S. agent, operating a radio in a little town near Chartres, reporting on troop movements." He said it casually, like someone reporting that he had turned on his television set to listen to the news. I felt a chill; for a flicker I was there with him behind the lines, and I was afraid.

A lady who had something to do with Versailles now had the general in a merciless half nelson. "Robert Lee, darlin', you are definitely comin' with us, and *we're* all goin' to the Crazy Horse." The general protested, but she began to drag him toward the door regardless and he was too West Point to shake her off or knock her down. I trotted along beside them all the way down the red carpeted stairs to the lobby and out onto the sidewalk—unwilling to let him get away from me.

We stood, finally, outside in front of the hotel waiting for taxis, the film producer and the film producer's addicted wife engaging the Versailles lady in a spirited discussion of everyone's ultimate rendezvous. While they were all talking, the general turned his back on them and asked me in a low voice "What did Winkworth Gaud say to you the day you saw him in the hospital?"

"How did you know I was there?"

"Watching—trying to guard. Not successful . . ."

"Trying to guard? Why?"

"Had an idea about Gaud . . . not at all what he seemed, I think. It was involved, very involved. Had an idea . . . tied up with Cathedral . . . that old scandal."

A corps of inebriated fun-lovers swarmed around him, separating us. The Versailles lady had her arm linked with his and was pulling hard. "Come with me, darlin' . . . my car is waiting. You'll never get a cab if you go with them."

I strained toward the general, trying to push my way to him in the maelstrom of swirling people. I saw his straight back recede as they drew him away.

"Wait, general," I called. "I have to know about Wink . . . I have to talk to you."

I didn't think he could hear me above the din, but evidently my voice carried enough to make him turn to look at me over his shoulder.

I called again, "Cathedral . . . what cathedral?"

"The club," he called back to me. "Or your hotel, if we miss connections. You ought to know about . . ." He was gone, swept up by Gregor and Pierre Richardson. I was swept up myself by, of all people, Jason Waldheim, who was suddenly there on the sidewalk and detaching himself from the crowd to come to me.

"Late," he said. "And I have to go back almost at once. But when Gregor called, I couldn't resist: had a bit of business to do here but it was mainly to see the look on your face when you saw me. It was worth it. You look pleased."

I was so delighted to see him that I wanted to fall into his arms, but it wouldn't do to let him know. "I'm glad," was all I said.

"Good. Then it's worthwhile."

Cool. Play it cool, Persis. "We're going somewhere," I told him. We squeezed into a cab with some other merrymakers and sped away. Somewhere turned out to be the Lido, and it was a zoo. There must have been a thousand people pressed into impossibly small spaces at long tables. I was practically sitting in Jason's lap, which wasn't all bad.

Before us, live horses thundered around a minuscule stage on leather-wrapped hooves to keep them from slipping off the stage and into our laps. Chorus boys dressed unconvincingly as cowboys shot off guns. Near-naked girls did acrobatics. Some of them swam in a tank full of water that appeared miraculously on stage. The uproar was deafening.

I couldn't see the general anywhere. I searched every face, but he did not appear. He must have been whisked off to the Crazy Horse.

"We have to go to the Crazy Horse," I whispered to Jason. Naturally, he couldn't hear me. All he did was squeeze my hand.

I stood up and beckoned him to follow. Without asking questions, he rose, paid the bill, and followed me. We squeezed and writhed our way across the huge room and out. "Where are we going?" he asked, reasonably enough, when we had finally achieved the sidewalk on the Champs Elysées.

"I have to find the general," I said. "Let's try the Crazy Horse. He must have gone there."

The scene at the Crazy Horse was, if possible, even more hysterical than that at the Lido. The other refugees from Gregor's party, including the host, were seated at tables next to the floor show, and as the floor show happened to consist of a tank full of leaping dolphins, they were all soaking wet. But their *joie de vivre* wasn't dampened in the least.

"Persis . . . Jason . . . come join us," they cried. Their faces were streaming: they looked like participants in a water ballet.

"Where is the general?" I called, refusing to sit down. They didn't know and didn't care. "Never got here, darling. Imagine. The lady must have made off with him—she's a man-eater, you know. Gobble, gobble—eating him up right now, probably."

I wasn't amused. "Where does she live? I'll call him there."

It struck them all as terribly funny and they roared with laughter. "But you can't do that, Persis . . . she won't have taken him home—she has a *husband* . . . the doddering old count. Oh, no, darling—you won't get to speak to the general tonight . . . not while that woman has him in her clutches."

I could cheerfully have strangled them all, silly frivolous creatures, but Jason laid a restraining hand on my arm. "Do you know what hotel he's at, any of you?"

They were bored with me now. It was no fun. "No idea, darling. Come—watch the show. Relax. You won't see old Robert Lee tonight."

I knew better. The general wanted to know what I knew: I wanted to know about—what had he said?—Cathedral. Why had he waited until we were in the middle of a howling mob to speak to me? Perhaps because it was the first howling mob we'd been in together since the opening of the Waldheim—the first chance he'd had to speak without seeming to make a point of it. Or maybe it had something to do with the deaths of Saskia and Blossom . . . maybe their deaths had stirred him to action. I would go back to my hotel and wait.

Jason was darling. We went to the bar at the Ritz for champagne cocktails and then he delivered me to the Vendôme, two steps away.

"Your room?" he whispered in my ear.

"No, Jason. I'm sorry."

"Damn," he said. "I thought maybe in Paris you'd go mad."

"Maybe sometime . . . but not tonight," I laughed.

"It's spring," he reminded me. "Remember what you once told me . . . about falling in love in April?"

I kissed him. "It's just March 15," I said.

So we said good night, and I went to my room with the gold and beige brocade curtains and the brown velvet chairs and the big brass bed where only one would sleep tonight.

I waited for the general. And while I waited, I called

Mrs. Howard, just to pass the time. She wasn't in the least bit astonished to hear from me and launched immediately into a tale about a pane of glass missing from the kitchen door, and when I finally got her off that one, she managed to remember that there was a letter from South America. I instantly sat up straighter and asked her to read it to me. In response to my cable, Meyer Freudenthal wrote from somewhere in Brazil, he awaited with eager anticipation the arrival of the drawings I was working on. They would, he thought, be of the greatest help in resolving the enterprise at hand.

After reading me the brief letter, Mrs. Howard assured me that Isadore Duncan was now in the best of health, after a morning of drooping about in unusual style. Would I, she wondered, be seeing Mr. Oliver Reynolds in Paris? When I said no, she didn't try to hide her disappointment. "If you don't get someone soon, no one will have you," she told me diplomatically. Then we hung up.

An hour passed. Two.

I realized that I hadn't eaten and ordered a quiche from the restaurant. It was soggy and horrible, also cold.

Just before midnight Gregor came and pounded on the door of my room. When I opened it, I found him pale and shaking. "Persis, there's been a frightful accident. They called me at the Crazy Horse—the hotel knew it was one of my guests."

My first thought was Jason, and my heart began to hammer. Something had happened to him. "Who was it?"

"The general. They found him right outside the hotel here, run down by a car—probably one of those crazy French taxis. Skull fracture and multiple assorted injuries."

"Dead?" I knew by the way he spoke that it was so.

"Yes. Hell of a way to buy it, after all those battles, don't you think? No dignity in it for a war hero." He sat down in one of the velvet chairs and put his head in his hands. "I mean, when you think of all the dangerous things he must have done and survived, it seems unfair to die of being hit by a car in a Paris street."

I mumbled something, I don't remember what; it didn't

matter because I was choking on tears, and whatever I said wasn't audible. Poor old General Robert Lee Scott—dead on his way to talk to me.

And then, I thought, maybe he died in battle after all.

29

It was during the brief services for the general at the Église Saint-Roche that it finally hit me about my head being above the trenches.

The general's body had been sent home to his children, but Gregor had hastily arranged a memorial service for him at the church near the Vendôme, in absentia, as it were, for the benefit of those of us who were in Paris and wished to say good-bye to him. We sat on the small rush-bottom chairs and listened to the choir's Gregorian chant—an Olitsky request—and to the words in Latin that eased the general on his way to a more peaceful place. Rosi was sobbing, her head hanging down and her long golden hair unpinned and streaming toward the floor like some da Vinci angel grieving. Diantha was keeping a stiff upper lip and even looked slightly disapproving of the medieval pomp and music. Pierre Richardson looked sad and distracted: he kept turning his head and staring into the side corridors at nothing at all. De Groot kept looking at his watch; he was apparently late for something and the general was to blame. David Lawless looked merely bored. Belle Sandringham looked invincible, as always.

And that was when, for no particular reason except that I had nothing better to do than think, it hit me that someone had undoubtedly tried to do away with me. Of course, I muttered, how could I have been so stupid! Somebody had wanted me dead enough to break a window in the kitchen entry door, open the door to the kitchen proper, close it carefully, and turn on the biggest gas jet they could get their hands on. By morning . . .

Why, I wondered? Was it my words with Wink as he lay in the hospital? Something I had seen at Blossom's? The sketches

I was working on? The letters from South America? The research on art thefts? Whatever the reason, it unquestionably led back to the Rembrandt . . . and to the fact that I had disobeyed my own cardinal rule: I had stuck my head above the trenches. And they were using real bullets out there.

For a moment I was more frightened than I'd ever been in my life. And then a strange thing happened . . . I wasn't scared anymore. I was angry.

I thought of the general, and Wink, and "Saskia," whoever she was, and even poor Blossom Rugge—why had they died? Didn't I owe it to them not to be intimidated—to try and see this thing through? What was it Aunt Lydie had always said? "Never be pushed around, Persis. Never. If you believe in it, do it."

I believed in it. I believe I could find out who had stolen the Rembrandt. I believed I could find out who had killed my dear friends and why. And I was going to do it, even . . . I grimaced . . . even if it killed me, which I sincerely hoped it would not.

"Persis, we're leaving."

I'd been so absorbed I hadn't realized that the service was over. They were all standing up and looking expectantly at me. I rose, and we all moved out onto the steps of the church, where flower sellers were offering their bright wares.

Gregor had already cast off the gloom of the general's death; his duty had been done inside the church. "Darlings, I hate to leave you, but I'm already late for luncheon at the duchess's château and she'll be furious." He leaped into his chauffeur-driven Mercedes and was whisked off.

The rest all scattered to a multitude of destinations—de Groot to Longchamp where he had horses in training, Lawless to see a European client, the rest to who knew where. Very few words were spoken.

I climbed into my little newly rented car and turned its nose in the direction of Amsterdam. If I wanted to find out anything about Rembrandt, that would be the place.

The Peugeot 504, rented from those nice people at Avis, flew along the highway. It was a mettlesome little car, and I gave it its head.

We barreled through Belgium. PARIJS said the signs now, meaning "PARIS." RIJSEL, they said, meaning "LILLE." Rows of drab brown houses of brick and stone flashed by, every window blooming inside with snake plants. Long narrow fields stretched endlessly on either side, accented with barbed wire or trees and populated by enormous horned cows in black and brown, their faces marked like Indians in white war paint.

Then it was Holland, finally . . . always raining in Holland, Jason had told me once, and it was: flat, flat fields edged now by water-filled narrow ditches . . . yellow and blue trains flashing by, like toys . . . three windmills in a row . . . surprising brown and white sheep . . . three police in helmets streaming by in a Porsche. I was very tired. It was dark, and I was finally, thank God, getting mileage signs to Schiedam. I hadn't eaten, of course, and I was getting very hungry. It would be late by the time I reached the hotel.

Finally, I could see the sign in the distance shining like a mirage in the night sky, HARGALAAN NOVOTEL. It took another half hour of circling around before I could find the right road to the hostelry, but finally I arrived, as dusty as the U.S. Cavalry. The welcome was adequate, the food likewise, the room agreeable, and the guest exhausted.

Actually, I didn't care. They could have stuck me in a broom closet and I wouldn't have minded. All that mattered to me was that there should be a bed and a telephone and there were both. The first would have to wait for a while, though. I had some telephoning to do before morning. Most urgently, I had to arrange to see a doctor.

30

I was standing in front of Rembrandt's *Night Watch*, the Rijksmuseum's most famous masterpiece. I had been standing with a crowd of people in front of the thick glass that protected the painting for over fifteen minutes, spellbound. A guide was giving a lecture in English, every word clearly heard above the murmur of the admirers gathered respectfully before the great work.

"A triangular piece measuring 11 by 3 inches was cut entirely out of the canvas in 1975 when a schoolteacher named de Rijk attacked it with a bread knife," the guide was explaining solemnly, like a surgeon explaining an operation. "He later killed himself. Seven famous experts worked on the restoration. Because they had to concentrate so hard, they could work for no more than fifteen minutes at a time."

There was a murmur of appreciation from the audience, and the guide looked properly gratified.

"It's a wonder there's anything left of this 335-year-old painting at all—it lost several inches in 1715 when they cut it down to make it fit inside the town hall and it was attacked just before World War I by a jobless shoemaker, an attack it survived with minor damage. Four times it was changed from one hiding place to another in World War II—no easy job when you consider the size of the painting: 11 by 4 feet."

I stared at *The Night Watch*, mesmerized. The masterpiece, so recently in critical condition from thirteen knife wounds, now appeared to be in glowing good health. Captain Frans Banning Cocq and his company were in absolutely top form, full of vitality, skin glowing. No wonder this museum had been built around it.

Today was Sunday. Outside, it was raining lightly. On this dark day Amsterdam was a city of tall gray governesses, very plain; even the people themselves looked pallid, like watercolors in which the artist had used too much wash. Only the paintings in the museum glowed.

I had been early for my rendezvous, so I had "done" all the paintings, lingering most lovingly over the Vermeers. *The Night Watch* had been last. I was lost in the study of it when a voice spoke in my ear. "Brilliant, isn't it?"

I turned. Standing beside me was a little man in a spotty frock coat and a moth-eaten beard. He was carrying yesterday's *International Herald Tribune* under his arm. As was I.

"It's called a *shutterstuk*," he said, "a commemorative portrait of a volunteer militia." He smiled. "A wonderful word, don't you think?"

"Wonderful."

His eyes sparkled. I noticed that they were as clear and free of guile as a child's. "You must be Mrs. Willum, young lady. Our recognition signal, this newspaper here, worked like a charm. What I don't understand is why a recognition signal was necessary."

"I'm sorry, Dr. van der Donck, but as you know from my letter, we had a great Rembrandt stolen a month ago. Since then, three, possibly four, people may have died because of it. I didn't mention that over the telephone last night . . . but it does seem that precautions are in order."

He studied me gravely. "I see."

"I'm very grateful to you for seeing me," I went on. "I know how many demands there must be on your time—"

He waggled his head energetically and held up a hand. "Don't speak of it, young lady. I'm intrigued. I wouldn't miss it for the world. We don't have a major Rembrandt theft every day, thank goodness, so I want to know all about it."

He took my elbow in a businesslike way and began to steer me out of the *Night Watch* room. "We will pretend that we have met by accident. Since I was one of the seven experts who worked on restoring this painting, it is quite logical that I should stop by to see it from time to time. I do, as a matter of fact." He was hustling me along now at a brisk pace. "Quite logical that we should meet and that I should invite you to join me for lunch in the museum cafeteria. As I am doing. Come along, now. I lunch here often. You will find the food not bad."

He padded along beside me, chatting away as casually as if he were not a world-famous scholar and a leading member of the Rembrandt Research Project that was causing trembling fits around the world.

The cafeteria was jammed with people jabbering in all sorts of tongues. Dishes were clattering, cutlery rattling. The doctor looked pleased with all the commotion and urged me through the food line and onto a banquette in record time. He had selected a pâté, a bottle of Blanc de Blanc, and a salad. I had snatched up a cold soup and a chilled split of Pouilly-Fuissé. It was all very civilized, barring the noise.

"What about this Rembrandt of yours?" the doctor demanded when he was settled. I could see from his spotty coat and trousers that he was a man who loved eating: he was, in fact, as round and fully packed as a sausage, with the moist, hungry eyes of a friendly but overfed beagle. "Tell me everything. I love a mystery. Have you brought me a photograph, as I requested?"

"No," I answered, unhappily. "There don't seem to be any."

It was one of the things that had baffled me from the very beginning of the affair, yet de Groot's explanation had been perfectly reasonable. The painting, he had said, had always been in private hands and had never before been publicly exhibited; therefore there was no reason for it to have been photographed before its debut at the Waldheim. And with the destruction of the cameras and film the day of the theft, there was still no photograph.

I explained this and gave Dr. van der Donck a copy of the press package de Groot had distributed in advance of the painting. "You will see, doctor, that there are certain ambiguities about this release . . . and that there is far more emphasis on Willem de Groot than on the Rembrandt."

"You say de Groot issued this press material?" Dr. van der Donck extracted a pair of gold-rimmed glasses from his breast pocket.

"He did, sir, at his expense and no money spared, as you will see. It came out under the museum's masthead, but it was prepared and supplied by him."

The doctor studied the full-color reproduction on the cover. It was the painting of Saskia as Flora that hung in the collection of London's National Gallery.

"Very snappy," said the doctor, obviously pleased with himself for choosing an up-to-date word.

He opened the cover. The inside left-hand flap contained a collection of items, including an 8-by-10-inch black and white glossy photograph of Willem de Groot and a five-page biographical résumé of his career and personal background. The back flap held four press stories ready for immediate release. All were variations of the same release, with minor changes adapted to the needs of different publications.

I selected a single page under the raised gray letterhead of the Waldheim Museum and gave it to the doctor. "This one is typical. It will cover what they all say." He began to read. I knew every word of it by heart.

Press Conference

Willem de Groot, chairman of Universal Gas and Anthracite and a famous sportsman whose Amsterdam Stables are known worldwide, will arrive in Gull Harbor on Thursday, February 10, 1977, to deliver the star painting for the exhibition *Masterpieces from Seven Great Private Collections* opening at the Waldheim Museum in Gull Harbor on February 12.

Mr. de Groot will personally deliver the great painting

from his personal collection in Florida. It is Rembrandt's portrait of Saskia van Uylenburgh, the artist's wife, considered by the world's greatest art critics to be one of Rembrandt's finest masterpieces.

The press is cordially invited to cover Mr. de Groot's arrival in his private jet at 1:00 P.M. on Thursday, February 10, at the American Airlines special hangar, LaGuardia Airport. *IMPORTANT:* Admission to the special hangar at the airport is subject to strict security measures. Please call Winkworth G. Gaud, coordinator of public relations and director at the Waldheim Museum, with names of assigned reporters by Tuesday, January 18.

Dr. van der Donck placed the paper back inside its flap and closed the packet's cover. "Interesting. Very interesting. Was the painting photographed when the plane landed?"

I shook my head. "No, de Groot was trying for maximum suspense. The only photographs were of the painting in its crate."

"And the 'world's greatest art critics' who proclaimed it to be 'one of Rembrandt's finest masterpieces' . . . who were they?" asked the little man who probably *was* the world's greatest Rembrandt critic.

"I don't know. I've done weeks of research on it and come up empty. De Groot won't discuss it—won't discuss anything about the Rembrandt since its theft."

"How long had the painting been in his collection?"

"Not long, I gather. My impression is that he bought it especially for this exhibition."

"You saw it, didn't you? Was it one of the best?"

"I would say so, definitely. I saw it just before it was stolen."

He worked on his salad for a minute, decimating the crisp greens with enthusiasm. Finally he looked up. "Curious story. Rembrandt did several such paintings, as you know. A photograph of this one is imperative, if I am to help."

"Well," I said regretfully, "there aren't any."

The doctor raised his shoulders expressively. "Then I do not see how I can be of specific aid to you. I cannot issue opinions based on generalities."

I began to dig around in my copious shoulder bag. It was big enough to hold a vast assortment of things and did; consequently, it was almost impossible to find anything in it. "I had a very good look at the painting," I told him, "because I was asked to describe it to the press just before it was stolen. Afterward, when you answered my letter and asked for a photograph, I called it back to mind and made some drawing 'notes.' "

It was no big thing. When we were students, we would-be artists were often asked to copy masterpieces in order to learn from them. The big thing was to find anything in my bag. Finally, just as I was about to get hysterical, I found it. It was always the same: search—panic—success. I passed the drawing and its color notes to the doctor. He slipped it inside his newspaper and began to study it carefully.

He seemed to take forever. I don't believe he even blinked his eyes, so intense was his concentration. Suddenly: "More details about the dress, if you please." I did my best. "Exact background colors." I tried.

Then there was a silence that endured for perhaps five minutes. It felt like an hour. I began to fidget, sensing the beginning of a bad case of nerves. I tried to look around the room to distract myself and stay calm. Everyone, I swear, was smoking except me and the doctor. My willpower is being tested, I thought nervously. I'd give anything to be lighting a cigarette at this moment. It would be so easy: all I'd have to do would be to rise from this seat, stroll over to the counter, and buy any brand of cigarette I want. They had every brand, even American. I'd seen them when I went by with my tray. . . .

When the doctor finally spoke I was so engrossed in a fantasy of smoking a cork-tipped filtered Tareyton from a white package with two red stripes that I literally jumped.

"I find this extraordinary," was what he said. He must have been talking to himself, though, because he lapsed into another long period of introspection. This time I waited patiently, senses alert. He shook his head several times, discouraging me once more. I began to feel like a metronome, pulsing between elation and despair.

Finally he spoke again. "I want to tell you a story about a family named Wiener in Amsterdam just before World War II. The Wieners did not believe that Hitler represented a threat to Holland—they were Dutch Jews. They didn't believe a man like Hitler could have anything to do with a civilized country like Holland. But it happened. They had refused, against all advice, to run away and when they were taken, their collection was confiscated, too. Everything was taken from them except one picture."

That prickly feeling of the bomb about to go off and soup about to be spilled was back.

"The Wieners," he went on, "went to Bergen-Belsen, where they perished. Their paintings went to the salt mines near Linz, where they were carefully stored away as part of Hitler's 'collection.'"

"Who were the Wieners? I've never heard of them."

"He was a wealthy Dutch importer who loved art and had a superb collection, which was almost unknown. After the collection was impounded by the Nazis, some of it was exhibited at the Linz museum . . . the paintings had Hitler's inventory numbers stamped on the back when they were recovered at the end of the war. Those salt mines were a treasure trove. But that's another story."

"Did the Wieners own a Rembrandt?"

"Indeed they did." He stopped for more introspection, like a balky engine that functions by fits and starts. I was getting a strong urge to scream. "Please, doctor, the Rembrandt."

"Oh, yes." He started up again. "There was a huge exhibition of paintings in Antwerp in late April of 1939. It opened with absolutely no regard for the fact that war was inevitable. Museum people are naive when it comes to politics." This was said with deep disapproval, almost with disgust. The doctor had no patience with idealists who ignored world politics at the expense of irreplaceable works of art.

"To continue," he said. "The Wieners were invited to send their Rembrandt, the prize of their collection, to the Antwerp exhibition. In spite of what they said, they may have had some reservations about Hitler, because they agreed. They may have been hedging their bets, as you Americans say, because ordinarily they never lent their paintings."

"And the exhibition was scheduled for late April of 1940?"

"Mark the date. The world—our world—was about to fall apart. But you couldn't imagine, could you? You weren't even born yet."

"Not quite," I admitted.

"That is the background. I was sure when you called me last night that it would be. Now read this newspaper clipping: it continues the story."

It was from Paris, 1940. The headline screamed at me: 20 TRUCKLOADS OF ART VANISH IN WAR ZONE.

The article went on to report that twenty truckloads of art treasures, including paintings by Rembrandt and Rubens spirited out of Antwerp during the German invasion, were missing. The priceless treasures had been taken from the Antwerp museum and placed in trucks, which had set out over the bombed and refugee-tangled roads of Belgium. They had departed before the fall of Antwerp, but had not been heard of since.

This must be the rest of Wink's 20 TRUCK clipping.

"The Rembrandt referred to was the Wieners'?" I asked. My heart was banging so hard inside me that I could hardly speak.

"Unquestionably."

"And it was an early portrait of Saskia van Uylenburgh?"

"Yes."

"Then it is the same painting that was stolen from the Waldheim . . . it was stolen from the Wieners and it was stolen again from de Groot?"

"It would seem so."

"Why couldn't I find a catalog record of it anywhere?"

"It obviously *was* cataloged, when it was exhibited in the Antwerp show, but all those records were lost in the war—there was never even a list of the paintings that were in the twenty trucks that disappeared. And before that . . . let me try to explain. Jews in Europe, people like the Wieners, were never very secure. Hard experience had taught them as a race that it was better to keep anything they had of value under wraps. They resisted having their collections documented; they knew from experience that documentation was a first step toward confiscation. The few of us scholars in the art world who knew joined the conspiracy of silence. It was to our advantage to keep the great treasures where they belonged. I suppose you will go to Antwerp now, because that was the last European trace of the Rembrandt?"

"I would be going there in any case—one of the people killed was from Antwerp. He may had something to do with a Cathedral. Does that mean anything to you, doctor?"

"It seems to me I have heard rumors, long ago. Was it— I think, yes—a clandestine operation? But I am not sure. I, you see, made the mistake of thinking I could bear arms for Holland. The result was that I was captured and performed forced labor all through the war instead. I would have done better to have joined the Resistance from the beginning. There must be somebody. . . ." He seemed to be rummaging through some ancient filing cabinet in his head. "Of course. Cherubim would know."

"Who?"

The doctor was pleased with himself for having come up with a good name. "A fine man. He started trying to save the treasures of Antwerp and was tortured for his pains. But he would know, if anyone would. Where are you staying?"

I told him.

"Good. He's no longer active, you know. But if it's anything to do with Antwerp, he will know. I'll see to it that he calls you. Oh, and one last thing . . . you asked in your letter if there is a descendant of Saskia van Uylenburgh alive today. The answer is no."

The doctor was standing. I tried to thank him for giving me so much time and information, not to mention lunch, but he brushed it all aside and, bending over my hand, he kissed the air just above it in the polite Continental fashion.

Then he was gone. I watched him disappear, rolling easily along on his rounded little legs. He had cut a vital thread in the Rembrandt tapestry—I now knew the origin of the picture. The unraveling had begun.

And tomorrow there would be Antwerp, and a man called Cherubim who had been "tortured for his pains."

31

The Middelheim Gardens were full of strollers: the pale, north European sun had made one of its rare appearances and everyone in Antwerp was taking advantage of it, enjoying the day in this particularly European way. The grass was seriously thinking of becoming green. A few birds were chirping optimistically. The sculptures, serene in their airy setting, caught and held the errant beams of sunlight like eager sunbathers on the beach ahead of season.

There were supposed to be some 200 sculptures here in this unique outdoor museum . . . everyone who counted in the sculpture world was represented including Rodin, Maillol, and Henry Moore, their work presented as it was meant to be seen—in the out-of-doors with the skies and the trees for a background. The eye was blinded by the splendor of them stretching on and on along the winding paths, an incomparable feast for sculpture lovers. But a feast I could not fully enjoy. Somewhere in these eighty-eight acres of magic forest, someone was waiting for me. Beside the Henry Moore, I had been told. Beside the king and queen.

The couple was not hard to find; they presided over the passing throng with regal dignity. And standing in front of them, seeming to study them with great interest, was a man who was almost as tall and thin as the figures themselves. He wore dark glasses and carried a walking stick. He also carried a three-day-old *Herald Tribune*. Cherubim.

"I am Persis Willum. Thank you for seeing me."

He turned sharply toward me. "Seeing you?" The voice was not friendly.

"Dr. van der Donck said you might be able to help me."

"With what?" Again the chilly tone. I began to lose heart, but I pressed on. There was nothing else to do.

"A friend of mine died. Just before he died he mentioned something about a cathedral or something called Cathedral. I'm not exactly sure." What *had* the general said, exactly, that night in Paris?

The thin, aristocratic face turned fully toward me for the first time, but it revealed nothing. I couldn't read the expression in the eyes behind the dark glasses. The nicely chiseled mouth did not condescend to smile.

"Please be quiet for a minute," Cherubim said, obviously not concerned about being rude. I felt myself blush, but I did not speak. Instead I concentrated on watching a wedding party that had gathered nearby. They seemed to come together, scatter, and reform again like a ballet in their long white dresses and black wedding suits. A harried photographer was attempting to group them next to a small, man-made lake. Occasionally a quixotic breeze lifted the bride's veil and wrapped it around now one, now another of the wedding party who laughed and called out to the rest to notice. The groom and his men were long-haired, ruffled, and booted like men of another century. Three small children darted giddily in and out among the grown-ups, threatening to trip them up while the photographer struggled to achieve order.

Finally, he lost patience and shouted commands. Everyone fell into place like cards dropping on a table. Click. Click. Click. A child burst out of the pattern and was quickly recaptured. Click. Click. Click. The pattern rearranged itself. More clicks. And suddenly it was over and they were drifting away in all directions . . . swirling . . . laughing. Nothing was left of the tableau but a laugh that floated on the thin spring air.

I looked at Cherubim. He was listening. All of him was listening. And I finally understood his need for quiet . . . he couldn't see the wedding party. He couldn't see me.

Cherubim was blind.

"We are alone," I told him. I meant that no one could hear us and he understood.

"It is old habit. The old habits persist."

I felt a surge of pity. The one thing I could not bear to be would be blind, the thing every artist fears most. But this man was proud. It explained his coldness. He would be afraid of being pitied.

He turned away from me as if he understood what I was thinking, and got down to business. "Tell me about your friend and I will try to help if I can, because the doctor has asked me."

I told him that Wink had come from Antwerp, grown up here. "What is Cathedral? Why was it important to my friend? And could it have anything to do with why he died?"

"Listen carefully," he told me, "and I will try to make you understand—for the doctor's sake." He was standing even straighter than before and there was a fiery pride about him now. "You sound young . . . are you? You would not know about the war or how things were then."

"But I would like to learn. Please."

America was very far away right now. The war was close, very close.

"From the first signs of World War II, all the nations formed art squads. In the case of the Allies, they were designed to hide priceless national treasures from the invaders and protect them from bombing and then after the tides of war finally turned, to search out and recover them . . . there was particular pressure to recover them before the Russians did, or they would disappear into Russia forever.

"The German art squads looted countless masterpieces and hid them everywhere. Allied art squads later found them in caves, vaults, castles, monasteries . . . one cache was discovered in a brick cave three miles long in the Austrian Alps.

"Cathedral was a covert action team formed in the first days of the war to save art from the Germans. Later its job was to recover what the Nazis had stolen.

"Cathedral was first formed under the British . . . the Americans didn't begin to be involved officially until 1943, reporting to the Commission for the Protection and Salvage of Artistic and Historic Monuments. Unofficially, however, American experts were involved from the beginning. One of Cathedral's first operations was the rescue of the collections of Antwerp and Brussels museums before they fell into the hands of the advancing German armies."

A bulb switched on. "May 18, 1940. The fall of Belgium."

"Just so. The operation of May 18."

"You were a member of Cathedral?"

"Yes. Code name Cherubim. I was working in the Plantin-Moretus Museum, pro tem. I preferred to be in the army . . . I was young . . . I preferred to fight. But my expertise was needed elsewhere, to help save the treasures of Antwerp. I was Cathedral's man in Antwerp, which didn't mean much at the time because it was in the beginning. Not very efficient . . . not the organization it later got to be. Bit helter-skelter in the beginning, although we did have enough sense to use code names for security. Felt a bit silly, I can tell you . . . we didn't really believe the Germans were coming, you know. Young idiots!"

He paused, tapping his stick impatiently on the ground. Very close, a family group passed . . . a great Amazon of a woman, a pinched, red-nosed man, and two capering children. Cherubim's acute hearing had marked their coming; I had been so absorbed in what he was saying I had noticed nothing.

"There was a kind of panic when it happened," he resumed. "All of Antwerp's treasures had to be saved. Mind-boggling." He spread his arms in an all-encompassing gesture. "Have you any idea of how many Rubenses there were here in the churches alone? Some of it we managed to store behind the false walls inside the churches and then banked them with sandbags—the Germans never thought to disturb them. But the museum . . . those all had to be removed . . . the minor things could stay, but not the masterpieces. I organized volunteers . . . the museum staff could never have done it alone. Women helped pack and move the paintings, helped pack the trucks. Some women even drove them . . . we were already short of men, except the very young and the very old . . . the others were fighting, or trying to. Hard to fight for a surrendering country."

Young men, old men, and women had driven the trucks . . .

the very trucks that had vanished on the way to France, the sanctuary so near at hand, however temporary it would turn out to be.

The Rembrandt had been in one of those trucks.

"Winkworth Gay Gaud . . . could he have been working on the operation to save Antwerp's paintings?" He would have been young, eighteen or so.

"I would not have known him by name. That's how we tried to protect everyone . . . no true names. In fact, our operation was organized to prevent anyone from even knowing the pictures' final destinations. One group of volunteers packed. Another moved the paintings to the trucks. The first set of drivers took the trucks to a set rendezvous, where new drivers took over. Four changes of drivers were planned in all. We lost the twenty trucks before the second group took over."

"How? What happened?"

"There was a roadblock . . . a bombed-out area ahead, the drivers were told. The rendezvous had been changed . . . a new set of drivers would take over at this point. The drivers switched places. The trucks were never seen again. All those paintings, your Rembrandt included."

"You searched?"

He laughed. "Who searched? We were overrun and occupied. All that interested me was getting away to fight and I did manage . . . almost. But I was betrayed to the SS and they were determined to find out where all the paintings had gone. They held me for months, and in the end they blinded me because I would not tell them about the twenty trucks because I could *not* tell them. I got away during a Maquis attack when they were moving me to a different prison, and the Underground got me to England."

I was silent for a moment, chastened. "Does Cathedral still operate?"

He didn't answer me directly, yet, in a way, he did answer. "Most of the countries involved in the war still have groups trying to find lost art. Thousands of famous paintings have not been accounted for, even though the statute of limitations has run out on most of them and they probably couldn't be reclaimed.

Everyone stole what he could: soldiers, factory workers, farmers, peasants, officers . . . everyone."

"You think something like that happened to your trucks?"

"Perhaps. But . . ."

"But you have another theory of what happened?"

With his acute hearing he had again remarked the approach of a group of people to within earshot of us and he stopped speaking until they had moved on.

"I do," he said then. "The twenty lost trucks were only one incident . . . there were others."

The prickly feeling. Was it a honing and tightening of his tone? Was I feeling, vicariously, his own excitement?

"Things happened. I noticed. I lost my sight but I never lost touch, you see. Paintings we should have found . . . gone when we got there. Masterpieces our sources had located . . . vanished when we arrived. One entire collection Hitler had hidden . . . vanished without a trace. The Munich State Galleries . . . the best of the collection was stored in Hitler's private air raid shelter, our sources said, and our sources were impeccable . . . only a handful were recovered. The Russians were as mystified as we were. No, no, there began to be a pattern."

"And you think . . ."

"I think . . ." He was, one might imagine, engaged in a private discussion with himself. "I think that most of the time when we failed to recover collections we knew about, it was because the Soviets had gotten there first—just tough luck. Like the famous Zwinger Gallery collection in Dresden. First the Russian soldiers found the pieces in the collection's underground shelters and helped themselves, then the Soviet officials transported the rest to Russia. Over 500 priceless treasures were lost.

"But these particular cases excluded the Russians: there wasn't a Soviet in sight in the examples I refer to. And they lead me to conclude that the original twenty trucks were not hijacked by some superpatriot who was hiding the contents in a supersafe place . . . oh, no."

"You believe . . . ?"

"That someone on Cathedral went bad."

It wasn't such a big sentence, only six little words. But the implications were enormous.

"Someone?"

"Perhaps several someones."

I thought of all the homework I had been doing, and a computerlike list ran through my mind of the cases where a ransom had never been demanded . . . when paintings had simply vanished. Did it all fit together?

"And that someone had something to do with the original hijacking of the trucks from the Antwerp museum?"

"I think unquestionably yes. And I think, furthermore, that whoever it was betrayed me to the Germans. And not just me . our whole Cathedral cadre."

"All?"

"An entire unit—wiped out."

"Is there anyone left who might remember any of the people involved in the shipment of paintings? Anyone who might have seen them?" I didn't want to make a point of it, but the Germans had insured that Cherubim would never see or identify anyone again.

"I wasn't involved in the actual shipping; I was in the planning. But I know that many people were involved, American students included. There is an old man still around who was there that day. Maybe he might recall something useful. One never knows—it was long ago, after all."

He told me where to go. I thanked him. We shook hands, American-style.

"Thank you for helping me."

"No, no . . . I do it to help myself," he replied.

"If I find who did it . . ." I started to say.

But he was leaving, very straight and military in his bearing, tapping confidently ahead of himself with his walking stick.

32

The entire city of Antwerp was in the throes of a gigantic birthday party for its most illustrious artist. Peter Paul Rubens had been born 400 years ago, and the Coordinating Committee of International Rubens Year had been hard at it planning things for over two years. Poor old Rembrandt must have been writhing with jealously in his grave to see the fuss they were making over his Belgian rival.

By the time I arrived at Rubens's house at 9 Wapperplein, where I was to rendezvous with Cherubim's man, the celebration was at its height. Through the leaded windows of the house I could see crowds moving from room to room inside, gawking at the sparsely furnished parlor, admiring the Flemish kitchen, streaming into the bedroom where he had died.

I knew the house by heart from former visits to Antwerp. It was a beauty. I also remembered clearly the inscriptions that were carved into the archways to the formal garden outside the studio: "Leave it to the Gods to give what is fit and useful," said one. "One must pray for a sane spirit," said another, in part. Both seemed extraordinarily apt to the situation at hand. I needed anything God could offer that was fit and useful and I most certainly needed a sane spirit. And a lot of luck.

The man I was to see, Cherubim had said, worked here as a tour guide. He had been a part of the museum staff that had helped pack the ill-fated shipment of paintings for transport to France in 1940. When the Germans came, he had joined the Resistance and been part of the group that had liberated Cherubim from his Gestapo captors.

The only old man in sight was herding an unruly and disrespectful crowd of British and American tourists, most of whom appeared to have overindulged in Belgian beer before arriving. Several seemed, in fact, to have no notion of whose house they were visiting.

Part of the problem was the old man. He was droning on in a monotone that showed clearly that he had long since lost the context of what he was saying, drowned in a lethargy induced by the ignorance and the indifference of the crowds.

". . . restored after World War II . . . lived here with his beautiful second wife, named Hélène Fourment. When he died, his relatives, friends, and fellow artists wined and dined nonstop at three huge funeral banquets, while 500 masses were sung throughout the Netherlands . . ." And so on.

The tour, one of several, all of them in different languages, dragged along. I skulked on the outskirts of the alternately thinning and burgeoning crowd, waiting for my chance to approach the leader. Two little boys, as bored with the monotone of the speaker as everyone else, livened up the proceedings by stepping on my feet and smearing my best new skirt with chocolate, then they punched at one another until one of them stumbled and fell down, screaming.

At last the old man ran out of steam and it was over. The crowd muttered gratefully, then broke formation and wandered away. The little boys tramped on my foot again for good measure before bursting out on the street to freedom. I tried to intercept the guide, but he pushed his way through the tourists and made his way to the entrance desk, where he drooped against the side wall, drained. He was trying to regroup his forces for the next assault.

"Christ," he said, dejectedly.

"They say we'll have 300,000 of them before we're through," the ticket seller told him. He groaned.

"I may have to kill myself before it's over—the war was never this bad. Even the Germans . . ."

"Don't say that," the ticket seller chided. "Take your coffee break and stop grumbling."

I stepped forward. "Maybe you would be good enough to

have your coffee with me—a beer perhaps, as my guest. I'm most anxious to talk with you."

They both looked at me in surprise.

"You are from the press? There is much press in Antwerp this summer. But this is the first time anyone has asked *me* for a story. 'A Guide's Eye View of Rubens' . . . not bad, eh?"

"Old goat," the ticket seller sniffed. "Who would read a story about you?"

But he was already snatching an old beret from a hook on the wall behind her and pulling on a coat. "Does it matter? When a young lady asks you to share a drink, you go."

Good, I thought. If he has an eye for a young face he may remember some other young faces . . . from the past.

Sometimes it seems to me I spend most of my life eating and drinking. We were at it again in a scene so mundane it belied the seriousness of what we were about to discuss. The old man (his name was Deroye) was happily munching on Belgium bread and drinking Stella Artois, his favorite beer, he told me. I had a small glass of Porto de Borgoygne.

"What I'm actually interested in is the story of what happened to the twenty truckloads of art that vanished in 1940."

He groaned. "That old story. Who would want to dredge that up again?" He downed a large swallow of beer, taking his time. "I've been asked a hundred times about all that and the answer is always the same—I know nothing. The people who might know are all dead—the SS saw to that . . . and the only survivor that I know about is blind. So who wants to know?"

"No one, I suppose." He looked surprised and his eyes suddenly lost their look of indifference as he stared at me over the rim of his raised glass. "I'm only interested because I'm trying to find out about a friend of mine who may have been involved somehow."

He shrugged. "I wish you luck. To begin with, everyone was helping out that day . . . people one had never seen before and never saw since. All of Antwerp, you might say. In addition, it was many years ago . . . people change . . . memories dim."

He was a funny old man . . . not so old, actually, I thought as I studied him, barely more than sixty, and still showing the sinews that must have made him an athlete. I mentally peeled away the layers of age-betrayed flesh and imagined him as he would have looked back then in all the panic and excitement of approaching war. He would have been tough and stocky, though today he was running to fat. He still had snapping black eyes, but only a straggly fringe remained of what must once have been curly dark hair. I could imagine him moving through the scene at the museum that last day with gaiety and bravado, too young and full of himself and unimaginative to grasp the full significance of it all.

"My friend might have been there that day. His name was Gaud, Winkworth Gay Gaud."

The beer glass trembled in his hand and drops of beer fell onto the table. "Gaud? He's dead. . . ."

"How did you know?"

"Well, I ought to know. I was there when he died." He looked at me as one might look at an idiot.

What could he mean? This man couldn't possibly have been present when Wink died.

"Look, miss, I don't know what you're after, but I can assure you that your friend Winkworth Gaud has been dead for many years. And he couldn't have been your friend—you're too young. So maybe you ought to tell me what this is all about."

Like someone in a daze, I did my best to explain about the person I had known as Winkworth Gaud and how he had died and why that brought me to Antwerp.

He listened without saying a word and was silent for a long time after I stopped talking. When he began to speak again he was brusque, almost angry, like a man who preferred not to voyage into the past on any account.

"After the paintings left Antwerp, the Nazis swept up everyone they could find who might have an idea what had become of them. I was gone by then . . . I'd gone into the Underground at once, along with most of the young men who could manage it. Gaud was swept up with the others; his mother had wangled him a minor job at the museum and he was a kind of a pet with some of the staff. Just a young kid—about eighteen. Didn't really know anything about art . . . just hanging around to be kept out of mischief. He was 'artistic,' if you know what I mean, without knowing art. A mama's darling . . . weak and effeminate . . . but the Germans took him along with the rest.

"He, and all the others, vanished into Gestapo hands. They were there for months . . . we never knew the exact location until finally we had word that they were only thirty miles away and, for the time being, under light guard. We always tried to save our own and we tried this time. The Gestapo turned their guns on their prisoners in the end, just as we reached them . . . we saw it all and were helpless to stop it. They got away, leaving their dead and dying prisoners. Only Gaud survived—and even he died very soon after. We never admitted that he was dead, preferring to let the Gestapo worry that there was a surviving witness to the torture and the massacre. In fact, he did identify some of the Gestapo before he died."

I waved to a waitress for another Stella Artois as he talked. He put his nose gratefully into his newly refreshed glass.

"You see, it was this way," he explained. "I was young—an athlete, though you may find it hard to imagine now. Soccer. I was good—not the best, but good enough—and I worked for the museum to pay my way to the sports events, doing muscle work like hanging pictures and packing. That particular day in May . . . it was a madhouse . . . a nightmare. How could I forget it? Everyone in Antwerp was running in and out. The directors and curators were beside themselves. The staff was crazy. It seemed to me that I had the whole responsibility of seeing that things got wrapped and packed and into the trucks. Those volunteers—useless . . . perfect strangers off the streets . . . students . . . artists . . . some staff . . . you name it. And there I was, in the middle of it all. Me, who really didn't know one painting from another, except that I liked those nudes of old Peter Paul." He smiled, remembering.

"Gaud was there?"

"Might have been. Must have been, in fact. Although I confess I don't remember seeing him—it was a madhouse, as I said."

"Would you remember anyone, if you were to see them again?"

He thought for a moment. "I doubt it . . . too many years ago."

"Would you remember Winkworth Gaud?"

"You have a picture?"

I did. It was one of the series I'd been working on and finally finished. Some were more successful than others, but they were all there as I imagined they would have looked all those years ago. Rosi and Diantha were just little girls, maybe on holiday from Swiss schools . . . Rosi with long blonde hair in pigtails and with a careless, laughing face even then. Diantha more solemn and very thin with knobby knees and elbows. De Groot— he would have been a very grown-up and self-contained lad—very sure of himself and of his golden future. Pierre Richardson—he and Brown would have been close to Wink's age, young men already ready to fight . . . short hair . . . slender . . . carefree . . . brave. And the general . . . by then he would have been in his mid-twenties and already soldierly, with a correct military bearing. He would have been a handsome fellow. Whereas H. Caldwell Ringwell would never have been handsome, even in his youth. He would have been beefy even then, and full of guile. Belle Sandringham—what a pleasure to draw her as she must have been then. She would have had the beauty and pride of an Indian princess, with flashing eyes that challenged each passerby and a forty-three-year-old appeal that would be breathtaking.

"Do you know any of these people—remember any or them?"

He picked up the drawing of Winkworth Gaud and held it the way a thirsty man in the desert holds a container of water.

"Jan Jacques Vignoles," he said.

"Who was that?"

"I couldn't be mistaken—not even after all these years. My God, just imagine—Vignoles. He was my hero, you know. I was afraid he might not have survived the war. But how dangerously he lived . . . you know, he was liaison operative between Allied Intelligence and people working behind the German lines. In

1943, the Gestapo arrested him and he was condemned to death. He managed to escape after six months of solitary confinement and torture and after that he resumed his activities. At the end he was organizing escape routes between Germany and Spain. A great man, I tell you . . . and he lives?"

I shook my head.

"I'm not surprised . . . he was a man who always lived close to the edge. He was Belgium's greatest soccer player before the war . . . a great, great hero. After the war he disappeared. Of course, he was then too old for the game. But I always wondered what had become of him. Such a hero. How did he die?"

"In the hospital."

He didn't believe me. "Not Jan Vignoles. Not him." He was flipping through the other sketches. Suddenly, he stopped at one that seemed to make him forget everything else. "It is not possible," he said in a whisper.

He had found something. I tried not to sound as excited as I felt. "Who is it? You recognize someone who was there that day?"

"So long ago . . . it's difficult . . . but yes, I think so. How very strange." He leaned toward me now, reaching for the pencil I had left on the table after I had put a few finishing strokes on the drawings before passing them to him.

"Well," said a voice with a very Long Island accent, "fancy meeting you here. What are you doing, missy? You come all this way to give drawing lessons?" H. Caldwell Ringwell had never looked bigger. And I had never been more surprised.

33

H. Caldwell Ringwell's voluminous presence overwhelmed our small table and overflowed onto the backs of the adjacent chairs as he seated himself. I tried to diminish myself and enlarge the space between us by flattening myself against the wall. In vain: the flatter I became, the more he overflowed into the newly vacant space. He was like lava.

And he wasn't alone. Already pulling up a second chair was his comrade-in-arms, William C. Brown.

"By God, it is a surprise to see you here," the county executive exclaimed. He waved a hand in the air. "Order us up something, Brown. That beer looks good."

Brown, looking his everyday, friendly self, hustled up a waiter. The slight diversion gave me a chance to get my mouth closed and my drooping jaw back in its usual location. Nothing could have astonished me more than the sight of these two, although I would never have believed anything could have astonished me after what I just learned.

"I suppose you're wondering what we're doing here, and we're wondering the same about you," H. Caldwell continued cozily. "As a matter of fact, it could be the best thing that ever happened . . . could be you might pull this whole thing together for us, eh, Brown? What do you think about it?"

I looked around nervously for the old Resistance fighter . . . now, of all times in the world, I did not want to be interrupted by these two, whatever their reasons for being here. But the old man had vanished . . . he must have left while they were seating themselves. I swept the drawings off the table and onto my lap to keep them from being seen.

"Yes, indeed, Mrs. Willum, I do just believe you could put this thing over for us. Right, Brown? As long as she's already here?"

Brown nodded with his usual lack of enthusiasm where anything to do with me was concerned. I stared at the county executive and noted, not for the first time, that he had eyes like raisins pressed into rising dough.

"So tell her," Ringwell ordered his second-in-command, and Brown, like a well-trained puppet, cleared his throat and prepared to obey.

"You probably know all the collectors withdrew their paintings . . . you probably even knew before they did it, in fact." He threw me a murderous glance. "Anyway, now with the show dismantled, we need something big . . . and we thought maybe a Rubens. It would be a tremendous coup to get a Rubens from Antwerp, and with all they have, they ought to be able to spare one. Maybe several." Well, they certainly didn't lack bravado!

"So we came over on a cultural mission, as it were. Why not?" Ringwell interrupted. "They say the museum here has over one hundred paintings and oil sketches and some sixty drawings . . . they ought to be able to lend a few."

Give them to a museum that had already had two robberies and a kidnapping? They were either mad or joking.

"You could always steal some," I said.

They both glared at me, but said nothing. The county executive took an extremely large swallow of beer, looking as if he would be perfectly happy to eat the glass, too. They say big men are jolly. This one wasn't.

"They're not giving us any cooperation," he told me. "I think you might get the job done for us. You're a nice-looking woman, an art expert, with lots of class . . . you know all the right people, the Four Hundred and all that. I bet you could talk them into something for us. You understand, don't you—we need a real blockbuster right now to make up for all the bad things that have happened." He groped under the table, found my knee, and gave it a painful squeeze. I moved away so fast I almost upset all the beer glasses.

"Mr. Ringwell, I don't believe the people here would listen to me, even if I were to ask them. They're in the midst of a great Rubens celebration and they'll want all their paintings right here, not traveling around. They wouldn't even send their Rubenses to big museums, let alone a new one like the Waldheim. I'd like to help you, but it just isn't a practical idea, really it isn't."

There wasn't the faintest indication that he would accept no for an answer; he had survived encounters with tougher opponents than me. "Don't give up so easily, Mrs. Willum. Where are you staying?"

I might as well tell him; he'd telephone around until he found where I was registered, anyway.

"O.K., now, you think it over and we'll call you. We're at the Hotel de . . . what's it called, Brown?"

"Hotel de Keyser."

"Right. Or you can call us. And listen . . . you do this for us and who knows? . . . could be a big job for you in the county. We could use a smart, loyal girl like you in our administration. So see what you can do about it, right?"

Brown was on his feet now, putting money on the table and helping his mentor up. Then they were off, followed by a cacaphony of scraping chairs and the complaints of banged and scraped patrons who had gotten in the way of their exodus. The total effect was like a small version of the retreat of the Mongol Hordes.

What had all that been about, I asked myself? Could they seriously believe, with the Waldheim's record, that they would land some Rubens paintings for their museum? Well, time to worry about that later.

I gathered up the drawings from my lap and prepared to put them back in their portfolio, which nestled safely inside my big shoulder bag. They felt lighter . . . I began to count them. While I had them spread out, one of the waitresses came up to me. "A gentleman asked me to give you these, miss."

She handed me two of my sketches and I thanked her and had started to add them to the rest when I realized there could be only one gentleman who could have sent them back to me . . .

the old Resistance fighter. He had been looking through them when Ringwell and Brown had made their appearance.

And what had he taken with him in his precipitous disappearance? After so many shocks today, I was not even surprised. What he had returned to me were the drawings of H. Caldwell Ringwell and William C. Brown.

Across the sketch of the latter he had scratched a big swastika in ink and there was something on the bottom of the paper, too. In a scrawling, passionate hand, he had written, "Suspected of being a member of the Nazi SS. Sentenced to death in absentia in 1949 by a Belgian court for taking part in the torture and shooting of six Belgian Resistance fighters."

34

Ed Simms—I suppose I had been expecting his presence all along, and here he was, slouched into one of the Novotel Middelheim's standard chairs. I wasn't even mildly surprised. Where the trail of the missing Rembrandt led, Ed Simms was sure to follow. To date, the trail had led us both to Antwerp and, at this exact moment, to the lobby of my hotel.

"I have a distinct impression that this may really be the Grand Hotel," I sighed, sliding into a chair opposite him. We were both nearly obscured by the potted palms that were suddenly in fashion in the hotel lobbies of Europe.

I looked him over with a mixture of admiration and astonishment. How was it possible for anyone to look so 100 percent stick-out American? He was like a neon sign advertising the good old U.S. of A. He was too big to be European. His suit hung too loosely. His features were too regular.

"Grand Hotel?" he asked.

"I mean, I really expect everyone in this whole Rembrandt cast of characters to come walking in here sooner or later. I've already had my big shock of the day from one member of the cast." I handed him the drawing of William C. Brown and watched him read the written comment on the bottom.

He took his time looking it over. Finally he whistled thinly through his teeth. "Well, I must say, this is a blockbuster. Who is your source?"

I shook my head. He was very nice; he didn't insist. "Can't say that I blame whoever it was. Afraid of retaliation, I expect. These people are always scared stiff when they identify anyone from the SS."

"But you don't seem too surprised." It was true, he didn't.

Simms laughed. "We're not completely naive, you know. We checked him out very thoroughly and we did discover that Brown had been in Germany all during the war, although we didn't know about this Nazi business."

"Why was he in Germany?"

"It seems his family was German. His father was a New York City fireman in World War I and the anti-German sentiment was so strong that he changed his name—he was afraid of losing his job. From Braun to Brown. The family seems to have remained staunchly German, though, and just before the outbreak of World War II they scraped together enough money to send their son back to the 'Old Country' for a visit. He went to stay with relatives in Munich."

"Wasn't Hitler in Munich?"

"Exactly. But the story we got is quite a different one from the story these notes suggest."

"What story did you get?"

"Fact, not story: Brown was rescued by our troops from a concentration camp—Ravensburg, I think. Now to the story . . . he said he'd gone into hiding when the war broke out because he couldn't get home and that he'd been caught and put in a concentration camp. And the concentration camp beatings had required plastic surgery. That's what we believed."

I thought I could actually detect a slight gleam of excitement in his eyes. It was catching. "And now?"

"And now," he said softly, "suppose—just suppose—that his German relatives were pro-Hitler. Suppose that he and his relatives were all swept up by Hitler's charisma and that Braun, using his relative's name and posing as a member of the family, joined the Nazi party. It wouldn't have been hard, in the beginning. Ultimately he wound up working for the SS, probably as an enforcer or a thug. When it became apparent that Germany was going to lose the war, he got himself placed in a concentration camp under his true American identity. It is probable that all of his German relatives were conveniently dead, either in the war or in bombing raids . . . or by murder; he wouldn't have stopped at murdering his own people, if he was typical SS. To make sure that *no* one could identify him, he then had his looks altered by plastic surgery. It was common practice."

A silence fell between us. I could hear the girl at the lobby desk talking in French to someone on the telephone . . . the clock on the entrance wall ticking . . . a chatter of busboys in the grille.

"Wow," was all I could finally think of to say.

"That about covers it, doesn't it?" Simms answered. "Do you have any more little tidbits like that one tucked away?"

I looked at him steadily. I was just opening my mouth to finally tell him about the Degas when, with a shock of recogntion, I suddenly realized what must have happened that night over a month ago. And I promptly closed my mouth again. I could not tell him that Mrs. Sandringham must have hidden the Degas under her robe before she was wheeled outdoors during the bomb scare at the Waldheim opening. Nor that Rosi must have helped her—she had been the one pushing the wheelchair the last time I had seen her that night.

"No, Ed, I don't," I said, smiling broadly to try and mask my confusion. "What about you? Surely your being here can't be a coincidence. You and I are both millions of miles away from where we'd ordinarily be found. It must mean something."

"Thousands," he corrected automatically, eyeing me. "Thousands of miles . . . no, I'm just here checking a few leads, that's all." His tone was deliberately offhand, so I knew he was lying . . . it must be as I'd suspected—he was following me. It was just too much of a coincidence otherwise. On the other hand, there were Ringwell and Brown. . . .

"Did you know that the county exec and his culture czar would be here, too?" I asked.

He smiled. "A little pleasure jaunt at the taxpayers' expense?"

Not quite, I thought: in Brown's case, now that the Waldheim affair had changed from theft to murder, it was obviously a little expedition to make sure that nothing pointed a finger at his wartime career. Further, "With an election coming up, I wouldn't think Ringwell would want to inflame the electorate by traveling around at their expense. Would you?" Brown was one thing, but why was Ringwell here?

"On the other hand," Simms pointed out, "there's been such a scandal at home that maybe the only way he can save himself is to come up with some sort of art coup here in Europe. He's desperate, you know . . . his career could be in a shambles. The one thing that can kill a politician is ridicule." He paused, then he changed tack. "By the way, speaking of your rich friends . . . where are they?"

I shrugged. "Who knows? You probably keep better track of them than I do. If you want me to do some guessing, though, I'd say that Pierre Richardson is checking up on his European affiliate banks—he could be here right now, for all I know. Diantha Lord is probably looking at paintings. David Lawless and Rosemary Craig-Mitchell are undoubtedly together in some little snuggery. De Groot is racing . . . and Mrs. Sandringham? She could be anywhere, wheelchair and all."

"I get the message. What you're saying is that the only one you're sure of is General Robert Lee Scott, because he's dead."

"Unfair." Thinking of the general, though, reminded me of Paris and thinking of Paris reminded me of Sogegarde, which in turn reminded me of a letter addressed to Winkworth Gaud. . . .

"Ed . . ." I said. I was thinking of stolen gas canisters.

"Yes?"

No, I couldn't tell him. He'd think I was crazy. "Nothing."

His usually bland face was suddenly grim. For the first time he didn't look like an all-American Campbell Soup child grown up.

"Go home, Persis Willum," he said. "This isn't a charity benefit. It's not a society ball or some fancy fashion show. This isn't even an art exhibit. It's dangerous—and no place for amateurs."

I could feel my feathers ruffling at once. "I'm not getting in anybody's way, am I?"

"That's not the question."

"Then what *is* the question?"

He leaned back, crossed his legs, and stared at me. Then, "Let me explain. Let me give you a for instance. Imagine millions of dollars in stolen art, 'collected' over a period of nearly four decades, 'liberated' from some of the world's greatest collections. Imagine these masterpieces in the hands of a secret art cartel, stored around the world in hidden, temperature-controlled vaults guarded by the most sophisticated security systems. Imagine artworks that have been missing for so long that all records are lost or the statutes of limitations have run out or the true owners are dead. The possessor of such treasures would have limitless wealth."

I felt my fingertips turn to ice. It was one thing for me to research all this; it was quite another to have Simms give it the stamp of reality.

"Imagine if you owned the greatest da Vinci in the world . . . the greatest Goya . . . the greatest Michelangelo . . . the greatest Titian. Imagine the power. Imagine."

Just to hear him saying it made me realize that everything I had been researching was fact. I began to tremble. I couldn't help it.

"So don't meddle, Persis," Simms was saying. "These people mean business. Leave it to *us*. There's been too much trouble already. Go home."

I suppose in some obscure way I was flattered that he cared what happened to me . . . but I wouldn't go home. Not yet. I owed it to Wink.

It was then that Ed Simms made a remark that showed what great insight he had. "It's Winkworth Gaud, isn't it? What you really want to know, once and for all, is whether your friend was a good guy or a bad guy. You want to know what team he was on, don't you?"

I caught my breath in surprise.

"That's it, isn't it? Well, if you'll promise to leave Antwerp, I'll tell you something that may help."

I just looked at him, dumbly.

"All right. The man you knew as Winkworth Gaud was one of the earliest recruits of a British-originated movement called Cathedral, formed for the safeguarding and eventual recovery of works of art in all countries affected by the war . . . an effort that eventually involved disparate units from many countries. He was also one of the youngest—Jan Vignoles, operating under the code name of Acolyte.

"He was recruited and began his special service even before the war broke out . . . the British government and the Europeans recognized that art safety would be a problem in case of war. Because he was a star European soccer player, Vignoles could move around the world easily and without being suspected. The work he did was invaluable. He was the right-hand man to the commander of Cathedral on the Continent. Vignoles was the field man; his superior was the brains, his identity a carefully guarded secret—an obvious necessity to safeguard the entire operation. Even Acolyte never knew the identity of his commander, as far as we know."

"And the commander of Cathedral in Europe . . . his code name?"

"Bishop. We know that. But what we do not know is who he was or why Acolyte was in the United States after all these years. We don't know why he took the job at the Waldheim Museum. Nor do we know why he took the name of Winkworth Gaud instead of his own. Those are the questions."

But there was another question as well. Why was Jan Vignoles—Winkworth Gaud—killed? It was, I was certain, the most important question of all.

And the Bishop—a vision flashed before my eyes of a doodle on a crumpled piece of paper. Wink had shoved it into my hand that day at the hospital, and I'd simply thrown it away. The drawing had been of a bishop, seated in the back seat of a car. And in his hand had been a gun.

35

That night, locked in my room at the Novotel, I wrestled in the dark for a sleep that would not come. My mind was assaulted by all of the events since the day of the "nuns." Finally I gave up and got out of bed. I turned on the light, sat down at the desk, and gave myself up to a total preoccupation with the matters of the Waldheim Museum and the Rembrandt.

More and more, I slowly realized, I had come to think of the affair in terms of an attack on the museum. Almost every episode could be translated into that term: the original theft . . . the revelation of Saskia as a prostitute . . . the bomb threat at the opening . . . the thefts of the Degas and Whistler . . . the demonstration against the museum . . . the fire scare at the museum . . . the delivery of Blossom's body to the museum. . . .

And then there were the four deaths—all related? And William C. Brown—apparently Wink had suspected him, or someone, of being a Nazi, and now Brown stood accused by the Belgian Resistance fighter. And Ringwell, a politician fighting for his life. And a bishop . . .

The thing that bothered me most about all this, I realized, was the disparity of the events. On the one hand, we had had thefts, armed robbery, kidnapping, and murder, a series of truly terrifying crimes. These made the rest—bomb threats, demonstrations, fire scares—seem trivial, in a whole other league. How did they fit together?

I thought for a long time. Finally I picked up the telephone and called Ed Simms at his hotel. Naturally I woke him up; it was now 3:00 A.M. His voice was thick with sleep. "Yes?"

"It's Persis. Can you get a search warrant and get into Mrs. Sandringham's house in Long Island?"

He was waking up fast. "What for?"

"I think you'll find the missing Degas there. You'll be told it's a copy—but it won't be. The Degas in Mrs. Sandringham's house in Gull Harbor is the real thing."

Simms was totally awake now, briskly professional. "Suppose we do find it—may I ask how you knew it was there?"

"Don't pin me down just yet, Ed. I'm not sure of my answers. But I believe you'll find I'm right."

"Mrs. Sandringham's still in Europe, I think. It won't hurt to have a look quietly. Then what?"

"Then, if you would, please, do nothing for the moment. And look in Rosi's house—all and any of her houses, including her château here in France. Though I'll bet you find her Whistler on Long Island."

He whistled, very low.

"Go back to sleep now, Ed. I'm sorry I disturbed you."

He muttered something about being wide-awake and wasn't it just like me to expect him to go back to sleep after startling him out of a sound slumber. I told him I'd always thought FBI meant the ability to fall asleep at the First Bloody Instant, and I hung up, feeling better.

It finally seemed so clear to me, here in the quiet of the night. Belle Sandringham and Rosi Craig-Mitchell were incapable of murdering people. Therefore, they could have had nothing to do with the events at the Waldheim, events which had led to death. Ergo, somebody was deceiving them, too. I still didn't know why they had taken their own pictures, but plainly it was time to tell Simms about the Degas. Belle Sandringham herself might be in danger. I loved the old lady, and Rosi, too. Now they would be in Simms's capable hands.

Tomorrow, I decided as I crawled back into bed, I would drive to Le Touquet. Alone. I had thought of telling Simms about this, too, but had decided against it—it was too fantastic a theory without facts to back it up. I would need to check it out first.

And yet, as I lay there, I was convinced it was not so fantastic. Canisters of gas, the kind used in Sogegarde, had been recovered in an accident on route Nationale 40 headed in the direction of Le Touquet, Boulogne, Calais, Dunkerque, Belgium, and Holland. The architect's plans for Sogegarde, the most secure plant in the world for the safeguarding of valuables, had been stolen or misplaced. And for the past four decades, some of the great art treasures of the world had been vanishing without a trace.

Had Winkworth Gaud been on the right trail? Was someone building a Sogegarde of his own—to safeguard *stolen* masterpieces?

I got up once more, still restless, and unfolded the map the man at the desk had been kind enough to give me earlier. Yes, Touquet was the place to start. It was an ideal location, accessible by boat, rail, highway, and plane, yet sufficiently small and remote not to be in the spotlight. Tourists and strangers passed through it all the time, creating a great deal of activity and bustle. People could go unnoticed. So could packages and luggage and unidentified crates.

The roads through Belgium would be swift and easy, I saw, but once I turned well north of Lille, conditions would deteriorate. I could not make a wrong move or I would waste hours.

I was just tracing the final leg of my journey to Touquet with my pen when a tremendous blast shook the room, causing my hand to jump off the paper. Then there was echoing silence. The sound seemed to have come from the front of the hotel.

Several seconds passed, then my telephone rang.

"Madame? This is the desk. You are all right?"

"What was that awful noise just now?"

"I regret to say, your car, madame."

"*What?*"

The desk was in a state. "We have been plagued with automobile thefts, madame, so we now have special guards at night. Someone was trying to get into your car . . . it was your license number. A thief. Before the guard could apprehend—an explosion. We have notified the police. Thank God you are all right. We couldn't be sure . . ."

I could hear shouts in the background and sirens.

Very quietly I replaced the receiver and sank down on the edge of the bed. Then I began to shake so violently that my teeth chattered.

There, but for the grace of some hapless thief, went I. The reception had been arranged for me. I had better hurry and find the answers I needed or there would surely be another reception somewhere, sometime. And this time it would be fatal.

36

If I were asked to build a movie set for "The Three Musketeers," I would build Le Touquet Paris Plage, France. It has timbered houses, oddly placed balconies that are perfect to leap from, narrow streets down which to retreat while fencing or galloping on horseback. . . .

But I would be wrong. Touquet is a movie set, all right but for an entirely different film. It would be about Edwardian Englishmen and -women crossing the channel in search of charming summer houses, about elegant denizens of the upper class strolling on in their white suits and boater hats, long muslin gowns, and parasols.

The English have long since abandoned Touquet except as a quick stop when the British Air Ferries prop plane lands from Gatwick or Southend and passengers board the Touquet Airport train for a two-hour trip to Paris. A few English still come, but it is mainly to meander along the streets, look longingly into the chic shops, and eat at the cheap restaurants like Le Restaurant de l'Atlantique, sandwiches six fr.

All the beautiful villas with the inexorably English names are today the occupied territories of French, Dutch, and Germans despite their names: By-Ways, Lone Pine, O'Malley, Airshot. The Forest (La Forêt), where English nannies in impeccable starched uniforms once wheeled their charges beneath the pines, is today the site of villas and yet more villas, until the forest has been nearly gobbled up and little else except the ancient pine needles remain.

By the time I arrived in Touquet after the inevitable delays in Antwerp caused by the bombing of my car ("lucky for you they tried to steal it . . . get out of here while you're still alive" was what Simms had said, easing the way), it was dinner time and dark. It had been raining off and on all day, and it was raining here, too. As I cruised down the Avenue St. Jean, I noticed the waiter from the Ascot Bar hosing down his sidewalk. It seemed excessive.

The rambling red brick and yellow sandstone Westminster Hotel looked welcoming. L'HOTEL EST OUVERT said a sign on the rainswept veranda in case no one could believe it. The red, curved awnings over the windows were streaming with rain, but the lobby was warm and glowing with soft light. And the management was delighted to see a traveler in this off-season.

Tomorrow I would treat myself to a sensational dinner, I vowed . . . maybe at Flavio next door where I had first made the acquaintance of the celestial coulibiac Craig Claiborne had almost seen me make in my dream. Just thinking about it made my mouth water.

But this night there was no time for self-indulgence. Tonight it would have to be a quick bite somewhere and then up to my room to plan tomorrow's chase.

Promptly at 8:30 the next morning I embarked on my search. I realized that it would require patience and I was even prepared for—half expecting—failure. If I failed in Touquet, however, I would simply move east along the Channel coast from town to town and try again until I found what I was looking for . . . or had to admit I was wrong. It had stopped raining, finally. The sky was clear.

I would be systematic, I had decided, in my effort to bring out the Cathedral people. I would go to the Gendarmerie, the Syndicat d'Initiative and to every garage and gas station in town, one by one. I would tell my story: I was secretary to a wealthy man who had bought a masterpiece in Belgium and needed transport to carry it safely to his villa in Touquet. It was so expensive he didn't trust the usual carriers—afraid word of it would leak out and it would be stolen. Was there a local firm that knew the back roads and could be trusted to be discreet? I was counting on the words *masterpiece, expensive,* and *discreet* to raise the art thieves. If they were in Touquet, word of what I had should bring them sniffing around, I thought.

Sometimes I wonder if I am simpleminded—I should know the French by now. The French are suspicious. They are suspicious of one another, not to mention foreigners. The very words I had counted on to flush out Cathedral worked on the local populace like the cry of hounds on the hare in hunting season . . . they figuratively took to the hedgerows.

It is quite true that everyone was very polite—I find that the French are as overwhelmingly polite as they are overwhelmingly on guard. But they were not about to part with information of any kind that would be useful to me. As I tramped through puddles of oil to interview dark men in blue coveralls and plowed through booklets and brochures to interview tourist bureau ladies at their counters and pressed through *pochards, inconnus,* and *malheureux* to query gendarmes in their bureaus, I realized that I was getting nothing in return for my labors. By the end of the day I knew every street by heart and the name of every villa in that charming little city, but that was all I knew.

I drove my car down to the beach and parked facing the water. A few indomitable strollers breasted the strong Channel wind that made all the beach flags stand stiffly horizontal. A fleet of landlocked sailboats, the *char à voile,* listed away from the gale in front of the Blériot Club. One or two boats passed on the horizon like dabs of paint in an Impressionist painting.

All I had to show for the first day was a flurry of polite handshakes, a soupçon of small talk, and a potpourri of pleasant smiles. They listened, but they did not talk. Still, they had listened. Perhaps when they thought it over . . .

I stared out to sea in what I felt sure was the general direction of Dover and tried to decide exactly how much I would give to be able to smoke a cigarette just then. I decided I would give everything I owned.

37

The second day I took a new approach: it was what you might describe as a matter of establishing my credentials for the local citizens. I telephoned a French friend of my Aunt Lydie's, Count Georges du Lavay. Du Lavay was one of her multitude of admirers. He spent a lot of time in his villa in Touquet because he raced his horses both in England and on the Continent, and Touquet was a convenient midway stop between both.

Ten minutes after my call he was at the Westminister to fetch me in his bottle-green Alfa Romeo, and for two days I let him entertain me. It was a good way to see the town and, more important, to have the town see me.

Since he was a contemporary of my aunt, the count was obviously no spring chicken. He was, rather, a sophistictaed, worldly, excessively rich, and altogether charming member of the international set de Groot was always talking about. In short, he was a cultivated and attractive companion. I indulged myself shamelessly in his hospitality for forty-eight hours.

The pace was terrific: tennis at the Club des Quatre Saisons, the Tennis Club, and at his own private court. Tournaments of all kinds, from stately bridge contests at the Palais de l'Europe to boisterous rifle contests between the shooting clubs of Calais, Bethune, Dunkerque, Touquet, and St. Omer. At night we danced. There was a ball for the benefit of unadopted French orphans at the Palais de l'Europe at which one of the Paris fashion writers asked me respectfully who had designed my dress and I did not confess that it was really my best nightgown, not having packed with a ball in mind. We also attended a swinging party at the Bip-Bip Club, after which du Lavay gaily proposed that we take his plane to England and go disco-ing in London. He rounded up a copy of the *London Times* to check out the current goings-on and I saw a headline about a small Matisse sculpture missing from the Queen's Collection. Scotland Yard was investigating.

"We could leave after lunch tomorrow," du Lavay said. "I have a *pied à terre* in London."

I declined regretfully. I was not on holiday: two days of fun were all I could spare. He would have to go without me. Surely by now I had sufficiently established my credibility in Touquet as a young woman who might conceivably work for a wealthy man who had recently purchased a priceless art treasure. If there were thieves around, they might surface.

The call came at the same time as my *petit déjeuner*. The caller was a man, speaking English in a heavy accent.

"Madame Willum?"

"Yes. Who is calling, please?"

"You are in need of transport for a work of art?"

"I am. I need someone discreet—that is very important. Do you know of anyone? The payment will be exceptional."

"There are two possibilities. Démanagements Dumas from Boulogne—but they are not for you . . . too big and too many people who may talk. Then there is Pas de Calais, Transports Internationaux, right here in Étaples. They are best for what you wish, I think."

"Thank you so much. Where will I find . . ."

"*On vous téléphonera, madame.*" My caller hung up. I understood perfectly: the man I had just spoken to had ascertained that there was a job to be done and a good fee involved. Now he would call the shippers, tell them about the job, and extract a finder's fee for his information. Then they would contact me. But how could I wait?

Pas de Calais, Transports Internationaux in Étaples, he had said.

Étaples is the small village separated from Le Touquet by a bridge over the Canche river. The simplest description of the relationship between the two towns is that the swells have always lived splendidly in luxurious Touquet, while those who attend to and make possible the high quality of Touquet life live across the river in Étaples.

I picked up the local telephone directory next to my bed and went through it carefully. There was no Pas de Calais, Transports Internationaux, listed in either neighboring Étaples or Touquet itself. I got out my car and began once again to search. This time it was in Étaples instead of Touquet and the object of my search finally had a specific name.

Étaples is a fishing village consisting mostly of two busy main streets, numerous narrow side streets, and a large quai where the fishing fleet pulls up to unload its catch. I spent the day driving those streets, block by block. I traced and retraced my own trail. I finally acquired a fine kink in my neck from staring upward to examine business signs. But that was all I acquired. If such a firm as Pas de Calais, Transports Internationaux, existed in Étaples, I couldn't find it.

Another wasted day.

38

By now my head was dancing with visions of trucks of all sizes and colors. But mostly, though, what I was seeing was white Volkswagen trucks, small, unmarked, and ubiquitous. They were, the hotel informed me, "the cleaning trucks, of course."

"You must understand," the desk explained, "that Touquet is largely a weekend town. People come from all over to holiday at their villas, from Holland, Belgium, Paris, even Germany. Most of them don't maintain a full-time staff, however, although there are always exceptions, so when the villa owners leave at the beginning of the week, the cleaning trucks come and clean up and take the linens to be washed. Before the next weekend the white trucks return, make the beds, stock the refrigerators, turn on the electricity, and so on. Without the white trucks Touquet would slowly run down and expire."

If ever I wanted to be invisible in this town by being *too* visible, I told myself, I would become a white truck.

It was while I was sitting at a table next to the window at Flavio, musing on this very thing, that I saw the white truck whisk by on the Avenue du Verger. This one was slightly different from the rest. On its side plate were the initials P DE C and the abbreviation TRANS. INTNATNL. The small nameplate was discreet in the extreme, scarcely visible, in fact.

I leaped up like a shot deer, scattered a handful of twenty-franc notes on the table, and took off for my car before the astonished *patron* could even protest my exit. The small white Volkswagen bus was dodging in and out of traffic with the expertise of a broken field runner. I revved up my little car and burst out of the parking lot, determined to cling to the Volkswagen's tail.

It was a nice day. Puffy white clouds sailed self-importantly in an azure sky. My stomach gave a rueful twinge at the thought of the lost coubiliac and then resigned itself to the chase.

The white bus flicked itself onto the Avenue General de Gaulle and I buried my car in the traffic behind it. On the left, the airport suddenly appeared, busy as always. Then we were on the bridge and soaring over the river Canche where it empties into the Channel, and we were in Étaples.

Now the white truck twisted sharply to the left along the quai where two dingy-looking fishing boats were tied up. Next, it hurled itself around a corner to the right and disappeared into a wall. It hadn't literally disappeared into a wall, of course: it is just the astonishing appearance French vehicles give of vanishing into thin air when they have actually driven into an inside courtyard behind a wall and slammed the gate behind them. They are invisible.

I tramped hard on my brake and skidded to a noisy stop several doors down. When the traffic permitted, I backed up to where I thought the truck had performed its vanishing act. Now I could see a sign. It was really nothing more than a brass plate set in the wall and it was so small that I had to get out of my car and cross the street to read it. No wonder I hadn't seen it before.

P DE C, TRANSPORTS INTERNATIONAUX, it said. I had asked for a firm that would be discreet; this was discretion carried to the point of near invisibility. The question was what to do next. Bang on the gate? Ring the bell in the wall? No, the answer was to wait. Wait and see.

I drove down to the quai where I would have a good view in my rear mirror of anything or anyone coming out of the gate, opened a copy of *Elle*, and prepared to wait. To anyone passing, I was simply watching the fishing boats and the activity at the airport across the river.

My mind idled on hold. Pas de Calais . . .
Transports Internationaux . . .

P de C . . . Pay de Say . . .

Suddenly I stiffened. My God. My mind flashed back to the Waldheim Museum, to the day Blossom Rugge had made her most dramatic appearance ever—dead, in a shipping crate.

That had been the name of the firm on the crate. Pei D. Sei. We had all thought it looked Chinese, but that wasn't it at all. Pay de Say was the French pronunciation of the letters P de C for Pas de Calais. Someone had been playing with us, laughing at us. One thing was indisputable: the people behind the gate and the people who delivered Blossom Rugge to the Waldheim were one and the same.

The brioche, so light and airy when it had made its appearance on my breakfast tray this morning, felt like a stone inside me now. My hands weren't shaking nor were my teeth chattering —none of the usual signs of nerves—but I was definitely in a state. It was like catatonia: muscular rigidity combined with great excitement, but mercifully without the mental stupor and confusion that went with it. My mind seemed to be sharp and operating at full capacity, thankfully.

I sat there for hours. Fishing boats came and went. Fishmongers dickered over purchases. Citizens wandered along the wharf, making their own private deals with the boatmen. Planes came and went at the airport across the way, disgorging passengers and freight with boring regularity. Traffic swirled by on the busy bridge over the river. The tide came and went and the boats tied to the quai rose and fell with its coming and going.

Finally the white bus reappeared, its nose poking cautiously out of the wall like an animal examining the terrain for safety's sake. Assured that the coast was clear, the entire vehicle emerged.

The Volkswagen set off briskly back across the bridge to Touquet. At the Avenue de l'Aéroport it swung to the right, with me not far behind. We headed into the airport.

Ahead of me, the white bus pulled up to the customs shed and parked. I swung into a space farther away, hidden from the bus by other parked cars, and waited to see what was going to happen.

A British Airways flight was already on the ground, its passengers swarming across the runway to line up before two harassed-looking customs officials. The baggage lifts were busy unloading the flight. Friends and relatives peered into the customs section, waving and calling to the arrivals. The airport teemed with people. I stayed where I was, watching.

Slowly the passengers moved along the customs line. Baggage destined for Paris was being transferred expertly onto the little Paris-Touquet train, waiting beside the airport. Passengers bound there hurried to the train as soon as customs released them; others streamed into the airport proper, some to eat, some to shower and change clothes, some to telephone; others moved into the parking lot, looking for cabs or their own cars.

There was a sudden bustle of activity around the white bus. I saw two coveralled men step into the customs shed and carry out a long and bulky package. Under its multitudinous wraps, it looked to me like a large altar cross. It was followed solicitously by a bearded priest who emerged from the customs line closing his passport and reaching up under his coat to slip it in his hip pocket. The movers placed the wrapped object carefully in the back of the truck and closed the doors, then all of them, including the man of the cloth, climbed into the front seat. The motor of the Volkswagen coughed rebelliously once or twice, then the bus started up, skittered swiftly across the parking lot, and headed for the exit road. I shadowed carefully. Immediately outside the parking lot gates, the bus stopped. The driver climbed out and moved swiftly around from one side of the truck to the other. To my astonishment I saw him remove the plates that carried the firm's name from each side of the truck. The white bus was now anonymous.

Once again the procession started up and we dove into the traffic on the main road. I had the swing of it by now and was prepared to follow at a tactful distance, praying that no other white bus would plunge into the line from a side road and confuse the issue.

None did. I contented myself keeping three cars back. We were briefly in Étaples . . . I caught a quick glimpse of the sea-scarred boats at the quai, their rich harvest of Channel fish long since unloaded . . . then the bus turned right, along the road to Montreuil.

I had to stay well behind now—there was not as much traffic on this road and it became a struggle to keep at least one car between me and the bus, which careened along carelessly, apparently unworried about the possibility of being followed. It was still daylight.

The road was edged on both sides with neat farms. Not old ones—there had been too many wars fought here—but they looked reasonably prosperous. I saw horses at pasture and cows and a few sheep. Occasionally there was a tantalizing glimpse of the tree-bordered Canche winding along on the right, always within hailing distance, like a good companion. On either side, occasional small roads wandered off to small unseen farms or villages.

The white bus didn't stray. It kept to the Montreuil road, whipping along N. 318 with the confidence of old acquaintance. I clung to its dusty trail with the single-mindedness of a limpet. Just before the slight bend to the right that would take it up to the walled thirteenth-century town of Montreuil, the bus darted to the left and plunged into the countryside that hugged the valley of the river Course. I plunged after it, praying it wouldn't disappear from sight behind one of the sharp turns in the narrowed road. I was in luck—each time I rounded a curve I saw its white *derrière* skittering along ahead.

I began to pick up signs to villages on the route of the Course: Estrelles . . . Montcavrel . . . Inxent . . . Bernieulles. We were now flying along D. 127. ENQUIN-SUR-BAILLONS, a sign announced. *Parcours de pêche communal.* The white Volkswagen left it swiftly in its wake . . . so did I.

Suddenly I rounded a curve and found that I was alone. There wasn't another car in sight. It had vanished as suddenly as if it had gone down the rabbit hole in Alice's Wonderland.

I drove on for several kilometers: nothing. I doubled back, moving as slowly as my car would tolerate. Nothing. I went back, retraced my route almost to Enquin. The white bus had totally disappeared.

On the outskirts of Enquin I reversed myself and followed

D. 127 northwest for a second time. About three kilometers after that small village with its "communal fishing grounds," I saw it ... a sign almost totally overgrown by wild flowers and bushes and rendered nearly totally unreadable by the rigors of many years. LA CATHÉDRALE DE LA VALLÉE DE LA COURSE, it said. I wheeled my small rented Simca off the road so swiftly that a hail of pebbles followed and came to rest with me in the tall weeds adjacent.

I may be the typical vague artist in many ways, but as a traveler I am always the very epitome of the well-prepared voyager. The Simca was almost listing from the weight of the maps and brochures that I had commandeered the very first day from the Syndicat d'Initiative in Touquet's Hotel de Ville. I reached now for the Syndicat's green guide to the Vallée de la Course, certain that the towns along D. 127 would be too small to be listed in my red Michelin.

Quickly, I flipped through the little handbook. "*La Course c'est d'abord sa rivière, ses truites, ses étangs, ses paysages, ses campings.*" Lovely, I thought. I'm delighted to know that I'm in a region of the river, its trout, its ponds, its lovely countryside, and its pleasant camping sites. But what about this cathedral?

Next came a listing of the towns in alphabetical order: Becourt, Bernieulles, Beussent, Bezinghem, and so on straight through Zoteux. No Cathédrale de la Vallée de la Course. There were maps. There were advertisements for hotels, restaurants, and even house-builders. There were English translations (discovered only after I had labored through the French); endless ads for stores and services at Le Touquet, quite obviously the nearest center of commerce; photographs of chateaux, moulins, museums, and churches of the Vallée. . . .

Finally I spotted it, in very small type underneath a photograph of a ruined shell of a church.

"Cathédrale de la Vallée de la Course," it read. "Eleventh-century church which suffered greatly in the fourteenth-century wars and was the scene of violent battles in the time of François I. Built at the junction of Roman roads, it had become an important trading town by the twelfth century, boasting a busy market and street stalls of various kinds. Partially restored by the Carthusian monks for use as a retreat, it was again totally destroyed in World War I and has never been rebuilt, although outbuildings occasionally serve as an overflow for the Hospice of Neuville-sous-Montreuil, situated at the confluence of the Course and the Canche. Not open for visits."

All of this was printed in type so small that I could scarcely decipher it, and in French only. No wonder it had taken me three or four trips through the booklet to spot it.

I put the book back in the map compartment. What next? Did I drive down this overgrown, unprepossessing road? Did I try to get back to Neuville-sous-Montreuil and ask questions? Did I abandon the car (as too eye-catching) and walk?

While I was trying to decide, I noticed the faint vestiges of an ancient cart road tracing its way through the fields in the general direction of the more regularly used road. It looked to me as if I could follow it in my little Simca, which was clever and roadworthy. With a profusion of undergrowth on each side I might be able to get fairly close to my objective without being seen or challenged. From the look of it, no one had ventured on the cart road for years. The main right of way to the ruined cathedral was bad enough.

I would try it. I had come too far to turn back.

It was slow and torturous going and several times, when I sank into a depression I hadn't seen or when my car struck a concealed rock or downed tree branch, I thought its insides had been torn out. But the Simca crept onward gamely, more clever and lively than many a more expensive automobile might have been. "You are a little beauty, Simca," I whispered, nursing it gently along. "Don't let me down now." What would happen if I had to turn around and flee, driving very fast over this same terrain? I shuddered to think. The one image that came to mind was of the shell of a car tearing along with vital parts of its anatomy flying off in all directions. It wouldn't, I felt sure, go far.

When Cathédrale de la Vallée de la Course appeared, it did so very suddenly: one minute there was nothing but weeds and underbrush and remnants of hedgerow, and the next minute there were the ruins. Before me were collapsed walls of what had once been a small cathedral and remnants of living quarters, a small part of which had been patched together for habitation on a simple level. Anyone who had not read the description in the handbook would never have dreamed that the place could contain life. Also, those who had not read the handbook and turned down the road to the ruins by mistake would have long since turned back . . . one glimpse of the depressing, overgrown rubble and they would have opted for a more gracious landscape elsewhere. I almost turned back myself. It was a forlorn, unappetizing, and demoralizing sight.

Then I saw the white Volkswagen bus . . . just a whisper of its chastely clean side neatly slipped into an empty space between the habitable building and the collapsed front wall of the original cathedral. No one coming up the regular road could have seen it. I wouldn't have noticed it myself if I hadn't come up the cart road. It wouldn't be visible from the air either, I noted . . . there seemed to be a kind of roof made of fallen slabs that managed to look natural. There was no other sign of life anywhere.

I left the Simca behind a thicket of thorn trees and what looked like 300-year-old locusts, after turning it around to make sure it was facing in the right direction in case I had to depart suddenly. I watched the ruins for a long time before I made a move, but nothing was to be seen . . . if there was anything going on, it must be somewhere out of sight. I didn't really want to go up there—it was, as a matter of fact, the very last thing on my list of acceptable pastimes—but there seemed to be no other alternative. What would Oliver say, I wondered? He would be furious, I knew, but maybe he would never find out. Now Aunt Lydie, on the other hand, would be all for it, and Gregor . . . hard to predict what Gregor would do, but it would be a safe guess that he would *hire* someone to go in and look around. Gregor was smart . . . a survivor.

With a suddenness that made me jump with fear, the white bus came to life, backing swiftly out of its hiding place and hurtling off down the road. There seemed to be three people in its front seat. I had a quick glimpse of black, then they were gone. Back to Touquet? On an errand to Montreuil? I didn't know. They were simply gone. And if I was ever going to find out what this place was like, it had to be now.

I left the shelter of the trees and stepped toward the fallen buildings, moving swiftly and quietly on my sneakers, half running through the underbrush, unconcerned with the branches that tore at my blue jeans. I can move fast when I have to and I was in the cover of the buildings in seconds. I paused to catch my breath and to listen. Nothing. I moved forward again until I reached the place where the Volkswagen had been before.

There was just room enough between the remnant of the cathedral wall and the living quarters for the bus to be concealed without scraping its sides. On the left was a shabby, temporary door. It led to the habitat. On the right was what was still standing of the vastly thick front wall of the cathedral. It was about all that was standing; the rest was rubble. I looked at it carefully, unable, in spite of my precarious position, to resist admiring the beauty of the ancient stones. There was a door here, too . . . one of two smaller doors that must once have stood on either side of the great central doors of the cathedral. This one was made of oak. Not thirteenth century, certainly, but doubtless very old. It fit snugly into its old stone arch. I looked again, surprised, my artist's eye alert.

Too snugly. It fit like a door still in use. But going where? Into an empty wall? Hardly likely.

I studied it carefully, all of my senses tingling with awareness. Surely this door, which in the natural train of events would not even still be standing, had a purpose. I concentrated. Thumb latch, no lock . . . no keyhole, ancient or modern . . . yet it couldn't just *open*, not in this place.

I moved my attention to the stone walls on the side of the door. Yes . . . that might be it. I ran my hands over the cold surface. My fingers felt a slight tremor. Quickly I pried and clawed, and one of the stones came away in my hand. Beneath it was a button. I pressed it. There was a slight humming sound and the oak door swung open.

Directly in front of me, set dead tight behind the door, were the gates of an elevator and its small cage. I opened the gate and stepped inside. It was very narrow, just wide enough to fit inside the deep walls of the cathedral's ruined front and to accommodate two persons at most. There were two buttons inside: "up" and "down." I pressed the latter. The cage trembled slightly, then went into motion so silently that it was only by the almost undetectable vibration at the end that I knew we had come to rest. I slid the gate open and stepped out. The light inside the elevator went out. I was standing in darkness. Before I had lost the light, though, I had seen a door to the left. Near the top of it was a narrow slit of glass, just wide enough for an observer to see what was going on in the room inside . . . perhaps someone who wanted to be sure the employees were doing their jobs without himself being observed.

It hadn't been installed there with people like me in mind.

I stepped carefully across the dark hall and stood on tiptoe. The glass pane was just the right height when I made myself taller. I looked inside the room.

39

I knew immediately what I was looking at. It was what I had been searching for all along. An underground version of Sogegarde.

It was an unlikely setting. Here, extending fully under the remains of the ruined cathedral, was a perfectly preserved original eleventh-century crypt. Like the Canterbury Cathedral crypt and many others of its time, it formed a complete lower church in itself, its plaster walls decorated with fresco painting and its ceiling aspiring to a comparatively modest Gothic arch. Stone columns divided the walls. On the nearest one I could discern faint carving which read *Les Évêques de la Course*. Beneath, fading into the ancient rock, were near-invisible tracings of the names of long-dead bishops. Some of these same bishops were doubtless interred right here, in a burial chamber somewhere beneath the original sanctuary.

But all of this was merely the casing on the package. Built inside the core of the original crypt without disturbing its ancient outer walls was a completely modern facility which fitted as snugly as a nut within a shell. All the indispensable accoutrements were there, in gray metal units adorned with dials and lights and colored buttons: what appeared to be temperature and humidity controls, lighting regulators, smoke detectors, and electronic surveillance equipment. Marching down the center of the room was an enormous unit of what looked like metal drawers, four units high, in vertical rather than horizontal position. Each drawer had two metal handles. Each drawer was numbered. There must have been several hundred of them, I guessed.

The door I was peering through, using the narrow glass slit, was a thick metal fire door. Between it and the room inside was a series of three closed steel gates. Next to each one I could see a microphone. Although it was too dark where I stood to see, I imagined there was such a microphone next to the fire door, too.

Stationed inside the crypt, beyond the last of the steel gates, was a man in a cassock seated at a table on which sat a console of complicated dimensions and occasional flashing lights. I assumed that it controlled the locking of the many doors and probably the elevator also. There was a battery of telephones on the table. I noticed that the man was wearing tennis shoes beneath his cassock. A submachine gun was near his hand.

I noticed the shoes before I noticed the three closed circuit television screens. One was monitoring the area between the living area and the cathedral side door. Another was monitoring the inside of the elevator. The third was black until the priest reached out and pressed a button on his console. There was a blinding flash as the hall in which I was standing lit up with several thousand watts and I saw what the third screen was monitoring: me, standing at the door on tiptoe, peering in. Between them, the screens must have picked me up the minute I moved into the area where the white bus had been, and they had been on me ever since. I had been *allowed* to enter, like the spider and the fly.

So the painful jab of the gun in my back was no surprise. "Open for number 7," a deep voice from behind me said to the microphone. There was a click and a black-clad arm reached around me and pulled open the door. The procedure was repeated for each of the steel gates. Then we were inside. Whoever was prodding me forward must have been standing in the darkness of the hall the whole time, waiting for me. I heard the doors lock automatically behind us.

I felt like a fool. I also felt very afraid. The gun urged me forward.

The man at the console table didn't bother to look up at me as we passed: my captor pushed me down the corridor formed by the wall of the crypt and the massive banks of perpendicular containers. I was thoroughly frightened, but not too terrified to notice that each section of the containers was monitored by some sort of scanning system—I could hear the click of the sweeping beam.

We marched for what was probably no more than forty yards or so, although it seemed like miles; then we turned to the left. Steel gates and another fire door halted us momentarily until the right words were spoken, then all doors unlocked. We stepped into a room that in the Middle Ages must have served as a special crypt, perhaps for the remains of saints.

There were no saints in it today. Only a bishop.

He was wearing a ski mask, brown wool, with the eyes and nose openings outlined in red. It was one of those that serves as a cap until you choose to pull it over your face.

"Welcome, Mrs. Willum," he said. "We have been expecting you." The voice was deeply muffled by the heavy wool and virtually unrecognizable. "Excuse the mask. A precaution."

Chess is not my game; I'm too impatient. But I did know this much . . . in this game, at this moment, I was the person of the lowest order. "The pawn has arrived," I said, trying to sound very cool. "I suppose it is now the Bishop's move . . . you are the Bishop, of course."

"Of course. Delighted you have heard of me. The pawn has arrived, as you say, because we chose to have you arrive. In fact, the truck thought it had lost you and has gone back to find you."

They must have been aware of every move I had been making. They had deliberately led me here. I thought I was so clever to have found them, but they had allowed, even arranged it. And that certainly meant they had no intention of letting me leave alive. I thought of Saskia, and I felt ill. I would have to keep my wits about me. I could not give in to fear if I hoped to survive.

The Bishop understood what I was thinking. "You should know this: if you touch the door behind you, every door in this entire complex will automatically lock. Every corner of the warehouse is monitored electronically. An alarm will go off should you touch a painting in the main area without taking the proper precautions—and my guards do not ask questions before they shoot."

"Like Sogegarde," I said. Why had they allowed me to enter?

To find out how much I knew and with whom I'd shared that knowledge, obviously.

"Just like Sogegarde. Better, perhaps," the Bishop said.

It was true. Here there was a special safeguard Sogegarde couldn't duplicate—guards that looked like harmless priests unless you saw the machine guns hidden in their cassocks. Who would suspect the clergy of thefts, kidnappings, and even murders?

I tried for a cool, conversational tone. "This must be where the saints were buried—perfect for the Bishop's command post. It is your command post, isn't it?"

"There have been others in the past. We move from time to time, as events dictate."

I looked around me. I saw that one whole wall was covered with television monitors; it looked like the screens in a TV network control room, and it was obvious that the Bishop could command the entire area without stirring from his desk. I noted the speaker he used to communicate with those outside this room. I saw, too, his bank of telephones and tried to work out the meanings of the code letters identifying them.

All the television monitors on the wall were dark. If the Bishop wasn't monitoring this interview, did it mean he wasn't allowing us to be monitored either?

Behind the Bishop there was another door: it looked more like the watertight door on a ship than a conventional exit. Above it was a light with a red T. My memory pricked me . . . if this was truly a duplicate of Sogegarde, then they'd have an exit tunnel which flooded with water at night and then was pumped out again in the morning . . . and this must be it. . . .

A square of black velvet hung to the left of the watertight door. The Bishop saw me looking at it and reached behind him to pull at the black material. It dropped to the floor, and I was looking at the missing Rembrandt of Saskia van Uylenburgh. I gasped.

"You must have really loved this painting to steal it twice," I told him.

The Bishop laughed. "Love? No, these paintings mean power. With one great work I can buy oil wells . . . diamond mines

... kings ... countries ... When you offer the best, no price is too high. And there is always a collector somewhere in the world who will pay the price, whatever it may be." This was no mad collector sitting in his room savoring stolen masterpieces. The Bishop was a businessman.

He had stolen this Saskia painting twice—first, when he had hijacked the trucks leaving Antwerp and a second time from the Waldheim Museum. I hadn't understood the double theft at all until I finally deciphered the meaning of the Haarlem Rembrandt in this whole affair. Without the Haarlem portrait the parts of the puzzle would never have fitted together.

The Rembrandt glowed on the wall behind him. Even in my state of fear I couldn't help admiring its beauty. "At the time you stole the Wiener Rembrandt, it was considered the greatest early Saskia portrait in the world," I said. If he wanted to know how much I knew, I would oblige by telling him. "Years later the fickle critics declared that the Haarlem Saskia was the greatest and you had to have it, so you arranged for it to be stolen. Meanwhile, it was noised about that de Groot wanted a top Rembrandt —no questions asked—so you organized the sale of the Wiener Rembrandt to him, the portrait you now thought was second-best." I could almost see the transaction ... a meeting in a parking lot at night ... a masked man exchanging the Rembrandt for cash ... de Groot's intermediary (probably David Lawless ... he'd have the right connections and wouldn't ask questions) taking the painting and driving off.

But then had come the bombshell ... the Rembrandt Research Project's declaration that they had been in the process of studying the Haarlem Rembrandt before its theft and had finally decided that it was not genuine. Right or wrong? It didn't matter —the reputation of the painting was permanently damaged and its value diminished. So the Bishop had to reacquire the Wiener Rembrandt. And he did, by stealing it from the Waldheim. One of these days the Haarlem Museum would probably receive a ransom offer and their Saskia would be returned.

"I suppose," I went on, "that you had to kill Acolyte—Winkworth Gaud, that is—because he had read in some museum journal that the Waldheim was about to open and thought he recognized you in a picture. He couldn't be sure, though, after so many years, so he came to the Waldheim and you had to kill him, although you hadn't anticipated it. Then you had to kill the girl, because it wasn't a simple kidnapping anymore when Gaud died. You couldn't afford to take any chances. Poor Gaud. He was lucky when he escaped being swept up and 'interrogated' by the SS, as you had arranged. He may have been lucky many times. But his luck ran out in Gull Harbor."

I could hear the note of loathing that had crept into my voice. I couldn't help it: I despised the man sitting in front of me. He had betrayed his own colleagues to the SS, knowing what their fate would be. He had pursued and killed Winkworth Gaud. He had ordered the murder of Saskia, who was really an innocent bystander. He had used Blossom Rugge, letting her harbor his men (it was surely one of the "nuns" I'd seen at her demonstration) when necessary, using her loft to kill Saskia, and finally disposing of Blossom herself when she had outlived her usefulness.

Just as he would now dispose of me.

Delay—I had to delay . . . I had to buy time. I looked desperately around the room. Across the top of three walls ran a frieze of medieval tapestry, marching in procession from wall to wall.

"Lost segments of the Bayeux Tapestry?" I asked.

The eyes were watching me through the slits in the mask. Back there, shadowed, they were anonymous, like the voice. "Why do you think so?"

Buy time, I thought. Keep talking. "They're embroidered, not tapestry. They're in eight colors, on coarse linen, and they seem to be about the Norman Conquest." All that trivia eternally in my head. What use was it now?

There was a sudden sound; it was the Bishop laughing. "Booty of the Hundred Years War. We 'acquired' it from the descendants of the original thief. Most scholars don't even suspect that it still exists." He shifted slightly in his chair and I noticed for the first time that the right hand in his lap was holding a gun. It was pointed approximately at my stomach.

Lying across the desk between the Bishop and me was a large gold altar cross. It measured at least eight to ten inches in diameter. The elaborately chased top section had been unscrewed and was lying amid brown paper wrappings on the floor. A still-wrapped object about a foot high stood at the corner of the desk near me.

I pointed to it. "The Matisse? It came inside the cross by way of British Airways today? May I see it?" He nodded. I suppose it was my reward for having recognized the Bayeux fragments, or maybe it was just pride of ownership. I didn't know . . . and I didn't care.

I reached for the sculpture, and all the while kept talking. "It's very funny, you know," I told the Bishop, as I began to take the padded wrappings off the little bronze statue, "I've just been with Dr. van der Donck and—you're going to hate this, I know—there's some very serious doubt now about the authenticity of the Wiener Rembrandt. All the top scholars are saying it was stolen from the Waldheim to prevent any authorities from examining it and pronouncing it a fake."

It wasn't true, of course. Dr. van der Donck had said nothing of the kind, but if I was going to live, I needed a weapon—and shock was the weapon I was counting on right now. And it worked. The Bishop couldn't help himself . . . his eyes went to the Wiener painting, which meant that he had to turn slightly in his chair.

"The Wiener painting has never been examined with today's sophisticated techniques—so they can't be sure if it's genuine until they do examine it." He turned a fraction more.

With a swiftness I didn't know I could manage, I hit him with the heavy little Matisse. It caught him on the side of the head, and almost toppled him off his chair. Before he could swing his gun up, I was upon him again, this time with the heavy cross that had been lying across his desk. He was out of his chair. There was blood running down from the side of his head. I swung the cross at his hands as he raised the gun toward me, sending the weapon flying across the room. He lunged and caught me by the throat, stumbling. I found the microphone on the desk and began to smash at the masked face. The fingers clutched at my throat, cutting off my breath. I began to feel faint. I smashed again and again with all of my strength. The Bishop stumbled against the wall. There was a lot of blood.

He was groping like a blind man for the gun. My right hand found and pressed the T on his control console—luckily, the button was clearly marked and I'd spotted it earlier—and the door behind his desk began to open, purring softly as it moved. Before it was wholly opened I hurtled through and into the descending entrance to the tunnel.

There was a strong smell of damp, and the floor felt slippery beneath my pounding feet. Once upon a time this must have been one of the famous medieval tunnels built to help disperse troops and bring in supplies during a siege. It would probably end somewhere near the banks of the Course. I would have to be very fast.

My feet slipped and slid under me with every step—three times I went down to my knees. My hands were covered with slime and dirt. Dim lights had gone on simultaneously with the opening of the tunnel door and I could see, as well as feel, that the corridor was rising slightly as I ran along. That would be to facilitate the flow of the water from the river when the flooding took place.

I could hear my own breathing echoing eerily down the space ahead of me. There must be an exit before the river was reached and surely the Bishop would have a fast car at the other end, probably hidden from sight of the road in some tumbledown outbuilding. With the keys in it, I prayed. But where was the exit? How far away?

I slipped again, and this time I felt a searing pain in my ankle. I stayed where I had fallen, waiting for the agony to subside. And in that moment of respite from the sounds of my own footsteps and my own labored breathing, I heard something else . . . the faintest of whispering noises in the direction of the Course . . . and I heard footsteps from behind me, clearly. The Bishop was following me.

My right leg had become a column of fiery pain, but I dragged myself to my feet and willed myself forward. After the first few steps, a merciful numbness took command of my whole right side and I moved along, crablike, in an awkward, hitching motion. I could hear the Bishop's footsteps loud and sharp above the sounds of my own halting progress. He was getting nearer.

And then, in heightening panic, I heard the most terrifying thing of all. The whispering in the distance had grown into a rushing sound—the waters of the Course . . . the tunnel was flooding. The Bishop must have stumbled against the control lever in our struggles and activated the flood.

My lungs hurt. My legs would barely move. It would be so easy to give up. The rushing sound of water was clearly audible now. I thought of the unlovely death and made a last effort to force my body onward. The tunnel wouldn't flood instantly, I promised myself hopefully; certainly it would be a gradual thing. Surely I would have time.

But it came fast when it did come. One instant the water was trickling forward along the tunnel floor, then it was up to my knees and rising fast, although I could still manage to move against it. The Bishop was almost upon me, just steps behind. I had heard his racking breathing before the water drowned out all other noise. I thought I would feel his hands clutching me at any instant. I would never escape him a second time. We would die together here.

Then I saw the ladder. It rose straight up along the side of the old stones to an iron hatch like that on a submarine. I reached for the slippery rungs. The water was all around me now, pulling at me. I tried to draw myself up the steps to wrestle the hatch open. So heavy . . . too heavy for me . . . I would never get it open.

As I struggled, clinging precariously to the side of the tunnel, I felt the Bishop's hands dragging me downward and back. I kicked back at him with my good leg and felt his grip loosen. At the same time my fingers finally found a release catch and I pushed. The watertight hatch swung open and I struggled up and out, fighting to escape the drag of the churning, boiling waters.

I fell to my knees, choking and gasping. The hatch stood open, waiting for my touch to force it closed once more. I reached toward it, then hesitated. The Bishop was in that tunnel—because of me. If I closed the one escape route he would die—because of me.

I threw myself across the open hatch and stretched my hands down into the foaming water. "Here . . . my hands . . . take them!" I reached back to wrap one arm around the hatch cover to give myself an anchor. The tunnel was almost flooded to the top.

In the water I felt a hand grasp mine, and I tried to pit my strength against the strength of the Course, pulling as hard as I could until my right arm wanted to come out of its socket and my left burned itself into the unyielding metal of the hatch. It was no good. I never even drew him close enough to see his face before I lost him to the relentless waters. I never had a chance against the power of the flood.

I felt him being swept away. I reached after him with both arms, my face streaming with the wetness of the Course and my own stupid tears of fear and exhaustion. "Please," I cried into the crashing water. "Please don't die." Because I knew then who the Bishop was.

But he was gone.

40

They had all come flying when I finally called for them. They had come saying, "It's just like you, Persis, to wait until it's all over before yelling for help." I suppose they were right.

Actually, it had been over very quickly after the Bishop was swept away. Just as I had hoped, there was a fast car (with keys) hidden near the tunnel exit. I'd driven off like a maniac, undeterred by a severely sprained ankle and collecting outraged police and gendarmes the way a runaway horse collects burrs, until I arrived at the Touquet Gendarmerie in a blaze of Klaxons and Gaelic oaths. If anyone from the cathedral had thought of following me, my police escort must have deterred them. Instead, they had cast off their cassocks, picked up as many paintings as they could manage, and disappeared into the local peasantry. The police were busy searching the area even now.

I had taken the first train to Paris and called for Aunt Lydie, Gregor Olitsky, and Oliver Reynolds, all of whom rushed to my side. At this moment we were in Lydia Wentworth's town house on the Avenue Raphaël, Paris. They were all furious with me in differing degrees and for differing reasons. There is nothing quite like being in everyone's doghouse simultaneously.

"*My* friends," Lydia Wentworth was saying to me crossly, "would never behave as you say they have, so there is no use in your telling me that they would, Persis."

"You shouldn't have driven all the way to Touquet to get the police, Persis. That was taking a terrible chance," Gregor lectured angrily. "You should have used your head and called on the local villagers . . . you'd have saved time enough that way to rescue all the paintings." Gregor had no sense of reality: Persis Willum and the local villagers facing machine guns?

Oliver was as much hurt as angry. "If you'd just once—just *once*—call on me before the trouble starts, I'd be most grateful."

I sighed. "Well, I'm calling on you now—all of you. I need you to advise me. Your friends . . . well, what do you think I should do about them? I don't know. . . ."

Aunt Lydie was going to be difficult. In all her sixty years of being a spoiled beauty and one of the richest women in the world, there had never been any way but her way. And her way of dealing with any troublesome subject was always the same . . . to ignore it. That was what she was preparing to do now. I knew the signs: she would suddenly introduce a totally unrelated subject into the conversation and stick to that subject like glue until we forgot whatever it was we had been discussing to begin with.

She did it now. "What is the name of a river in Russia that flows northeast to the Volga?" she demanded.

"Oh, no you don't, Aunt Lydie," I said. "You have to be serious about this. And it's no use your saying that your friends wouldn't behave in such a way, because they have."

Oliver was tamping tobacco into his pipe with furious vigor. "It is *not* possible."

Gregor wasn't so sure. "They're a pretty spoiled lot, after all. They are used to getting what they want and all that."

"Well, really, Gregor—you can't blame them for not wanting a bridge, can you? None of us wanted the bridge." It was obvious that my aunt was on Oliver's side in this matter. "Not that I truly understand it. Suppose you explain, Persis."

I drew a deep breath; this was not going to be easy and I wasn't looking forward to it. But it had to be done. "They knew that to stop the bridge they had to stop Ringwell, so they did. They all got together behind my back—they didn't want to cause me any trouble since I was the outsider—and planned his ruin. They would destroy his credibility, once and for all, in the most public way they could think of—through the museum. They made a pact that each of them would do something to discredit the museum (in other words, Ringwell), each keeping his contribution to the operation a secret from the rest for safety's sake."

It all began to click together for me in the last few days . . . all the things that had been bothering me about the disparity in the crimes and the Seven's seeming involvement in so many of the lesser ones. I didn't refer to them as the September Seven, though. Aunt Lydie, Oliver, and Gregor wouldn't have known whom I was talking about.

"Pierre Richardson was the first," I went on. "He arranged to set up an out-of-town neophyte actress to look like a prostitute and then be brought in to be photographed with Ringwell and the Rembrandt—and then later to be exposed as a prostitute to embarrass Ringwell."

All three of them stirred at the same time, preparing to interrupt. I held up my hand. "No, please." They subsided, but watched me nervously. Just wait, I thought . . . you'll see.

"Then the Rembrandt was stolen and the girl kidnapped. They were horrified—they thought one of *them* was responsible. They held a meeting, probably before the opening night preview, to decide whether or not to go on, but as everyone naturally denied having anything to do with the Rembrandt affair, they decided to continue, doing their best to protect me while also doing their best to destroy Ringwell and Brown.

"That night there was a bomb threat—David Lawless, I'm sure. That same night, two small paintings disappeared, but turned up later safe and sound in their owners' houses: Rosemary Craig-Mitchell and Belle Sandringham stole their own paintings during the bomb scare. Illegal? Probably, but not terribly."

Oliver Reynolds and Gregor Olitsky were looking more and more appalled. My aunt's expression was beginning to change from one of cold disapproval to one of tentative amusement.

"Those anonymous phone calls and letters defaming everyone else's paintings—Willem de Groot, obviously . . . since his Rembrandt's pedigree was shaky, he was denigrating everyone else's and keeping the pact at the same time. Pretty shifty footwork, don't you think? Then there was the demonstration. . . . Diantha's contribution by way of Buffalo Horowitz by way of his former mistress, Blossom Rugge. The fire scare—the general. Seven disgruntled collectors bent on saving their community—seven episodes designed to destroy the opposition by ridicule and loss of credibility."

They had been well designated the September Seven: if they had ever decided to turn their varied talents toward real terrorist activities they could well have devastated the universe among them.

"But there were eight episodes, at least." My aunt never forgot anything.

"More, if you consider the deaths of Wink Gaud, Saskia, Blossom Rugge, and the general. But they had nothing to do with your friends . . . their deaths were part of the theft of the Rembrandt and the involvement of the Bishop and Cathedral—something else altogether."

"Cathedral?" asked Oliver.

My aunt held up her hand. "In a minute, Oliver. What you're saying, Persis, is that our seven silly friends had nothing to do with the kidnappings and deaths. Am I correct?"

"You are, Aunt Lydie. It was the Bishop."

"Very well. We know what they have done . . . and there's no real harm in it, I say, except mischief to the museum and to those two dreadful men, which doesn't upset me in the least—they deserved anything that happened to them. I suggest we pretend we never heard a word you said about our friends. For example, the poor old general is dead, and it wouldn't be nice to say he went around setting fires, would it? We will forget what we have heard. Do you agree?"

"Agreed," said Oliver and Gregor in unison.

"If only," my aunt continued thoughtfully, "Belle Sandringham hadn't insisted on lending her Rubens to the anniversary exhibition in Antwerp. I didn't approve of lending paintings, you know . . . it always leads to trouble. Her Rubens is exquisite, by the way. It's a portrait of his second wife, worth at least 3 or 4

236

million, and a very fashionable picture this year. They would surely have kidnapped *it* and then maybe the girl wouldn't have been involved at all. Maybe Pierre wouldn't have found anybody appropriate. . . ."

She was probably right, but we would never know now. "Ah, well," she said sadly, then she put it aside. She did not like to think about sad things. "In any case, we will say nothing about the foolishness of our friends. It's the best thing, isn't it, gentlemen?"

The gentlemen nodded gravely.

"And now, Persis," she said, "what about this Cathedral?"

I explained it all as best I could—about the twenty missing trucks and the organization known as Cathedral and Wink's part in it and the international operation for the theft of great works of art.

"Winkworth Gaud saw a photograph of someone associated with the Waldheim when the museum was being planned. He'd always suspected that some member of Cathedral was the brains behind the theft ring and he thought he recognized that person in the photograph. Thirty years had passed, he couldn't be sure, so he came here to find out. But—" I paused. Was I really right?

"But?" they asked.

"But the Bishop—that was his code name—recognized that Wink Gaud had to die before he blew the whole operation. So Wink was killed. And the others, too. The girl had to die because she could identify the kidnappers. Blossom Rugge knew too much. The general suspected too much."

"I suppose there's no doubt in your mind, Persis, that they were murdered?" Gregor always looked for the bright side of things.

"No doubt at all."

"Then who did it? The Bishop, you say. But who is the Bishop? Let me see if I can guess." Aunt Lydie loved puzzles. "Someone smart, obviously, if it was a big international operation . . . someone who was at home all over the world . . . someone who knew art . . . someone who could have been in Belgium in

1940." She was ticking the qualifications off on the fingers of her left hand, and then pondered deeply. "Why, it's absurd: everyone qualifies. They all could have been the Bishop. I suppose he could have been a 'she'?"

"Could have."

My aunt looked at me searchingly. She had always known how to read me. "You didn't want it to be anyone you cared about, did you, Persis? And you cared about them all. You feel betrayed, don't you?"

She was right, as usual. "You could say that, Aunt Lydie."

"Poor Persis." Then her brief attack of sympathy was over. Pity wasn't her suit; puzzles interested her more. "You say the tunnel hadn't been pumped out by the time you left Touquet, so the body hadn't been found yet. But I'm sure you know—or think you know—the identity of the Bishop. You do know, don't you?"

"I think so."

"Then tell us," they all said together.

My aunt's French butler had come noiselessly into the room, entering, the way butlers do, as if drawn smoothly by a string. "There is a telephone call for Mrs. Willum, madame." They always call Aunt Lydie, who has never married, madame, just as you call a queen madame. It's because of her great style and presence.

My aunt motioned for the phone to be brought in; she was frankly planning to listen.

It was Ed Simms, calling from Touquet, where he had set up a command post immediately upon his arrival. The connection was perfect; his voice was loud and clear. "We pumped out the tunnel and we found the body. I thought you'd like to hear that you were right about who it was. I'd give a lot to know how you knew."

How had I known? It hadn't been difficult. If the Bishop was responsible for Winkworth Gaud's death, then it could only have been one person . . . the one person Wink hadn't laid eyes on before the theft of the Rembrandt . . . someone in the back seat of a car at the airport the day the Rembrandt arrived . . .

unseen by Wink, unseen by me . . . in a vapor-wreathed limousine.

"I should have guessed sooner," I told Simms. "And what about the paintings?"

"They couldn't take the big ones." He sounded triumphant. "And we'll probably recover a lot of the rest before we're done. The Rembrandt's O.K.—the door to that room closed automatically before the tunnel was completely flooded. The paintings we've found! There'll be celebrating in the art world tonight." He began to list the masterpieces.

I stopped listening after the first fifty or so names. There would be other caches of paintings stolen by Cathedral: the search would go on and on. But with the Bishop dead, there was at least a chance of finding them all.

As for the rest of it, Ringwell was definitely through—the discovery that his right-hand man had been an SS murderer was the coup de grâce. He was discredited. Finished.

And the Bishop—suddenly I heard the rushing waters of the Course. It was a very real sound to me. I shuddered, and handed the telephone to the butler.

"Who did it?"

I turned to Lydia Wentworth and Oliver and Gregor. They were watching me with pleased anticipation etched on their faces and I realized with a shock that for them everything that had occurred had little, if any, reality. They had never known Winkworth Gaud. Nor had they known Saskia.

"Who did it?" Their eyes were big and round like those of children expecting presents.

"It was Jason Waldheim."

Nobody spoke. I felt sick, hearing myself say the four words. Finally—"Why?"

I explained again about Cathedral. I explained about the Rembrandt.

"But why did he kill Winkworth Gaud? Why did he steal when he could have *bought* paintings like the rest of us? Why did he turn bad?" Oliver and Gregor bombarded me . . . they couldn't understand.

239

Why? I wasn't sure myself. Because he was brilliant, cynical, arrogant . . . and bored? Because he loved danger? Because he couldn't resist the challenge—or the promise of power Cathedral held? All I knew was that when Jason saw Winkworth Gaud sitting in his car while we waited for Willem de Groot's jet to land, he recognized Wink instantly—and knew he had to die before he could put it all together.

"But he seemed like such a fine fellow," said Gregor, who liked everybody in the world.

"It is inconceivable," said Oliver. "A man like that . . . educated . . . all the right clubs. A philanthropist. A sportsman. The Harvard Club. Inconceivable."

"Why did he do all those things?" Gregor demanded.

It was Lydia Wentworth who answered. She had thought it over and had grasped it all. "It is quite obvious, Gregor. It ought to have been obvious to everyone from the very beginning. It was because of his grandfather, Jacob Waldheim, being turned down by the Metropolitan Museum of Art and snubbed by everyone for being not quite a gentleman in spite of his collection—in spite of his money—in spite of everything. Not that I agree, you understand. What, after all, is a gentleman?" She glared at the two men challengingly. When they didn't respond, she went on. "Yes, it's obvious. All those Waldheims were born in New York City, you know. That was the problem, in the end."

Gregor and Oliver were having trouble following her train of thought. "We don't see—exactly."

"Well, they were born in New York City. Now, if he'd only been born in Gull Harbor, even though people often weren't in those days . . ." She let the sentence trail off.

"Which one? Jacob? Jason?"

"Both, of course. So it's quite obvious, isn't it?"

It was, as far as I was concerned. She had made her point. My aunt always reasons by a sort of convoluted, lunatic logic that frequently maddens people and is, at best, not easy to follow. In fact, seldom. But in this instance I think she was right.

She was still talking. "Don't look so downhearted, Persis. It's bad for your face—it will make permanent lines. Think upbeat hings. For instance, Ringwell will never get to be governor now—not in a million years. For another instance, it's almost April. And you know what happens to you in April."

It won't happen to me this April, I thought.

Then I saw Aunt Lydie. She was rolling her eyes in great exaggerated circles in the direction of Oliver Reynolds, her favorite contender for the role of my roommate. It was a typical Lydia Wentworth hint, delivered with all the subtlety of a tank battalion crashing through a row of greenhouses.

I couldn't help it—I began to smile, unable to resist her idiotic charade. All right, I thought. Maybe not this April.

But there's always next year.

Clarissa Watson is co-owner and director of The Country Art Gallery *in Locust Valley, New York, which she helped to found, and author of* The Fourth Stage of Gainsborough Brown, *the first Persis Willum mystery. Her interest in gourmet cooking has also prompted her to edit a collection of artists' recipes from around the world called* The Sensuous Carrot. *She lives on the North Shore of Long Island, with her husband, a television executive.*